SHIFTING SANDS

Not all treasure is made of gold

Jana Sun

Cover Art by @1enary1 | Cover Layout by Amber Paige | Hardback Art by @ambgrrrdesign

1st edition 2025

Table of Contents

I

William

NEVER DRAW TO AN inside straight. Basic rules of poker. I knew this. I knew better than to risk two grand on praying for my lucky number eight to show up, but this was the game of a lifetime. I'd been prowling around these players, the Spice Traders, for weeks now—ever since I arrived in Cairo, ever since my friend hooked me up with a new dig. I knew the Spice Traders were loaded, and winning my next few months' rent here was a helluva lot more appealing than digging in the dirt for god knows how long. Archaeology was my passion at one point, but I wasn't stupid enough to think it would pay the bills. Any bill, really.

But none of that mattered now. All that mattered was this next card. It was a shit hand, really, but I took just one card anyway, and my heart damn-near stopped when he slid it across the table. Two thousand dollars was a lot of money. Maybe not for the assholes sitting around me reeking of sweat and sweet smelling tobacco, but it was for me.

Especially when I was *already* in debt a solid twenty-thousand.

Never draw to an inside straight.

I had a seven, a nine, a ten, and a Jack. No matching suits. No pairs. Just the fools bet to go for the straight.

Annatto–the dude smoking a shisha pipe with sickly, sweet tobacco–blew a puff of smoke across the table making my eyes water. I fought back an eye-roll at this guy's chosen name: a spice used for food coloring, and nothing else. He should have taken that hint at uselessness as a warning, and yet here he was, sweating bullets.

The dealer dealt the last cards and the group of men grumbled and shuffled through their hands like that would make the round any better. I picked up my lone card, not daring to cast a glance at it yet.

I needed to study each of the players quickly, just a fast glance to judge their prospects and figure out if I needed to make a run for it before someone pulled out a knife. The other three players gave nothing away, their faces still as stone. I took a swig of my whiskey and let it burn all down my throat. Could one even call that swill *whiskey?* I wasn't a snob by any means, but there had to be some standard. Rubbing alcohol with a bit of *annatto* in it, was more like it.

I glanced at my draw.

In an out of body experience, I heard a narrator narrating my stupid choices: *William Ford was, indeed, a fool.*

"So, what will it be? Fold or call?" the dealer asked the man on the leftmost side of the table. I was sandwiched between two other men, and while that might have been a fun night should I be pressed against them with club music pumping in the air, this decidedly was *not*.

I didn't catch what the player said because he mumbled it in very accented Arabic, but the tone got the point across. He slammed his cards on the table, and the dealer asked the next player, "Fold or call?"

He tossed the cards on the table, face down, and shot up from the table to flee. Annatto snapped his fingers a few times and several large, vicious men came from the shadows. It was like they materialized from the darkness, covered head to toe in black. They all had scarred up hands and dragged the fleeing player away.

No one got away without paying their debts to Annatto or his boss in the Spice Traders, Cardamom.

The dealer turned to me now, his old, lined face completely impassive. His hands were scarred too, but they weren't the obviously violent knicks and cuts, but the scars of age. I always noticed a person's hands: a smile was easy to fake, but the tremble in their hands or the flush in their palms? That's where the truth lay.

"Call," I said, pushing the rest of my chips into the pot. I held those cards like my life depended on it, and maybe it did. The guys in black were back, and they crowded around the dealer. The small back room felt like an inferno from all the body heat, but I didn't flinch or move. I didn't dare breathe, either.

The player to my right, Annatto, grinned that smug, asshole grin and grunted out, "Call, Willy. Let's see what you've got."

A good poker face only went so far, and the lowly deuce I drew did nothing for that inside straight I prayed for. But I sat down each card, one by one, ever the showman.

"A straight! I can't believe it–" Annatto swore, but as I set down the deuce, it turned to raucous laughter.

"A busted straight, actually. Worth a shot, I suppose," I said and Annatto shook his head.

"You're already in debt twenty-k and now you've just added two more! Cardamom will be pleased, I'm sure. And of course, you are good for it, yes? And the interest–"

"No one ever said anything about interest," I protested. The room felt overheated now. *Interest*? I was already up shit's creek without interest added.

"Yes, of course. You're already late paying Cardamom and I back, and now you've lost even more. Consequences, William, consequences." Annatto blew another puff of smoke in my face, and I smacked the pipe out of his mouth. Instantly it felt like a mistake, but I didn't care.

"Temper, temper. Your interest just went up. Ten percent for every day that you're late."

I slammed my hands on the table as I jumped up, "Ten percent! What kind of crook–"

"Best not to defame Cardamom in these parts of town. The Spice Traders have eyes and ears everywhere. You'll find a way to repay, or we will cut a pound of flesh out of you. A kidney, a liver–something will sell nicely."

"You're joking," I choked out, paling. My blood pressure spiked and I felt faint as I noticed the very large knife hanging from Annatto's belt.

"You'll find that I rarely joke," Annatto said, his words turning cruel. "I'll come find you in three days to collect."

"I won't have anything by then–"

"Then you will find something else to pay with, won't you?" Annatto nodded his head and the guys in black grabbed me, throwing me out into the street. I landed hard on my face, blood dripping down my chin on my mostly-white shirt.

"That could have been worse," I mumbled to myself, and just as I sat up, one of Annatto's goons turned and kicked me in the ribs. I grunted through the pain, crawling up on my hands and knees, bracing for another blow that didn't come.

"Oh yeah Will, great job. You just had to tempt fate, huh?" I muttered. Flat on my back and staring up at the night sky, I stayed on the dirty street trying to catch my breath. The stars were brilliant tonight, even though there was so much light pollution in Cairo now. People weaved around me, staring at the random American lying in the gutter, and hurried past. It was late, but Cairo never slept: Khan el Khalili still buzzed with life even past midnight. I'd spent so many hours in this bazaar, usually in the seedier parts, but the beauty of it never stopped to amaze me. People walked through living history everyday, immune to its charms and I would do anything to stay in the beating heart of it.

The stars twinkled and I blinked–stars couldn't truly twinkle, and I worried that I had a concussion now too.

"At least you're not face down in the gutter," a woman said, sauntering up to me.

"Hi Zahra," I said. Zahra's black hair was chopped short, with her fitted linen pants and shirt, she seemed out of place here. She kneeled next to me, poking my face and ribs.

"That has to hurt," she said.

"Your observation skills are astounding."

"What did you do this time?"

"Lost a card game."

Zahra grunted, yanking me up to my feet. The world spun, but I stayed mostly on the ground. When I finally hauled myself up, I leaned heavily on Zahra. She was about a foot shorter than me and a solid sixty-pounds less. Where I was large and lean, chocolatey brown hair and soft green eyes, Zahra was thin with black hair and brown eyes. We met shortly after college, the friendship blossoming while we lamented our post-grad choices. Her Egyptian heritage made her beautiful, but she inherited her British father's demeanor: logical and assessing.

"And how much more are you in debt now? You couldn't have possibly been stupid enough to gamble with Annatto again. God, how much do you weigh?"

"Are we talking about actual weight or the crushing weight of my bad decisions?"

"Is that even quantifiable?"

"Cardamom would say it's twenty-two thousand dollars plus ten-percent interest starting tomorrow. Maybe today, I wasn't clear before getting kicked in the ribs, and was even less clear after that." Everything ached and I wheezed as I breathed.

Zahra dropped him, and my knees hit the gravel-lined road hard. "Twenty-two thousand dollars! How! How are you possibly–"

"Can we do this later? Broken ribs and all," I said, flashing her a megawatt smile.

"That crap doesn't work on me, William Ford. What exactly are you going to do about it?"

"Leave the country?"

"Will, the Traders are everywhere, you know that," she hissed out.

"Any bright ideas?"

"One, but you won't like it."

"I don't really have the personality for being an escort. I catch feels too fast."

"I think you'd prefer escorting," she said, as she led them from the bazaar. I cast one final glance up at the sky, staring at the moon. I'd still be able to enjoy looking at it without a kidney, probably. Maybe.

"Let's get back to my place," Zahra said. My head finally cleared enough that I didn't need to lean on her, and we moved much faster now that she wasn't half-dragging me through town.

Zahra's place–my unofficial crash pad–was a small apartment not too far from Khan el Khalili. The building was older but still in good condition, and even though neither of us were romantically intertwined with each other or anyone else, we wore wedding rings to stave off any unwelcome attention. Zahra couldn't care less, but I invited enough trouble on my own, and at least tried not to make it any worse.

"Let's see the ribs," she said.

"Tell me about this bad idea of yours."

"Well, you know my cousin is working on a local dig site right? He could get us jobs on the site. We've already got the archaeology and anthropology degrees, so I'm sure we could just slip in."

"Slip in and do what?" I asked as I grabbed some frozen vegetables to hold against my ribs. God, I hoped they weren't broken. Zahra had that look in her eye that usually meant trouble. For everyone involved, but typically me. I wasn't sure if it was a migraine or a concussion, but my head throbbed. Every heartbeat felt like a dagger in my head.

"You know, just... delicately acquire a couple little things that no one will miss–"

"Zahra, no. We are not thieves–"

"I'm not the one stupid enough to gamble with literal, actual thieves." She threw her hands up in mock defeat, derision melting through my protests.

"There has to be another way."

"Before or after you rack up another twenty-thousand dollars of debt?"

My ribs hurt. My head ached. How did my life get to this point?

"I have to draw a line in the sand somewhere, Zahra. I'm not a thief. So, new plan: we join the dig. Earn a little cash. And, I'll just find another game somewhere and win what I need–"

Zahra groaned and opened her small fridge, pulling out a beer. It tasted like sour water, but it did the job. She winced through each sip and I'd had enough pain already so I passed.

"And then I'll keep my eyes peeled for something small and profitable."

"I like my idea better," I muttered and Zahra laughed. I pulled my shirt up examining the blossoming bruises on my ribs. Probably not broken, just bruised. My tanned skin took on a purplish hue, and I sucked in a breath as I poked each spot.

"I'll call my cousin tomorrow. We'll be on that dig by the end of the week."

"Great, so I'll wrack up a solid forty-percent in interest."

"Good thing you're cute or you'd have nothing going for ya, huh, Ford?" Zahra flicked my nose, and headed into her room, closing the door behind her.

I did the same, stripping down to my boxers, sweat and dirt clinging to my skin. I didn't even have the energy for a shower, so I fell asleep soon after my head hit the pillow. It was already tomorrow, and this mess could wait a few more hours.

II

Arthur

I STEPPED OUT INTO the busy street in the heart of Cairo. I'd been here for a week already, and nothing, nothing, *nothing* would ever dull the magic of seeing the Great Pyramids rising in the distance, brushing against the city sprawl. It was magic—pure and simple. A marvel of human invention, a treasure that stood against the brutal weight of time, the marker of genius—

I ran right into an older gentleman that shouted at me in Arabic, which finally shook the cobwebs from my head.

Ah, Cairo.

Even when I made an ass of myself, I knew I'd never be happy anywhere else in the world. My PhD program was in its final legs with just more field work to complete and a thesis hanging over me like a death sentence.

But still, I was in Cairo, living my dream of being a real, live Egyptologist. One day my work on this dig would be considered required reading for future scientists. Imagining a room full of bright eyed students who loved history as much as I did made my heart swell.

Once I found something worth talking about.

Which I would.

I hoped.

I buzzed through the city, weaving between people and headed to Khan el Khalili to meet Dr. Wesley Carrington for a quick coffee and chat about the expedition.

Expedition.

I loved the idea of going on another dig; I did one once in Belize and while it was lovely, it wasn't *Egypt*. In the depths of my heart where I'd never admit to the larger academy, I pretended I was Indiana Jones, going on my next daring adventure.

Except I had asthma and hated confrontation. And snakes, but even Indy agreed with me on that.

I spotted Dr. Carrington almost immediately, sitting at a small table outside, sipping from an even smaller coffee cup. Dr. Carrington was a handsome man; in a few years, he'd be a silver fox, and even though that wasn't my type, I could appreciate the scenery. Dr. Carrington had the easy confidence of a man who lived his life exactly as he pleased–he was my role model in more than just Egyptology.

One day, I would be living that same life.

"Arthur! I ordered you a coffee too. I know you like them strong like I do," Dr. Carrington said.

"Ah, thank you! What are we doing today?" I pulled up a rickety chair next to him, and leaned over to examine the mound of papers he had.

"Today, we are finalizing our contracts with the local officials so we can start searching by Monday. We still need to hire more day-laborers, and the rest of our team won't be arriving until next Thursday, so we've still got a week or so to get the site prepped. I'm glad you're here for this part of the work though. It's not all digging in the dirt! Archaeology has an unfortunate amount of paperwork." He grimaced through the word *paperwork* and I stifled a laugh. It was hard to picture Dr. Carrington behind a desk filling out forms and clicking through endless pages of bureaucratic nonsense.

"I'm on board to help however I can," I said. The grin nearly split my face in half; I knew that I was selected for this dig because I was in the final leg of his doctorate program, but still. I was selected. I was here, and this was everything I could have dreamt of and more.

Every sense was nearing overstimulation, but I didn't care. Cairo was where I was meant to be.

"How are you finding the city?"

"It's perfect," I replied.

"Hardly, but what city is? There is something grand about Cairo though. I spent most of my twenties in

Egypt, as you know, and it does feel like I'm coming home."

"I don't think I want to live anywhere else in the world after seeing it. My specialty aside, there's more life in this city than I've ever seen. It's life-affirming." The coffee was strong on my tongue, another jolt of that life-energy I felt.

"Arthur, you are truly an idealist. We all start out that way, but I do hope that you never lose that spark. It will serve you well, I think."

I didn't know what to say to that; I had rarely met someone that praised my idealism, but maybe it was just another sign that this was exactly where I was meant to be in my life.

Good company, good coffee, good views.

This was perfect.

"Anyway, once we get all of this dreadful paperwork settled, we should be good to go. Now tell me, what are you expecting to find?" Dr. Carrington said.

"Oh, I don't know, I'd be happy to find anything–"

"Wrong answer, Arthur. We must continue to strive for greatness!" Dr. Carrington adjusted his gold, wire rim glasses and the sunlight made his gray eyes come alive.

"Greatness? But I thought this was a simple burial site, nothing like a Pharaoh or anything." I sipped my coffee, letting the wonderfully bitter drink fill my mouth. Black coffee was not for the faint of heart, I thought, and now that described me. I took another swig just to prove to myself that it was true.

"I don't think this is a simple burial spot. I've been digging," he paused to laugh at his own pun, "and I rather think we might be at the site of one of the old gods. One we don't know much about. I kept seeing *east wind* in some of the initial photographs of the site. The photos are hard to place. I can't tell if I'm looking at a wall or a floor, or what. But 'east wind' is clear as day. You know the story of the east wind, right?"

I shook his head; I knew about every myth there was but I'd never heard of this one. How thrilling–I hadn't even stepped one foot on site and was already making new discoveries. Adrenaline, and likely too much caffeine, flooded my system. I felt so very alive here.

"The god of the east wind is known for destruction. It's a common enough theme for the east wind; for some reason or another, eastern winds are not a good thing. It's unusual to see it referenced so blatantly, so I'm thinking some of this god's followers might be entombed here."

"Would they have proper mummies?" My pulse spiked. A mummy! What I would give to discover a real mummy. To touch the ancient wrappings, and look at that shrunken, shriveled face. I loved to imagine what their lives had been, who they loved, what work they did–sometimes I felt as though I could wander through the past in my daydreams so clearly that it felt real. I felt that familiar tug, the need to daydream, at the back of my mind and forced myself to stay in the present.

"I think so. I think we will find a lot more than just some mummies, Arthur. If this turns out to be a temple, we'd have a whole new avenue of research to pursue. Now that is worthy of a thesis if I ever heard of one!"

A whole new temple? Goosebumps prickled along my arms. Even though I was notoriously dreamy, even I had no illusions about actually finding some long lost temple. But if Dr. Carrington thought it was possible... Well, that was a different story.

"I can't wait to see the site. How many more are joining us?"

"I'm hoping we will have three more lead archaeologists, and a few more students. Although, aside from you, only William Ford caught my eye back in the day. Maybe my colleagues will have more promising pupils. I swear between the TikTok and th-the twerking, all you young people have just lost the ability to concentrate for more than a minute!"

My mood soured at the mention of William Ford. We spent our undergrad and graduate programs together–hunched over books, studying dead languages, listening to endless lectures–and it killed me that William was the better student. Just *barely*, but still. A 3.99 would always be less than a 4.0.

Not that I ever held a grudge, but that British literature class was utter *bullshit.*

"I don't think William even entered the post-graduate program, Dr. Carrington." I was aware that my tone was too clipped and that I clutched my coffee cup too tightly, but noticing emotions was not one of Dr. Carrington's strong suits. If it hadn't been dead for at least a thousand years, he wasn't interested.

"Please call me Wes. 'Dr. Carrington this, Dr. Carrington that,' it's quite the mouthful. Besides, we will be peers soon! Perhaps we need another coffee to drink to that!" Dr. Carrington–Wes–flagged down a server and ordered another coffee in perfect Arabic. At least it sounded perfect to me; my accent was atrocious.

"So, shall we get going?" I asked, dragging the conversation away from myself. Of course I wanted to finish my degree, but it was still daunting. This was the part I didn't want to end: the chase, the search.

"There's no rush, Arthur. The desert is eternal." *As was this conversation, apparently*, I thought.

"I can hardly stand waiting to see it."

"Well, don't get too excited. The first days of a dig are a lot like a construction zone. Setting up our tents and workstations, prepping the search areas. And this isn't a well funded project, so we will most certainly be in tents. If you have enough savings, I suggest looking into some hotels for your off days if for no other reason than a proper shower."

"Will we be sharing tents?" The thought of having to spend *that* much time with Wes was exhausting.

"Oh not me, no. Perks of being the senior on site. The students will be paired up though."

"Any idea who my roomie will be?"

"The desert will be deciding that too, I think."

I finished my second coffee and made my excuses to explore the city. I watched how Wes's features softened as I muttered my terrible excuses to get away, and he waved me off. I hoped he remembered what it was like to experience Cairo for the first time, because as much as I loved being with my favorite professor, I needed this freedom.

I snaked further and further into the Khan el Khalili, stopping at every shop, looking every bit the tourist that I was. I bought trinkets everywhere. I knew I should haggle, but the thought of doing it made my stomach sink. If I paid a little extra, so be it. It was worth being here and soaking in the vibrancy of Cairo.

I bought beads and replicas of the pyramids, little Sphinx statuettes and a little golden scarab beetle. I picked up a lovely scarf for my mother and a golden lamp for my father. There were spices I'd never seen before and little baked sweet potatoes that smelled divine.

My backpack was nearly overflowing with things by the time the afternoon had come and gone. As I wound my way back through the bazaar, I touched the stone walls. Excitement zipped through every neutron as I touched the walls that had stood for six-hundred years; the stone was worn but still deeply grooved and textured. The city was an artifact, and I needed to see every etching, every corner of it.

I studied the cornices of every building I passed, and wanted to climb the walls to get a better look.

My camera was going to be maxed out with photos by day three if I wasn't careful.

The heat of the day bore down on me along with the weight of my backpack, until I finally decided to head back to the hotel. It would be another twenty minute walk, and I was sorely tempted to take a taxi, but that would mean less time walking the streets.

So I walked.

Scanning the faces of everyone I passed, I wondered if they felt as in love with Cairo as I did.

A flash of sun-bright hair caught my eye but when I looked up, there was no one there. I walked into the hotel foyer still wondering what that flash of light could have been. For a split second, I thought of William Ford. It had to be because Dr. Carrington brought him up.

That sour feeling rolled through my stomach again–it always happened when I thought of William.

Who I didn't think about. Not much. Not often. Not any more than would be considered a normal amount. I certainly didn't dwell on how full his lips were or how his shoulders stretched the fabric of his t-shirts just so.

That would be nonsense.

I cast one more glance back at the street, looking for that hint of sun-kissed hair, before heading up to my room. The hotel was quaint but lovely; it was clean and fresh-smelling, with the scent of mint lingering in the air. The queen sized bed was lush with crisp, white sheets, but more importantly, it faced toward the Great Pyramids. I could stand at the window and enjoy this private view where the silence of the hotel room intensified their majesty.

I opened a bottle of water and turned on my laptop. It was morbid curiosity, and nothing else, I assured myself as I typed *William Ford* into the search bar. Common enough name, it wasn't like he would just pop up–

But there he was and all of the non-feelings I had for William came surging back. An absurd little crush from a lifetime ago. When William said he wouldn't be pursuing his doctorate, I told myself I wasn't disappointed.

To clear the thoughts, I flopped on my bed.

Except I *was* disappointed. William was infuriating but he was smart–I could spar with him and we'd be on equal footing. It was nice, having someone to keep up with you, if I allowed the thoughts through.

None of it mattered though because William Ford was still in America, doing God knew what. And it was for the best, because William being here would be a disaster. I didn't need or want the competition on this project; it was my dissertation, my research, and if Wes really thought there was something more out there... This would be one hell of a career launch. I dreamed of being asked to join other, larger digs at more prestigious sites, working with the best of the best in my field.

It would happen one day and I was just beginning. The sun had already set without me realizing it. Another afternoon spent dreaming and I didn't mind at all. Thoughts of holding history in my hands lulled me to a deep sleep.

III

William

ZAHRA WOKE ME UP too early; she bribed me with coffee and the promise of a greasy breakfast, but I still didn't want to *move*. My body felt better after sleeping, but I wouldn't venture to say that I felt *good*. My ribs were purple. The knot on the back of my head had gone down and I didn't have the urge to black out or throw up, so that had to be progress.

The split lip and busted cheek were tragic though; not much could be done to hide that.

"So, my cousin called this morning. He said that the site he just got hired on is looking for a few more people. He knows the site leader, so he's going to get us hired! All your money troubles will be history soon, my friend!"

"Assuming we actually find something. And assuming that I have the balls to steal an artifact."

"If you don't, I do," she countered. Zahra's energy practically sparked off her as she fluttered around the kitchen. It was awful to watch someone be so perky at such a hellish hour.

"Don't you care that you're robbing from your own heritage?"

"William, I'm Egyptian by blood. I grew up in Chicago. My first time in Cairo was last year. And no, I don't care if I steal a piece of crumbled pottery. It's not like we're robbing a Pharaoh or something. Trinkets, that's all we're looking for. Something big enough to pay off your debt and keep all your happy little organs in your body where they belong."

"But–"

"Would you care if you stole something from, like, insert random European country here? I don't even know what your heritage is."

"Mutt, mostly. But okay, point taken, I guess. I still don't like it."

"It's not like this is our gateway into the seedy, criminal underworld. In and out. That's it."

I folded my arms across my chest and instantly regretted it. It would take weeks before my ribs actually healed. "Zahra, I don't know if I can even lift a shovel right now. I don't think anything is broken, but look at this." I pulled my shirt up and Zahra didn't even blink at my toned, muscled body. She inspected the bruising with expert, detached care. She looked at me like I was another specimen for her to study, not her best friend in need of painkillers.

"Nothing is broken that I can tell. Obviously you'd need an x-ray to confirm, but considering you can move and breathe without crying, I think you lucked out."

"Tell that to my face," I muttered.

"Listen, chances are we won't find a damn thing, or we won't even be able to get close to anything juicy. But at least we're doing something? Yeah?" She had to reach up to brush the hair out of my face. I was a mess; I needed a shower and shave badly, but considering Zahra was already up, hair braided, and purse secured, I doubted there would be time for a shower now.

My phone rang and we both turned. The phone buzzed on her counter with a blocked number. We both knew who was calling: the Spice Traders.

"Don't answer," she said.

"They will just keep calling."

"Turn the phone off. Let's just get you a cheap burner for a bit."

"And what do I tell my mother if she calls?"

Zahra flashed that smile that promised trouble, "Well Will, you could always tell her the truth."

God, hell would freeze before I'd stoop that low. Ever since my father died, I tried to keep the stress in my mom's life to a minimum. She was finally living again, and I'd hate myself if I somehow ruined that slice of joy she'd found.

"You win. I need an hour to get ready," I said, walking into the bathroom before Zahra could protest.

"We're heading out of the city. The site is south of the Al- oasis, so I'll pack a bag."

"How long are you thinking we'll be gone?" I asked. The shower steamed up the small bathroom, and I breathed it in. It soothed my aching face.

"At least a few days. We're going to be working on this site for a while, besides the longer you're out of Cairo, the better."

"I'll bring everything then." I'd been living out of a suitcase for the last seven months. After my mom was settled, I couldn't face staying in that house another day. A gap year, I insisted, but really it was just an excuse to get away from the grief.

Now look at me, I thought.

"Let's put these overpriced college degrees to use," Zahra said.

I grunted my approval and let the shower beat away my thoughts.

***

By the time we were on the road, my mood improved. Driving in Cairo was nightmare inducing, but Zahra had spent enough time behind the wheel to navigate the traffic. Cars and scooters and pedestrians zipped in and out of each other, and the constant stop-go flow made me remember the bumper cars rides from childhood. I wasn't a fan then, and even less so now.

I watched the city slowly slip away, and the suggested two hour drive was closer to three.

The desert greeted us in full force with Cairo fully in the rearview, and something in my chest ached. Desolate and haunting, the sands called to me. I watched the wind blow the sand like a gentle caress, and it reminded me of why I fell in love with history all over again.

I searched the horizon, letting the desert enchant me further.

"You look faraway, you okay?" Zahra asked. Her voice sounded hoarse from being silent for so long. We rode mostly in silence, aside from the occasional frustrated cursing from Zahra. Everything in me ached, most of all my heart. What the hell had I gotten myself into? The wind howled and picked up, like it heard each crack deepening in my heart. Or ribs–they were probably cracked too.

"Yeah, just watching the desert."

She made a humming sound, but let it drop. I knew the melancholy was written on me in neon, but I should have been starting my doctorate and traveling the world looking for more glimpses into the past. Instead I was up to my neck in debt and praying for a way out that wouldn't land me in prison or dead.

"Want to visit the oasis? We don't have to meet up with my cousin until tonight. I just didn't want to wait to leave Cairo and get stuck in traffic," she said.

"Yeah, let's do it."

Zahra redirected our route and within twenty minutes we pulled up to Al-Fayoum oasis. Lush, shining blue water stretched out before us. It could have been a painting; the stark blue water was crystal clear, reflecting the cloudless sky. Tourists from all over were here to take in its beauty, and I found myself walking toward the water's edge. Reeds and grasses I didn't know the name of sprang up near the edge of the oasis. The sun's rays were relentless but I didn't mind the heat; the kiss of sunlight, nearing a burn, on my face made me feel alive. The palm trees provided bits of shade that people seemed to gravitate toward. Why come to the desert if not to experience the feel of the sun on your skin? I turned my face up to the sun.

We walked along the water until my muscles started to burn with exertion; I still felt weak from last night, but it didn't matter. This was what I came to Egypt for–not just the allure of the Pyramids or the museums, but the nature. I wanted to see how the sands swayed with the wind and how the oasis seemed to spring up from nothingness. My mind marveled and demanded to learn about the past, but my heart was in the dunes. The air was hot but every deep breath healed some tender ache in me.

"Will, look," Zahra said, pointing in the distance and I saw the entrance to the small park with the waterfalls that it was known for. Excitement lit up inside me as I watched the water cascade down. The heat mirage made the falls glitter and I desperately wanted to touch the water. The falls weren't the largest ones I'd seen but something about seeing water rushing down in the middle of the desert was powerful, life giving. Here in this little oasis, life flourished. The sounds of the tourists faded as I listened to the water, leaning against the wood and stone railing. There was a circular, rounded building that drew my eye. Everything here was purposeful and interesting to look at from the oasis lake to the waterfalls themselves and the square surrounding them. I imagined how finding this place must have felt like more of a treasure than any piece of gold.

This place seemed unreal–all of Egypt did, really. Zahra walked through the oasis like she had been here a thousand times and knew where we were going. The city of Fayoum was not far off, and that's where we were going to meet her cousin. Zahra found a spot to plop down in the sand and watch the waterfalls.

"Have you learned anything about the dig?" I asked.

"Rami said that it was led by some American guys, but he forgot their names. They don't exactly go into all the details when hiring people. He's got a clean background check and has worked on like four other sites, so he got hired quickly. We can ask him tonight at dinner. I booked us a room for the next couple of days, so be sure you wear your ring."

"Never take it off, Zahra," I said, kissing the back of her hand. She yanked her hand away so fast that I was almost offended. Or would have been if I'd been remotely interested in women.

"Gross, please stop." She pretended to shudder, laughing.

"One day we will both find good men to settle down with," I said, stretching my legs out in the sand. Everything was still so sore, but stretching eased the pain.

"I can't imagine you settling down with anything."

"Let's get me out of debt first, and then we go man-hunting."

"Deal," she said, bumping her shoulder against me. We stayed there, letting the sun bake us, until she spoke up again. "Hey Will, are we gonna talk about why you're gambling again? Because you know you can tell me anything–"

"We should get going, Zar. Your cheeks are pink, which means I'm already burnt."

"Nice deflection," she muttered, but didn't press. This was why I loved Zahra so much: she saw the cracks in me but didn't try to excavate any nuggets of emotion or information. She knew I'd crumble, and she'd be there to sift through the rubble.

The walk back to the car felt twice as long; I didn't grab an extra water bottle and now regretted it. I was dehydrated and Zahra slowed her pace too.

"I keep forgetting how damn hot it is," she grumbled. It was only late May, but the sun was out in full force. Summer bloomed across the desert, and my shirt stuck to my sweat-lined skin.

"This hotel has a nice shower, right?"

"God I hope so, I call dibs," she said. Her phone rang and she answered in Arabic. I saw her cousin's name flash on the phone and listened while they chatted. I understood more than I could speak but I didn't like to advertise that. A lot can be learned by playing ignorant.

"Rami is already in town, he arrived early. You ready to head into the city?"

"Absolutely," I said, casting one more glance at the waterfalls. I thought about the debt hanging over me like a curse and for one fraction of a second, wondered what drowning in the falls would be like.

"Dinner first, I'm starved."

***

The city was bustling when Zahra and I made it there. From seemingly endless deserts, the city sprang to life around us. The buildings were modern and sleek but the culture Egypt was known for was imprinted on every aspect of the city. There were sandy colored mosques and gorgeous museums, people buzzing with energy. It reminded me of a cozier version of Cairo. I immediately missed the vibe of Cairo; Fayoum felt like a homecoming and I certainly wasn't ready to face those emotions.

Zahra parked on the street and looped her arm through mine as she used her phone to guide them to the restaurant. *Dinner* was a stretch; it was barely three in the afternoon, but I was planning to eat until my stomach wanted to burst.

Rami was a good looking man in his late thirties with black wire-rim glasses. He flagged Zahra and I down when we entered the small, family owned restaurant and I had to look away from his stunning face. Zahra failed to mention that he looked like *that*.

Rami was tall and fit, and I noticed every clean, sharp line of his shoulders and arms. He had a working man's hands, and I'd bet the entirety of what I owed to the Spice Traders that those calloused fingers would be maddening hot if he were to rake them down my spine–

"William, this is Rami. Rami, Will. Thanks for getting us on the dig."

"Of course, it's good to see you again. Pleasure," he said, gripping my hand in a firm handshake. *If only someone took that bet about his hands*, I thought and let go before it became awkward.

He gave Zahra a side-hug, and they sat together at the small table. He spotted the rings on our hands and I caught the raised eyebrow as Zahra mumbled the truth about the rings. The worn fabric of the chairs were baby-soft from age, and I sank into them. The last couple of days crept up on me and I was practically asleep in the chair when Rami turned that intense gaze to me.

"So, Zahra tells me that you've been met with some bad luck recently."

"That's a polite way to say I'm an idiot," I retorted. I sipped some water, letting the coolness coat my mouth.

Rami's laugh was rich and warm, and something fluttered in my chest. *Bad idea, William, get a grip*, I scolded myself. "She said you were funny too."

"Zahra loves to chat, that's for sure, but thank you very much for getting us positions with the dig site. Have you heard what we're looking for or who is operating the site?"

"Not really, it's been very quiet. Typically there's more information given, but I've worked with several of these scholarly types before and some of them are secretive about their research. We'll find out soon enough."

"Will here went to school with me," Zahra said. "He majored in Egyptian history and I went the anthro route."

"And how are those job prospects, cousin?" Rami laughed.

"Well, considering I'm here and about to join an archaeological dig, I'd say I'm doing great for myself," she said, that razor sharp grin nearly splitting her face. The challenge, the dare to push her crackled in the air and I wondered how stupid Rami was. He smiled, their eyes locked in a silent battle. Must be a family trait—that glare.

"Easy Zar, no need to go for the throat," I laughed.

"I see why you two are friends," Rami said, the smile on his lips making his voice even softer. His English was perfect, but I'd heard Rami and Zahra speaking Arabic earlier. I catalogued that detail: at least bilingual, likely knew more than that judging from the intelligent, confident air about him. Rami was full of himself for sure, but he was damn good looking too.

"Did you grow up in Egypt or in the States?" I asked.

"Both actually, I moved to the States when I was around ten or so, and stayed until about four years ago. I missed home," he said, looking fondly out the window. Fayoum was full of life, and I understood how he would miss this compared to the States.

"This is home?" I asked, and Rami nodded.

"Yeah, I grew up here. My dad took a job in the States and my parents and younger sister still live there. Colorado is beautiful, but too cold for me."

"There's something beautiful about the desert," I commented and–was I imagining that light in Rami's eyes?

The moment broke before I could make more of an ass out of myself as the food arrived. It took every ounce of willpower not to moan at the smell of it. Rami had ordered a feast: falafel, baba ganoush, bread that smelled like heaven on earth, ful medames, roasted vegetables with rice, a spiced chicken kebab dish, and large koftas. My stomach growled and Rami grinned.

"Is Zahra not feeding you?"

"*Zahra* is not his keeper, and he should be feeding himself," she snapped, reaching for the pitcher of water. Rami heaved piles of food on each plate, passing them to me and Zahra.

Rami said a quick prayer, and I dug in. My body demanded fuel, and now that I thought about it, I hadn't actually eaten since before I got my ass handed to me after the card game.

"How is it?" Rami asked, watching my response.

"When we were in college, I used to make Zahra cook for me and I thought it was the best food in the world. This is better."

Zahra punched me in the arm. "I'll remember this when we're back in Cairo."

"And you two aren't... together?" Rami asked carefully.

"Oh gross, no," Zahra added. "Will is my best friend. And besides, I'm not his type." She said with a wink. *God kill me now*, I prayed. I squeezed my eyes shut, willing the moment to pass without any additional commentary.

"Tell me about the other sites you've worked on?" I asked, as I took a bite out of the falafel. It was to die for. Hopefully Rami took the bait to change the subject before Zahra shared any more details about my lack-luster love life.

"Mostly I do the day-labor, but I've helped clean some pieces of pottery and once I found a necklace. It was lovely–the chain was broken, but the medallion was still in good shape. Huge emerald encased in gold. I can't read hieroglyphics, but the team was quite thrilled about it. Then they swooped it away into some lock box."

And just like that, all of my hopes built up and crashed in an instant. Of course there would be safes. There had to be some kind of security at the site so no one did exactly as we were planning.

"Oh wow, it's good that they kept everything locked up," Zahra added, but there was something in her tone that I didn't recognize. She was the reasonable one, but she toyed with the edge of her plate, not quite meeting Rami's eyes.

"Indeed, too bad they whisked it away before I could even really see it. The lead on the site took credit for the find, of course." Rami rolled his eyes, but I noticed that same shift in him too.

"Not surprising, really. A lot of the archaeologists are in the fame business more than anything," I said carefully. What was this dance we were doing? I scooted up in my chair, leaning in, leaning toward this kernel of danger.

"Perhaps you will find something on this dig, William. Hopefully you have longer to examine it than I did," Rami added as he added another helping of the roasted vegetables to his plate. He took stock of Zahra's emptying plate and added more to hers too.

His phone chimed and Rami answered in Arabic. I caught his side of the conversation: lots of *yes, I see* and *of course, okay, no problem*, before he quickly hung up.

"Looks like the setup is starting tomorrow. The site leader wants to hit the ground running. I'll take you back to your hotel so you can rest. You should get some rest, you look dead on your feet."

"Thanks, that's about how I feel," I muttered. My side was aching and I needed to lay down.

We finished our meal, chatting about anything and nothing. I missed this easy, no effort interaction. Everything in my world felt so heavy, so dire. When my phone rang, I looked at the unknown number and declined the call.

When it rang again, my stomach sank, but I declined it again.

On the third call, Zahra took the phone and shoved it in her backpack.

On the fourth call, Rami demanded to know what was going on.

"Calling about extending my car's warranty? Someone trying to get me a lower mortgage rate?" I quipped, sipping some hot tea. It was boiling outside, but the tea still seemed to soothe me.

"What mess have you brought here, cousin?" he asked Zahra, and she gave him a tight-lipped, all-tooth smile.

"Just dear William here," she replied and the challenge in her eyes was for both of them: it promised another black eye for me and a ruthless tongue-lashing for Rami.

Rami didn't back down, and I couldn't decide if this made him incredibly brave or stupid. Probably both. He snatched her bag, and fished the phone out. It was ringing again, and this time Rami answered.

"Hello?" he said and I wanted to melt into the floor.

"Who are you looking for? William Ford? You have the wrong number," he said. Did his accent suddenly turn British?

"Well Annatto, I'll let this William character know you're trying to reach him if I bump into him." Rami ended the call, pinching the bridge of his nose.

"I believe that's mine–"

"You're tangled up with the Spice Traders?" he hissed, trying to keep his voice down. He tossed the phone to me and it knocked into my glass of water, spilling it all over my lap. Fucking peachy.

"Yes, and I'd rather not talk about it," I snapped, my anger bubbling up and threatening to boil over. I hated my temper and how much I sounded like my father when it came out, but there was no stopping the geyser now. "Zahra didn't mention that you were just as nosy as she was, otherwise I would have said no to this whole damn thing. I'm already in a shit ton of trouble, I don't need to drag anyone else into it and I don't need someone just *inserting* themselves in my shitshow. I'm running it pretty damn well on my own."

"Yeah, at ten percent interest a day," Zahra jeered.

"Send me the name of the hotel, I'll find my way there on my own." I stood, muttered my thanks for the food and left. I needed air. I needed to get out of that restaurant before I did something really, truly stupid. Like hurting Zahra even more than I already had.

"Will, wait–"

I didn't stop though, even as she followed me out to the street. "Will, stop, you're being ridiculous."

"I'm being ridiculous? Seriously? What did you think this whole plan is? Genius? You said it yourself, Zar, ten percent a day. I'm fucked. Let me sort it out."

"But–"

"Send me the hotel details, I need to clear my head." Zahra grabbed my arm, but I yanked it away from her. People on the street were starting to stare at us , but I didn't give one singular fuck. Anger shimmered in my veins–at the gawkers, at Zahra's crazy plan and the judgment on Rami's attractive face, but mostly at myself. Twenty thousand dollars. I could not have been more stupid.

"Don't be reckless," was all she said before going back into the restaurant. Rami stood at the door, quietly watching. He ushered Zahra back inside, and I took off.

I had very little cash in my wallet, maybe twenty-five hundred Egyptian pounds. I wasn't planning on a shopping spree, so I just wandered through Fayoum. The city sprawled out along a canal of the Nile, and I followed the trail of water. The water seemed to soothe my frayed nerves, but when my phone rang again and again, I nearly chucked it into the water.

Zahra's text came through with the name of the hotel and address and I paused at a bench to look it up. The sun lashed out against my burnt skin, but I didn't move. The bench drained whatever energy I had left, and a sudden whoosh of a sigh came out of me.

"You look like you've been hit by a truck," a familiar voice said. Of course Rami had followed me; Zahra was nowhere to be seen, but that didn't mean she wasn't lurking. Lurking could have been her profession.

"Feels like it," I said as Rami sat down beside me.

"What happened?"

"Zahra didn't tell you?"

"No, she didn't. Just said that you were in some trouble."

"A lot of it, actually." I leaned back, letting the sun beat down on my face some more. My skin was overheated and red, but at least this was my doing. My cheek ached and so did my eye. I touched my eye gingerly, feeling how far the bruise actually spread down my face. I felt like my whole face was one giant bruise, but I did have a flair for drama.

"Hell of a shiner," Rami commented. He started to reach up and touch me, but then dropped his hand.

"I don't bite, unless you're into that kind of thing. I'm not, but you do you."

Rami laughed so hard it startled me and he leaned forward. "I see why Zahra likes you so much."

"Yes, you'd think she would be smarter."

"Tell me about the Spice Traders." I paused, and studied Rami. The carefree, easy-going facade faded in record time, and was replaced by this stony faced man. The air seemed to shift around us, and alarm bells went off in my head.

"What do you want to know?" I asked.

"You're already in contact with Annatto. Anyone else?"

"I've had... brief encounters with Cardamom and Anise."

Rami swore, raking a hand through his hair. It was thick and silky; I had an insane thought about touching it, touching him. Instead I scrubbed a hand over my day-old scruff. It made me feel a bit roguish, a bit wild. How different that was from the college prep boy I once was.

"Define encounter," Rami said and crossed his ankle over his knee. He was poised to look at ease, but it reminded me of the panthers I saw at a zoo once. Comfortably lethal.

"Meaning we've chatted briefly, but I didn't stick around to get fucked over by them too." The words felt like chalk in my mouth; I should be more grateful for Rami's help, but what was the cost? There was *always* a cost.

"I've never met Annatto but Cardamom is cruel. You should be careful. You're running with a very dangerous crowd, William."

"Aware of that nugget, thanks. Why did you follow me?"

"Zahra was worried. You're a good thirty minutes walk from the hotel, and I get the feeling that you're lost."

"Not lost, just wandering. I need some space to clear my head." I massaged my temples. Maybe I could just leave. How would Annatto know? I could always change my name–

"How do you feel about earning some cash another way?" Rami asked, still the picture of nonchalance. I felt my cheeks heat; he couldn't possibly be suggesting this.

"Another way? Look, I'm flattered but–"

"Cards, William, cards."

The laugh that came out was short and bitter. It caught in my throat and I felt how my anger at myself choked me. "That's how I got into this mess."

"Here's the deal. I'm not looking at digging in the dirt until my back is too hunched to stand up straight. I'm trying to find my way out of this rat race, just like you are. Zahra told me you're a skilled player."

"Skilled when the game isn't rigged," I muttered. I *was* a good poker player. I'd gotten into a tournament before, but left when my dad got sick. I could have been a professional player one day, but that felt like a lifetime ago. Now I was just some regular asshole with a gambling problem.

"Play for me."

"What do you mean?"

"I bought my way into a game. It's full of rich players, more money than sense, looking for a little thrill. Sometimes jewels pass hands. Sometimes it's a key to a car or house."

"And you're in this game? Are you dumb or just greedy?" The dark look on Rami's face made my heart pound. I started to stand, but Rami grabbed my wrist.

"Sit down. You haven't heard my proposition yet."

"I think I liked it better when I thought you wanted me to sleep with you," I huffed, but sat back down. Rami was tall and lean, but I was taller and had more muscle on him. The cracked ribs would slow me down, but if I really wanted to, I could leave. But *did* I want to? I hated that secret part of my heart that was thrilled at the prospect of another adventure.

"I'm not good enough to tangle with this crowd. They're actually good players, and there's a few items up for grabs in this game."

"What kind of things? A house?"

"An emerald the size of my fist and a few ancient Egyptian trinkets. The trinkets alone would pay back your debt to Annatto."

"You think this shit would be worth like thirty thousand? That's what it's gonna be in no time."

"William, some of these will be priceless. I get the emerald. You take whatever else you want to pay off your debts and a little something for your time."

"Is it the same one you said you found?"

"Perhaps," Rami said, and the way he reclined, controlled and slow confirmed my original thought: Rami was panther, trotting around with men pretending he wasn't a threat.

"What's the catch?" This could be the break I needed–I wanted to find another game, something out of Annatto's reach, and this could be it.

"You can't tell Zahra about this." I felt like someone had punched him in the gut again; I hated the idea of keeping things from Zahra. She'd see through his lame excuses; for as good of a poker player I was, I was a terrible liar. Especially to her.

"She doesn't know about your little plans?"

"No, and I want to keep it that way."

"Why?"

"Because Zahra is headstrong, and a headstrong woman has no place here. She's going to get herself killed." Rami's tone offered no room for argument, and I could see it: Zahra blazing into the game, wild and cursing at everyone there, until she was dragged away. My chest ached thinking about anything happening to her.

"Fine, I'm in. I won't say a thing to Zahra."

"Excellent, I told her that I was going to take you out for a while, and she seemed so relieved. Let's not let her down, right? We both want to keep a smile on my cousin's sweet face." He rose, indicating that I should follow. Rami slung an arm around my shoulders, patting me hard. The contact made my ribs ache, but I said nothing.

"You've got money for me to spend? Because I'm not spending a cent of my cash on this game." Not that I had any money to begin with. Annatto owned every penny to my name at this point.

"Yeah, I've got you covered there. Let's get going, the game starts in a couple hours and I need to make a few stops beforehand."

Those couple stops were Rami doing his normal, day to day errands. We went to the grocery store and the pharmacy. He picked up something from a safety deposit box at his bank; I had to stay on the plush velveteen chairs in the lobby of the bank while he attended his business. The bank was shaped like a dome with a sky painted on it. The crisp blue was nearly too bright to look at, and the oddly shaped clouds removed any feeling of whimsy that the mural was going for. I imagined that the painter got fired mid-job and took his frustration out on those unfortunate clouds.

When Rami finally emerged from the vaulted room, I had nearly dozed off.

"Ready?" he asked, not stopping to wait for me.

"Are we doing any other errands? Picking up the dry cleaning too?"

"Cute," he replied.

We walked side by side until just the noise of the city was too much for me. "Where are we going?"

"Does it matter where the game is held?" Rami asked. As the day went on, his tone grew colder and colder. I followed him as we bobbed and weaved through the city; the streets were narrow and crowded, and I'd completely gotten turned around in my head trying to stay with Rami.

"Yes, I'm not trying to get stabbed when this shit goes south. I've already got enough injuries."

"No one is going to stab you. Probably." Rami said, a wicked smile in place. The road turned desolate, and I slowed my pace. The life of the city had died out, and the eerie, unsettling silence weighed on me like a death sentence.

"Where are we going?"

"The back route, you'll see soon." The sun had set, but the city was still bathed in light. Between the street-lights, headlights, and the light pouring from little shops and stores, night felt like a far-off thing. There was smoke in the air and smog clung to his skin. I felt like I had wallowed in the sand but it was the weight of the city pressing down on him. The weight of this game, this meeting.

I was going to fuck up again, I could feel it.

The alley reeked of piss and vomit. The light pollution of the city was mostly hidden, and we walked in the dark. My pulse thundered through me, shooting adrenaline through my veins hot as lightning.

"Are you ready William? Try to act like you aren't scared shitless, please," Rami said as he stopped abruptly. The door was practically hidden, and at first I didn't even see the outline of the door frame, but then I took stock of where we were.

We were at a museum; it was too dark to read the Arabic, but I could spot a museum anywhere. Rami pushed open the door easily and we were greeted by a large man with a grizzled face. His beard was thick with lots of gray through it. He looked like a wall of a man, all meat and muscle. My ribs started aching as if to remind me not to screw up again.

I listened as Rami spoke slowly, like he was giving me time to translate. *"Code?"* the burly man said. His voice rattled like gravel.

"Jewel tones. I've brought my associate with me; he will be playing for me," Rami replied.

"The associate is fluent in Arabic, don't slow down on my account," I said, inwardly cringing at my accent. I'd rather just read instead of having to speak–even I knew how terrible my accent sounded.

"This way."

Rami led the way and I stayed silent. We walked through the empty museum, and I immediately knew I was about to commit a crime. Another one–on top of the breaking and entering I just did.

In a fucking museum.

"Well, we don't have all night. Let's begin." The burly man grunted and opened a door to a small storage room. There were locked cases everywhere; items that

were currently off exhibit, ready to be shipped, or prepped for restoration.

We wouldn't possibly be betting on those–

Rami pulled out a wad of cash and dropped it on the table in the center of the small room. I didn't recognize any of the players until a woman with cropped black hair looked up at me.

Cardamom.

"Hello William Ford," she said as she took a drag from her cigarette. Her long, sexy legs were on display, and the thin, sheer dress left little to the imagination. The men ogled her like she was an object or a prize to be won. As she leaned forward, the curve of breasts bulging together, I watched the intelligence leave their bodies.

"Hi," I replied, keeping my eyes focused on her dark, kohl lined eyes.

"Your company hasn't improved, but that's all the better for me." She blew a puff of smoke toward me, and I held my ground, not even flinching at the acrid scent.

I pulled out a chair and Rami squeezed my shoulder.

"What are we playing?" I asked, reclining in the chair. They wanted me to fuck up, I could feel it, but this was where I thrived: under the dim light of a poker table, surrounded by people who saw me as easy prey. I willed the predator in me to lay low and smiled too wide, letting everyone see my teeth.

"Blackjack," Cardamom said, and she put her cigarette down to shuffle and deal. "I'm the dealer."

"I trust you'll be fair?"

"William, are you insinuating that I am less than honest? And I thought we were all friends here."

"Friends, sure," I said, cracking my neck and rubbing at my cheek. Cardamom's lips curled up in a thin, venomous smile.

"Shut up and deal," I said. Rami's head snapped toward me but he said nothing. He wanted me to play?

I was going to play.

Blackjack required more skill than most people thought; all poker games did, really, but Blackjack was about the micro-expressions on people's faces. I knew I needed to learn them fast all while giving nothing away myself.

That much I was always good at—had anyone really seen behind the mask I wore? Maybe just Zahra.

Maybe someone else, once, a long time ago. For just a second I thought of Arthur Lewis and his nerdy glasses that accentuated his dimples. I was great at making casual friends, but Arthur was never casual about anything. His intense, serious gaze assessed every detail and analyzed every word—especially the ones I dared never to say.

He'd be a helluva Blackjack player, come to think of it. Assuming gambling passed the sniff test for him. Arthur was a judgy little shit, but it did make him kind of cute.

As Cardamom shuffled the cards, I watched her hands carefully, but casually. No one liked a player that studied the dealer too much, but I wouldn't put it past her to slip in extra cards or remove a few.

"You do know how to play this game, right?" Rami whispered.

"Blackjack? Never heard of it," I said. The sarcasm was so thick in my throat I could have gagged on it. Rami's cologne and the scent of his skin was overbearing, but I didn't react. Everything about him was overbearing now, but leaving wasn't an option. Not with Cardamom here, watching my every move.

"Now is not the time for jokes."

"Shoulda thought about that before you *recruited* me. Zahra likes my jokes."

Rami lowered his voice even more, "Don't say her name here." The threat made my skin prickle, but I didn't move. Cardamom watched the scene with that irritating, serene smile as she started to deal the cards.

One card for all of the players, and one for her.

I glanced at my card–a king of hearts–and quickly scanned the faces around me. There was a man who was clearly drunk practically waving his shabby three of clubs around. The smoker's upper lip twitched at his measly five of diamonds. The chubby guy that was already sweating in the air-conditioning just got an ace; his eyes widened and darted around, trying and failing to look cool. The last player was a man with salt and pepper black hair and crows feet around his eyes. He didn't talk or twitch or react when a jack of spades landed before him.

This man was the wildcard at the table, and I instantly decided that he was a plant for Cardamom. She dealt herself a queen. Fitting, I mused.

Cardamom dealt the next round of cards as I made a show of adjusting my seat, leaning forward, leaning back, like I just couldn't get comfortable. "Surely our chairs are not that uncomfortable?" she goaded.

"You know, after getting the snot kicked out of me it's just hard to get comfy," I replied.

Drunk guy got a nine.

Smoker got a six and he smiled.

Chubby got an eight and he sighed so heavily that he nearly blew his cards off the table.

Her mole got a ten.

I got an ace. Blackjack.

"Blackjack already, good job, William." I pulled the winnings to my pile of chips, stacking them quickly as the chips slid into place with a satisfying clink. Cardamom's feline smile unnerved me, but I refused to let it show on my face.

After a few more hands, I learned the rhythm of each player. Smoker tapped his fingers when he was excited. Chubby sweated more when he was doing well and got gutsier with his hits. The mole purposely made stupid bets and hits, and I wondered why he was so obviously bad.

When Cardamom added the first ruby to the pile of chips, the players groaned, leaning forward, staring at their cards with renewed hunger and desperation. The ruby glittered in the dull light, and I assessed how the game shifted. The air was charged and Rami hovered like he wanted to pluck up the gem to look at it. His energy darkened and I felt that rush I got every time I sat down to play.

One ruby like that would solve all of my problems.

My skill couldn't control the cards, and the hand I was dealt was shit. A twelve was always a shitty hand, and predictably judging from the little smirk on Cardamom's lips, I got a king. Busted.

The chubby guy won the round, whooping and yelling like his favorite football team just won. The ruby glittered and Rami swore. I wondered what trouble Rami landed himself in to have wound up at this game–the Spice Traders were not a friendly batch, and Rami seemed to have a good head on his shoulders. At least good enough to fake it most of the time.

But that didn't prevent even the smartest man from being tied up with them. I should know; I was an ivy league graduate, and now here I was, breathing in day-old sweat, tobacco, and the musty smell of rancid alcohol.

Steadily, the pot grew with each game. Two rubies. A diamond. A chunk of solid gold. Egyptian tile work. An antique, real Persian rug.

Rami's fingers dug into my shoulder when two necklaces were placed on the table. The smaller one with fine, detailed craftsmanship caught my eye. I recognized the ancient hieroglyphics, but they were too small to read from here and I wasn't stupid enough to reach for it.

Oh, but how my fingers *itched*.

The larger necklace had an encased emerald in gold hanging from a golden chain. The pendant was large and pretty; I imagined some ancient princess wearing it to a party or function. The delicate chain was most certainly not ancient, but no one seemed to care or notice.

I glanced at it again, and realized that the pendant wasn't all that ancient either. The tool markings on the golden inlay were crude but purposeful–this was a lovely fake.

Cardamom noticed my attention and I turned to Rami.

"I'm nearly out of money–"

"No, you aren't," he said, pulling out more cash.

"I don't think this is a good idea, Rami."

"I'm not asking you to think, William. I'm asking you to play," he hissed back.

"And what happens if I lose?"

"Don't." He clapped me too hard on the shoulder, and the athletic figure I admired now seemed menacing. The overeager slap reverberated down my chest, sending sparks of pain through my torso.

"I want that little one. The necklace," I whispered back. Nerves and excitement prickled along my spine. Something about that tiny pendant called my name and I needed it. I needed that damn thing.

"Done. You win, and I'll be sure your debt gets paid and you get that little trinket."

Lightning zipped through me–could I really have found a way out of this mess already? This was exactly what I needed; no need to steal or swindle anyone except these assholes here.

My first card was an ace.

Anticipation hummed around me. My whole body went taunt like a string, ready to snap. When Cardamom laid down the second ace, I nearly cursed. I'd have to split them–it was the best chance I had.

Calculations and strategy tumbled through my head. I wasn't a fucking blackjack player. Of course it took skill, but *I* wasn't skilled at it. Not in the way I was at regular five card draw or Texas hold 'em. But still, I could win this. I had to. That little pendant glittered in the low light and I needed that thing. I just did.

Two players busted and I didn't even let myself exhale too hard in case it shifted the direction of the cards.

A queen landed on my ace.

Then a ten hit the other one.

Double blackjack.

I smiled.

"You're on a roll, William Ford," she said and the threat was laid bare. She pushed the small pile of chips and trinkets toward me . Rami scooped up the emerald and requested to cash out the chips. I palmed the necklace and shoved it in my pocket.

Cardamom *tch*ed, turning to her mole with a nod. He stood instantly and retrieved an old, army green lockbox. She fished a key from her bra and the other men stared at her breasts like they held other secrets. It took every ounce of self control not to roll my eyes at these assholes.

The mole opened the box and counted out my winnings, promptly handing it to Rami.

"That's only ten thousand, I should have twenty-five," Rami protested.

"And what do you think that pretty little gem is worth, hm?" she replied.

"But we won that *and* the cash–"

"Are you so greedy that you don't tip the dealer for her incredible work?" Cardamom's nails tapped against the scraggly table and Rami's jaw tightened. Surely, he didn't just expect to leave here with all of that cash? Maybe he wasn't as smart as I thought he was.

"A fifteen thousand dollar tip?" he pushed, and I placed a warning hand on his arm. Rami shrugged me off and I took a step away. If he was about to get his ass kicked, I planned to bolt before anything else got broken, sprained, or bruised.

"I'm an excellent dealer," she replied.

"If you are done playing, it's time to leave," the mole spoke in clipped, heavily accented English. Was that for my benefit? I didn't know or care; the message was received.

"Lovely to see you, Cardamom," I said, inclining my head but never losing eye contact. I knew better than to lower my eyes to a predator, especially a pretty one.

"I'm sure I'll see you again soon," she said, and returned her focus to the game, shuffling and dealing–clearly dismissing them. Rami pulsed with rage, but I simply stepped back. I felt the shift in everyone's moods and knew what was coming. I took another step back,

"That's it? I want my money–"

Rami got punched right in the jaw and I bit back a smile. Someone needed to take him down a notch, and honestly, I was just happy that it wasn't my jaw getting clocked. We stumbled out into the dirty alleyway we came from and Rami spat blood in the gutter.

"I can't believe that bitch–"

"Has incredible hearing with ears everywhere, shut up." I strode off, not waiting for Rami to follow.

"Don't you want a ride back?"

"I don't think I want anything else from you, Rami. You don't have the money to pay off your own debts, much less mine."

"Listen, William–"

"I don't know what Zahra told you, but I don't need your help to save my ass. And I don't need hers either. I'll take care of myself without dragging her into it."

"She's already in deep shit, William. Why do you think she came to me to begin with? Because we're the best of friends?" Rami laughed, and it was cold and bitter. I paused, turning back to him. Rami looked mean as shit in awful, sickly lighting.

"What do you mean?"

"Of course she didn't tell you. Why don't you go ask her about her little problems too?"

"Leave her the fuck alone," I growled. Rami held his hands up, but he didn't back away. "I'm serious. Don't fucking bother her. We don't need this bullshit dig–"

"You might not, but she does," he said as he turned and left. The words cut deep and left me wondering what secrets Zahra had of her own, and why she wouldn't share them with me. My fingers were still wrapped around the little pendant tucked in my pocket, and the ancient metal felt warm to the touch.

When I pulled it out, the faded hieroglyphics seemed to glow and I rubbed my eyes, trying to clear the tiredness. It couldn't glow.

My thumb rubbed across the etchings and each groove reminded me of the thousands of years between the crafter and me. How would they feel to know their creation lasted so long? Would they be happy to see it in my hand? I couldn't make out any of the words–they were too faded just like my memory of the language.

It had been years since I studied in earnest, and these days the only languages I spoke were Arabic and lies.

Shuffling along the alley, I followed the moon hoping it would bring me back to the hotel. My phone's battery was low, and I needed to save it until I was closer to the city-center to find my way back. The soft ring of light around the moon made it even more ethereal, and the subtle summer breeze brushed against my chapped skin.

A text from Zahra came through demanding my location. I sent her a middle finger emoji back and shoved the phone back in my pocket.

I wanted to wear the tiny gold pendant, but I didn't take it out to look at. The metal was weirdly overheated, even through the light fabric of my pants. Honking and the noise of evening life brought me out of my haze as I wandered back to my next temporary home.

IV

Arthur

WES AND I RODE together to Al-Fayoum. The dig site was another ninety minutes outside of the city, but we needed to meet up with our colleagues that would be joining them. I didn't know their names, which was shocking; I'd read nearly every article or journal published on ancient Egypt, so I was confident that I should know who these researchers were.

But the world was vast, and I recognized that my ego was likely bruised that I didn't know them.

Wes was behind the wheel of our rented SUV–some massive thing that I knew I'd seen before, but couldn't name. Cars all looked alike to me: small ones, large ones, and trucks. I'd long given up learning the names of them.

So I flipped through my notebook, trying to parse together what I could about east winds. There wasn't much on the subject, not from Egypt anyway. It would be another mystery for me to sink my teeth into and the prospect was nearly as exciting as being here.

Nearly. I didn't think there was anything in this world that could be more beautiful than Egypt.

The ride through the desert felt like the dunes were lulling me to sleep. Wes chattered on, but I didn't hear most of it.

I wondered how many got lost in the desert, the swaying of the sands like the notes of a song. How many ventured off for treasures or in self-discovery? I wondered what my spiritual journey would be like trekking through the desert looking for a miracle.

The radio seemed to hum in my mind and I let the noise carry my thoughts away. My journey was historical, not spiritual, but it would still be fulfilling and important. I'd wipe away years of sand and grime to find something long forgotten–that was worth something.

"Arthur, did you drift off? Wake up, we're nearly there. We're staying in Fayoum tonight, so we can continue on tomorrow. My colleagues arrive first thing tomorrow AM and I want us to get a lay of the land. I haven't been to Fayoum in about a decade, and I'm anxious to see how much it's changed. Progress–that's about the only thing you can count on to keep going these days."

"Isn't the line about death and taxes?" I said, and Wes laughed.

"Ever the scholar, I love it. Yes those too. Certainly the taxes, but here in Egypt death was not always that certain!"

"You don't actually believe in the afterlife and reincarnation and all that, do you Professor?"

"Myth and history, they aren't so different, Arthur." The older man's eyes sparkled, and I imagined him to be quite handsome in his day; he was still a good looking man, but that jawline could have stopped traffic in his youth.

"I think I'll need some solid proof before I start believing in magic," I scoffed, but the hidden part of my heart that still wanted to be Indiana Jones skipped a beat. The wind howled and my arms were covered in goosebumps despite the heat.

"Magic is all around us, Arthur. You just have to be brave enough to *look*."

Wes abruptly turned and I had to grab onto the handle bar inside the old SUV. My heart rammed in my chest, but Wes laughed and gunned it.

"Adventure, Arthur! That's where all the magic is!" He drove us off road and over a couple of smaller sand dunes, making the old car leap over the dunes. The car bounced and rocked and I thought I might throw up, but I couldn't help but smile at Wes's wide grin. The years seem to fade from his handsome face, and I grinned back.

WWID - what would Indy do?

I let out a whoop and cheer, and we drove over the dunes like two reckless teenagers.

***

The hotel was lovely and a tad on the gaudy side, but the decor added to the charm. It was covered in strange hieroglyphics that I could discern no real meaning from. It had a working elevator and air conditioning though, so frankly, it could have been covered in clowns and he wouldn't have cared.

The large elk head on the wall was jarring though. Were elk even native to Egypt? I didn't think so–

"Ah, I see you've met Wallace," the front desk clerk said. He was young, probably close to my age, and would have been handsome if he didn't look like a teenager.

"Wallace?" Arthur asked.

He pointed to the elk and laughed. "He was a gift to the hotel many years ago. No one really remembers where he came from," the clerk said.

"He's quite large," I replied, reaching a hand out to pat the creature's nose. Taxidermy always struck me as overly morbid, but the elk's intelligence was captured in the bust. The shiny eyes and well preserved fur made him seem almost loved–as loved as a stuffed elk head could be.

"Hello! We have two rooms booked for the night?" Wes said as he appeared with his luggage. The worn leather satchel screamed researcher to me—one day I'd have my own weathered set of tools.

"Of course, let's get you registered and your rooms prepared," the clerk replied. I took an extra minute to study the animal before catching up to his professor.

"Wonderful," Wes said. The clerk gave them the standard rundown and handed keys to both of us. Our rooms were across the hall from each other, and the clerk led Wes and I to them on the third floor.

"Well, I'm going to get cleaned up and then we can go find some dinner? I'll meet you downstairs in the lobby around seven?" Wes asked, stretching. That ride across the dunes must have done him in with the way he stretched and cracked his back.

"Sure, although if you'd like to just rest, I'll be fine—"

"I'll text you after a quick nap. This jet lag has still got its grip around me."

I pushed open the door to my room and smiled as I saw the warm yellow room with a very plush, very soft looking bed. My back would probably hate it in the morning, but sinking into a feather-soft bed was always divine.

I quickly showered and shaved—I loved scruff on other men, but not myself. Instead of looking sexy and manly, I looked scraggly and wild. The shower was full of steam when I finally got out, toweling off. The steam cleansed my thoughts and my lungs, and now that I was thinking about it, a nap would be nice—

"What the hell are you doing in my room?" a man said. His voice was hoarse but familiar, and I nearly dropped my towel when I noticed *who* the man was.

William Ford.

"William–"

"Arthur–"

"What are you doing here?" we said at the same time. I pulled the towel around my hips a little tighter. Of course the scruff on *his* face was charming and sexy.

"Why are you in a towel?" William asked.

"Simply *astonishing* that you were the valedictorian when you can't piece together that I was taking a shower," I snapped back at him.

"In my room," William added slowly.

"This is *my* room! Why are you even here?" I gripped the towel as tight as I could. I wanted to cover my chest and torso, but couldn't seem to move. William's eyes raked over me, and I felt my cheeks heating. Was there a slight flush on his too?

"Long story," he replied and flashed that smile that used to make my knees go weak. I remembered every little moment in college when we'd pass by one another or sit nearby and that smile would send little shocks through my system.

God, his lips were red and *split*–

"Oh my God, William, what happened to your face?" I said, stepping closer as if I was brave enough to touch him. I raised my hand but didn't reach.

"Like I said, a long story. Is this room 302?"

"304," I replied, and the realization ran over him.

William was in Egypt. In Fayoum. In his hotel room.

And I was in a towel.

His eyes darted south to where my towel sat across my hips and I might have squeaked. I wanted to die; did I really, actually squeak? I prayed that I imagined it. This was not how this meeting was supposed to go. If–*if*–I ever ran into William again, it would have been at a conference, discussing research over fancy cocktails with silly names and hors d'oeuvres. I'd ask William to grab another bacon-wrapped scallop and he'd agree because we were colleagues and maybe even friends.

It wasn't supposed to be with me half-naked in a towel.

"You're in the wrong room, then," I added. My bare feet made me feel more vulnerable and I felt myself start to fidget.

William's smile made me squirm. "So it seems. Well, I'll be going then Arthur, but we should catch up, once you have some clothes on."

"You are absolutely insufferable–"

"Let's get some dinner together? I'd like to catch up." The softness in William's voice made me pause. His eye was swollen and he wasn't standing to his full height; I remembered exactly how tall he was and how I fit in his arms those few times William had hugged me. There was a hopeful glint in William's green eyes that melted my defenses. What happened in the years since we had been study mates, jockeying for the top spot in our classes?

"I'm free tonight, I was going to go out and explore the city some," I said, throwing him a life line.

"I was looking for a night out on the town too. Has your phone number changed?" he asked, pulling his cell phone from the back pocket of his khaki shorts. God, even his knees were cute.

"No, it hasn't changed. You still have my number?" I said, and William flashed that infamous grin. It had gotten him out of trouble quite often in their college days, and even now, I couldn't even be mad that he barged into my room.

"Yeah, why would I delete it? Who knows when I'd need a brilliant archaeologist on speed dial?"

"Oh, now I'm on speed dial?" I laughed.

"Yep, you've been on my favs list since college. Meet you in the lobby around eight?"

"It's a date," I said, my eyes flying wide as soon as the words left my mouth. "I mean, yes, that's a good time. Mutually agreeable–"

"Some things never change," William said, and turned to leave. He ran a hand through his brown locks and I noticed the ring on his finger. William was married? My mind swirled, but I tried not to gawk at his hand. William slowed as he opened the door, and I felt the pressure change. He was waiting for me to say something more.

"William, how did you get in here? The door was–" I blurted out the words, needing something to say.

"Unlocked. Just like I was expecting. I'll see you later, yeah?"

"Yeah, of course." William nodded and left me there confused and cold and utterly exposed. What the hell was William Ford doing in Fayoum of all places?

***

William was early, sitting with his ankles crossed in the foyer of the hotel reading a newspaper in Arabic. He always had a knack for languages that I had to work for, and it was another reason to find him so damn attractive.

Which I didn't anymore.

Because it had been years since we'd seen each other.

And because it would be ridiculous to be holding onto any feelings for that long.

And mostly certainly not because of that delicious, fevered kiss shortly before graduation. We were drunk and William was just happy, and I was truly *certain* that him grabbing my ass had been a spontaneous alcohol-driven act and there was *absolutely no reason for me to be hung up on this years later.*

So of course I took an extra minute to study William before the smile and the charm came back, blinding everyone around him with that courteous shield. I remembered once, when we had been studying for what felt like days on end, when William confessed that he'd love to just not smile for a whole day. I hadn't caught his meaning back then–what could possibly make William Ford unhappy–but seeing him now, with the warm lighting making the dark circles under his eyes exaggerated, I saw the sorrow in William. I wondered how the years had changed him, and what made him not want to smile these days.

The little slice of exposed ankle was also enjoyable–good lord, was I actually getting aroused from an *ankle*? It had been too damn long.

"Hi, William," I said, forcing myself to get this dinner over with. I felt terrible for canceling plans with Wes, but he confessed that the off-roading actually made him quite tired so at least I didn't have the weight hanging on me.

I didn't want to see William, if I was being honest. The darkest parts of me hoped I never saw that beautiful face again. It stirred up too many complicated feelings–desire and jealousy–and I hated feeling like such an asshole toward him.

"Arthur, you came. I was worried you'd stand me up," he said, extending a hand. I shook his hand awkwardly. Remembering how that hand felt tangled in my hair made my cheeks redden.

"When have I ever stood you up?" I huffed, laughter edging my words. It sounded a tad hysterical to me, but William didn't call me out on it, thankfully. Oddly.

"There was that time we were going to have pizza and then you–"

"One time! I fell asleep! We had been studying for fifteen hours straight!"

"You wound me," he said, holding a hand over his heart, and I laughed again.

"You have always been an overdramatic ass," I said and now it was William's turn to laugh. He held his side when he did and my attention instantly darted to his side.

"Oh, don't make me laugh, it hurts," he said, still laughing.

"Are you going to tell me what happened to your face? And your side?" I asked, and a flash of that sorrow crossed William's face so quickly it shocked me. I took a half step back, looking him over.

"Let's have a drink first before we start trading war stories," he replied, his arm around my shoulders now. "Good to see you have some pants on now."

"You're lucky I had a towel on, I don't normally walk around in one after a shower."

"And how, exactly, does that make me lucky?" he said, sending a dash of heat right down through my belly.

"You are ridiculous," I managed to say, slipping out of the light grip. William let me flee, but had that hazy look still around his eyes. "William, have you been drinking already?"

"Drinking is an overstatement, I had a singular drink at the bar here."

"Maybe we should skip drinks then–"

"I like it when you're not all buttoned up. Come on," he said, tugging my hand and pulling me out into the night. We walked side by side, and I wondered where we headed. Not that I cared, but it would be nice to know how to get back to the hotel.

"You look good," William said, and I nearly stumbled.

"Thank you?"

"Happy, Arthur. You look happy."

"Oh, well, yes I am, I suppose." When William stopped, I thought maybe I shouldn't have admitted that I was happy, but as usual, I was reading into the situation. William stopped to peruse a menu, before flagging my attention.

William got us situated for a table for two speaking flawlessly in Arabic. My language skills excelled at the dead ones–where I didn't have to interact with another living person.

"Should I ask what you ordered?" I asked, settling into my chair. The last week was catching up to me, and I felt the combination of jet lag and shock wearing me down. William Ford sat across from me looking totally acclimated to life here, aside from the black eye, split lip and cheek.

"When did you become picky? You ate everything in college," he said, sipping his water. I watched as he swallowed, his Adam's apple bobbing with each sip, and I felt heat staining my cheeks.

I needed to get a fucking grip.

"I was merely asking–"

I was cut off as the appetizers were brought out. Food was another reason I loved history: it was a physical thing brought from years past to the present for all to enjoy. I wondered what making baba ganoush was like in ancient times and how the spices were traded, how the recipes were passed down through the generations to someone's grandmother today.

"You have that dreamy look again. Thinking about some random historical fact that literally no one knows or cares about?" William asked. He smeared a bit of the dip on some bread and took a bite. I studied how the creamy, savory dip clung to the corner of his lip and quickly made myself a pita.

"Just thinking," I replied and William laughed.

"Definitely a fact no one knew or cared about."

"You loved hearing my random factoids, as you used to call them," I retorted.

"Still do if you feel like sharing." The air was charged with some kind of tension that I couldn't name. It surely wasn't sexual, because that would mean William was actually gay. So that left *delusional*. Yes, the energy around us was completely delusional–*that* I could believe.

"I was thinking about how recipes are living history passed on from ages ago."

"I've never considered food like that before."

"That's because you don't think, you act."

"Is that so?"

"Always has been."

"And a man can't change?" William leaned forward, his elbows on the table. His creamy white shirt was rolled up on his forearms and as the muscles shifted I became painfully aware of that fact.

"Historically? No, men do not change."

"What about me?" he asked, and I heard the shift in his tone, the subtle wobble and I studied those green eyes that I could get lost in.

Braver than I should be–braver than I had any right to be, honestly–I reached up and lightly touched the healing scrape on his cheek. "You tell me."

To my surprise, William didn't flinch or move away. A moment passed, then another, until we were venturing into the unknown area of awkwardness, but even then I was reluctant to stop touching him. His face was warm and cheeks were flushed from whatever he had been drinking earlier. The scrape marred his lovely face and the black eye made the shadows under his other eye more pronounced.

"Nothing escapes you, huh?" he finally said, leaning back in his chair.

"It's what makes me a good archaeologist," I replied, leaning back also. I needed the space, needed the air to not feel so charged.

“So what are you doing here? Are you working or on vacation?”

“Working. I’m here with Dr. Carrington, and we’re going to be heading to a dig site. I’m finishing my field work for my PhD program,” I said. This was truly awkward–telling William about the work that he should have been doing too. After we graduated, I was expecting to see William in all of my PhD classes, ready to continue that mostly-friendly rivalry that drove me nuts in the best ways.

But he didn’t show up, and it made the classes a little less fun. No one wanted to spar with me; the conversations were overly agreeable and I wanted to be challenged. William would disagree with me just for the hell out of it, just to get me riled up and thinking.

“A dig? That’s great. What are you looking for?”

“Anything, everything.” I didn’t want to bring up Wes’ research on the east wind; it seemed more like a fairy tale than anything substantial, and I didn’t want to see the smirking amusement on his face.

It made him utterly too kissable looking.

“What a non-answer. Top secret, got it,” William laughed. The rest of our dinner was brought out and I sighed happily as I tasted each item. A comfortable, familiar silence settled over us as we ate, and I caught myself staring at William whenever his eyes were unfocused and faraway.

“Well, what are you doing in Egypt?” I finally asked.

"Do you remember Zahra? She invited me out. We're both taking a bit of a gap year. Well, years, I suppose," William said.

"And the gash on your face? Is that part of the gap year?" My words came out biting and cruel. I flinched at my own tone.

"Not exactly, no. I got into a fight. You should have seen the other guy," William responded. He didn't hear or respond to the crankiness in my tone, and somehow that made it worse.

"A fight? What happened?"

"Relax, Arty, I'm fine. I'm sore, but that's what happens when you get jumped by four guys with more muscle than sense."

"Four men! Did you go to the police? Or get checked out–"

"Let it go, okay? I promise I'm fine."

"So no, you didn't get checked out. Glad to see you're still stubborn," I muttered.

"There was something I wanted to show you, actually. Since I have a resident expert on hand, I might as well use that knowledge." William speared a grilled piece of chicken and popped it in his mouth. My eyes should not have been glued to his mouth, but I couldn't help it.

"What did you want to show me?"

"Not here, let's check it out tomorrow? How long will you be in town?" he asked.

"I'm here until Monday, then Dr. Carrington and I are headed to the site."

"What a coincidence, that's when I'm leaving too," he said. I was sure it was anything but a coincidence; fate smiled on William like he was the favored, golden child of destiny, and knowing that we had the same itinerary only made my gut twist.

"And where are you heading?"

"I'm working on a dig site too, actually. Day labor, not as an archaeologist."

"But you have the credentials–"

"I don't have a doctorate, and I'm not enrolled in a program. Just a guy with a degree, like everyone else in the world."

"What's the name of the site that you're working?" My heart raced; I already knew it was going to be my site. I could just feel it in my bones.

"I'm going to be at a site about two hours into the desert from here. Zahra and I will be working it. Her cousin got us the jobs."

"Who's running it?" I asked.

"Zahra didn't know. Where's your site?"

"About two hours into the desert from Fayoum."

"Interesting."

"That's a word for it," I muttered.

"I think I'll be seeing you in the desert, Arty."

"Stop calling me that, it sounds weird." *It sounds like that time you drank too much and kissed me senseless.*

"I think it suits you."

"Fine, *Will*."

"Actually, I've been going by Will more often now–"

"You're insufferable."

"There's the Arty I know and love," he laughed and I nearly choked.

"Are you ready to head back to the hotel?" I asked, trying to change the subject. Of course William Ford would be here, on his final dig, aged like fine wine. The lines around his eyes only made him more attractive, like instead of living his life in a library, he was outside in the sun.

"Trying to get me back to your room already?"

"Wh-what are you talking about!" I sputtered and William cackled.

"I'll do my best not to barge into your room. I'll try to knock."

"I'll do my best to be sure I have pants on at least," I replied and that wicked, devastating smile curled on William's lips.

"Now where's the fun in that?"

V

William

Once Arthur was back in his room, I made a beeline for my *actual* room where Zahra was laid out on the bed like a cat taking a nap.

"Where the hell have you been?" she demanded, sitting up. Her hair was a damp, curled mess.

"I've been with Rami and then I ran into an old friend."

"Who?"

"Arthur Lewis is in town. He's going to be working at a dig too. With Dr. Carrington. Do you remember him?" My heart raced as I watched recognition flit over her face.

"You've got to be kidding," she replied, plopping back down on the bed.

"Nooope. Of course the one fucking dig you find and we're gonna be neck deep in dirt with our old college friends."

"*Your* friends. I hardly knew Arthur, and Dr. Carrington annoyed me. Why are they here? Are they seriously on our dig?"

"It's *their* dig. Arthur and Dr. Carrington are running it. There's no way Carrington is here just as a day laborer. He's looking for something."

"Any idea what they're looking for?"

"Arthur didn't say."

"How's your face?" Zahra asked, poking my cheek and lip.

"Still hurts, thanks for checking." I slapped her hand away and headed for the fridge to grab some more water.

"Why were you gone so long? I know you needed to blow off some steam, but like, you've been gone forever."

"Rami took me out for a while."

"Glad you two are getting along," she said and the warmth in her tone made my heart seize. What was she hiding from me? I studied Zahra's carefully, calm face and wondered how I missed her telltale sign of stress: her refusal to smile. Joy radiated out of Zahra like she was made of sunlight, and when she didn't smile–couldn't or wouldn't–something was wrong.

"Zahra, why are we doing this?" I asked, gently, carefully. Her shoulders straightened for just a fraction of a second before she forced that mask of neutrality back over her features.

"To get you out of debt–"

"What's the other reason? There's something you aren't telling me."

"Just because we are best friends doesn't mean I owe you every detail of my life."

"How bad is it?" I asked.

"Get some rest, tomorrow we're meeting up with Rami to get the details of the dig. Whatever's left to learn after running into Arthur-fucking-Lewis, anyway."

"What's your issue with him?"

"Goodnight, Will," she said, and closed the door of our double room. I surveyed the rest of the space: a large-ish couch with a dated accent chair, with a coffee table and a counter by the sink. Couch or floor were my options, and judging how lumpy the couch looked, the floor might be the smarter choice.

My thoughts drifted back to Arthur, back to just being able to laugh without feeling the crushing weight of my stupid decisions hanging on me.

I pulled out my phone and typed out a message to Arthur.

Hey

Hello William

What're you doing?

Resting. Jet lag is awful

My lips curled up in a smile. I liked thinking about Arthur finally relaxing, letting the tension drain from his permanently bunched shoulders. His shoulders hadn't been drawn up after that shower though. He packed on a little muscle too; a little more weight than his rail-thin college days. I noticed the light hair across his chest and the color of his nipples, and how that blush went from his cheeks to the tips of his ears and down his fair neck.

Shoulda slept on the plane

Travel expert, are you?

Gap year, remember? I've spent more time in airports than I have back home

Gap four years, you mean

Ouch, right for the jugular Arty

Why must you call me that?

Because you squeaked when I called you Arty and I grabbed your ass and had my tongue down your throat, I thought. We never talked about that night; I had too many drinks and I'd never told Arthur that I was attracted to him. That massive brain and heart of gold made him utterly fascinating. His slight frame and gentle features didn't hurt either. Arthur's warm brown eyes and soft brown hair weren't really unique, but it gave him a softness that I found intriguing. He had the sharpest tongue of anyone I'd ever met but had the softest eyes. I loved getting Arthur all worked up and frustrated. I could practically hear the huff from his text messages.

Suits you I guess

Please don't call me that around Wes

Wes? Who's that?

Did he have a boyfriend? A girlfriend? I was fairly confident that Arthur was gay, but sometimes my attractions to men were more hopeful than accurate.

Dr. Carrington. Last thing I need is him calling me Arty all around the site and that sticking. Have you ever heard of a professional Egyptologist called Arty?

I think it's kinda cute

The minutes ticked on before Arthur responded. He typed. Then stopped. Then typed again, and I grinned. Oh yes, Arthur had to be positively flustered.

Cute is not how I want to be known in my field

Could be fun

We have different definitions of fun

I bet there's a few things we have in common

Such as?

This felt like a tipping point. Should I push further? See how brave Arthur could be? I remembered the feel of his hand against my cheek tonight, how it lingered. I wanted to lean into that touch but I was sure it would have sent him running.

I can think of a night that we had a lot in common, Arthur

I had to shoot my shot–what was the worst that could happen? I got rejected? It couldn't be any worse than the shit I was in already. I stared at my phone screen, waiting to see the little dots telling him Arthur was responding. It felt like ages before his next message popped up.

Oh

Oh. I grinned so hard I thought the scrape on my cheek was going to reopen. The slight sunburn had my skin overly warm, feeling tight. Of course the sun had nothing to do with why my pants felt that way too.

Mm. Are you blushing yet?

I don't blush that much

Arty

Lying doesn't suit you

You are the worst

You don't mean that?

Of course I don't

Did you miss me at all? You never texted or anything

Neither did you

Fair point, I conceded, but I felt Arthur looking for a way out, and I wasn't ready to give him one. If I never got to kiss him again, I at least wanted to be honest about how good it felt to have Arthur in my arms, pressed against the wall of his studio apartment. I loved that apartment; it was completely Arthur, from the green and blue tones everywhere to the dying houseplants he swore he didn't neglect. I loved the scent of mint in the air and how it always clung to his skin.

Didn't want to scare you after that kiss

Oh

You say that a lot

It's an adequate response, William. Esp over text when you can't tell what someone is thinking

What are you thinking?

I'm thinking about how I thought I had imagined the whole thing, because how the hell was I possibly kissing William Ford in my shitty apartment?

That apartment wasn't shitty

It had roaches and black mold, but you're dodging the subject

Wait, did you want to kiss me?

What do you think?

I thought I was about to go knock on his door to have this conversation in person, but that might not be smart. I needed to start being *smart*. I put my phone down for a second, trying to gather my thoughts.

Arthur wanted me to kiss him. I didn't misread or write it off as a mistake. Arthur wanted me.

I think I should have called you the next day

Yeah, you should have

VI

Arthur

MY SKIN WAS BURNING up and it had nothing to do with the desert heat. I stared at my phone in disbelief. William remembered kissing me. He regretted leaving things where they were?

That was... unexpected.

Something like hope stirred in my chest and I shoved that down. I missed my friend, and that's all that it was. The strain in my pants was just a normal, human reaction to intense emotion–

Knock, knock, knock.

I practically jumped out of my skin at the knock on the door but I didn't get up. I didn't move or breathe. My phone buzzed and I saw the message pop up on his screen.

Arthur, answer the door

I didn't move. This was a horrible idea. William was just going through something. His messed up face was clear evidence. It would be wrong to assume anything at this point–

My phone buzzed again.

I can hear you overthinking

I tossed the covers off and realized I was just in his boxers and a loose, ratty t-shirt. I didn't have time to change, because William was outside of my door, and I could picture it: leaning against the door frame, the muscle in his forearm taunt. His green eyes would be softened by the dim hallway lighting–

Arthur

I dropped the phone and nearly ran to the door, and there he was, leaning against the doorframe just like I knew he'd be. William had excellent posture but was a chronic leaner; the habit hadn't changed since college and I found that detail to be endearing. Maybe things hadn't changed as much as I thought.

"Hi."

"Hi," I said, clinging to the door handle. This wasn't like him coming over to study. There were no books, nothing for me to pin this moment on other than the desire flooding my system and the glint in William's eyes.

"Can I come in?"

I nodded, opening the door wider to let him pass. He scanned the room with my mess everywhere—the clothes, my laptop, an old leather journal I bought because of the aesthetic, and pamphlets from every place I'd been.

"Please," I said and I hated that I heard that note of desperation in my voice. Hopefully William didn't. He wore the same pair of basketball shorts he'd had in college; I recognized the paint stain on the hip from when we painted my apartment. His black t-shirt was fitted across his broad shoulders and the memory of William playing soccer shirtless flashed in his mind.

"I'm sorry I never called," he said, closing the distance between us. When had we moved to my couch? William grabbed my hand and guided me to the sofa, our knees nearly touching as we faced each other.

"You disappeared completely," I said, and there was no masking the hurt. I'd relived that night so many times—the good and the bad—and the only thing I could ever come up with was that William regretted stepping over that line so much he had to flee completely.

"My dad died. I found out the next day, and I disappeared from everyone. It was a year or so before I ran in Zahra around town and she called me out on it. By then, it felt like too much time had passed—"

I held his hand, interlacing our fingers. William stilled, waiting for my response.

"I'm sorry for your loss."

"Thanks, but it wasn't a reason to vanish."

"No, but you've never been one to make rational choices."

William laughed, a sound that I could have plucked from a memory, and he hissed as he held his side.

"They did a number on you, hm?" I asked.

"Could have been worse, they could have stabbed me or something." William smiled, and now it was my turn to lose all rational thoughts. My eyes darted back to William's lips and his pupils were blown even in the low light. I could smell his freshly washed hair and my hands moved on their own, touching his arms and sliding them up to his shoulders before I realized what I was doing.

"It's okay," William murmured, pulling me closer. I was practically on his lap, and I tried to readjust before William situated me on top of him. Reclined against the arm of the couch with me straddling him, I felt like this was just a dream.

"But you're hurt–"

"Not dead though. I'm here," William leaned up so our chests were together, snaking arms around my waist. Desire and need thrummed in my blood and when I shifted, I felt that William was hard beneath me.

Our noses brushed.

"We don't have to–"

"I'll stop when you say stop," William breathed against my ear. A chill shot down my spine making me shiver, and William caressed the smooth skin of my waist, running his hands up the back of my shirt. I sucked in a breath, leaning into his touch, and William's fingers kneaded into my shoulder blades.

"I want to kiss you," I said, the words tumbling out so fast I didn't even mean to say them.

"Then kiss me."

It was all the encouragement I needed, and I cupped his face reveling in the feel of that day-old scruff he hadn't shaved. My thumb stroked across his cheek until William tilted his head back, giving me access to his lips, his neck.

The first press of our lips together was electric but tentative.

Chaste, despite the need between my legs and the hardness at my back.

The next kiss brought us closer, William's hands still exploring the planes of my body. I nipped at his bottom lip, trying to be careful not to hurt him. William groaned so softly I thought I imagined it, but I moved to kiss his neck, up along his jaw, until I grazed the space just below his ear that had him breathing harder and groaning again. I remembered that; I remembered the sensitive place just at the base of his skull that drove William wild. I sucked there for just a moment, just long enough to tell William I knew and remembered him, before coming back to his lips.

William tugged the hem of my shirt, a silent plea, and I lifted his arms to let him pull it off.

"You've always been beautiful," William murmured against his lips and I tipped my head back to kiss him again.

This wasn't chaste or timid, I nipped at his lip again and when his mouth parted, I deepened the kiss. William's tongue met mine and we traded playful, exploratory strokes until I could hardly breathe. I pulled back just to catch his breath, but William pulled me closer again.

But instead of capturing my lips, he kissed my bare chest, peppering kisses along my collarbones and raking a hand down my stomach, stopping just at the waistband of my boxers. He snapped the band lightly, another question, another line to cross and I shook my head no, but just barely.

"William, I–"

"Your body, your rules, Arty. I'm here for whatever is being offered," he responded, sliding his hand away and along my chest, a light tug at a nipple.

"Then kiss me again," I said, rocking back to put more pressure against William's length.

"I feel like you aren't playing by the rules," he gritted out, moving just enough so I felt his body's reaction to me, but didn't push any further.

"There are rules?" I asked, nuzzling William's ear and delighting in the goosebumps that appeared on his arm.

"Don't play dirty," he said, that warm, deep laugh rustling something hidden in my heart.

"Is this allowed?" I asked, returning to that spot that made William melt.

"Mmm, is this allowed?" William replied, pulling back to kiss the same spot with a little more zeal, rolling his teeth against my skin. I shivered, pressing myself against William's chest, trying to get as close as I could.

"And this?" I said, reaching for William's shirt, but feeling him tense. "William?"

"I'm not really all that nice to look at right now, you know because of my side–"

"Let me see you," I replied, and William nodded. He lifted his arms and I removed his shirt as swiftly and gently as I could, and let my eyes drink in every inch of him. William's muscled chest was more filled out now, the lines of his body were deep and defined, like his body was etched from stone. The ugly, purplish bruise splayed across his entire left side, just under his peck to the top of his hip.

"This looks painful," I said, grazing my fingers over the healing injury.

"Only when I breathe or move," he said, that cocky smile splayed across his lips.

"Should we–"

"Please don't say stop. I've wanted to kiss you for the last four years, and I'm not going to ruin that chance because I got my ass kicked in a fight."

"You will be telling me exactly what happened, you know."

"I know. But not now. Right now I want to pretend that nothing has changed except this time I'm sober, and you know exactly what my intentions are."

"And that would be?"

William bucked his hips, his erection digging into my backside. "To be right here with you, however you'll have me."

I wrapped my arms around William's neck, and I felt him shift, until William lifted me up in one smooth motion groaning from the movement.

"Your side!"

"If I have to get the shit kicked out of me to get you to wrap your legs around my waist, it's a worthy trade off." William plopped us on my bed and leaned down to kiss me again.

We were a tangled mess of limbs and kisses, and I couldn't be happier. William nibbled on every inch of exposed skin until I was practically writhing.

And then my phone rang. It didn't buzz, it rang. Which meant that it could only be one person calling: Wes.

"Please tell me you're going to ignore that," William said.

"Can't, it's Dr. Carrington." I got up and grabbed my phone from the couch to answer the call. I felt exposed standing there in just my boxers with William's eyes glued to me.

Dr. Carrington was already babbling by the time I answered, something about how he just found another excerpt on the god of the east wind, but he needed another set of eyes to translate the name. It didn't sound quite right as he toyed with the pronunciation, and he wanted me to look at it now. Right now.

"I was just about to climb into bed, I'll look in the morning with fresh eyes."

"Oh yes, of course. That makes sense. You're probably still quite tired. Yes, yes, first thing tomorrow morning. Breakfast, seven am? Perfect, yes," Wes said, disconnecting the call before I had the change to agree.

"Glad to see he hasn't changed either," William said, propped up on his uninjured side.

"Talks a mile a minute, but he's actually great to work for," I said, sitting on the bed next to him. The spell of lusty kisses seemed to have broken but William wasn't making any moves to leave.

"What does he need you to do?"

"Translate something. He said it didn't look right to him, but honestly, if he can't figure it out, I'm not sure why he thinks I could," I said.

"Because written language was your jam and you're too modest to admit it."

"I don't know about all that."

"Actually, here, there's something I wanted to show you earlier, but I didn't want to bring it out in public." He reached into his pant's pocket and I had a moment where I thought he was going to show me his cock.

I was only mildly disappointed when he pulled out a necklace instead.

The chain was fine and thin, but the gold faded with age. There was a small pendant that dangled when he held it up, and my heart froze. The oval-shaped pendant had to be solid gold, and I knew immediately that the etchings were ancient. The air around us buzzed with energy, and my hands itched to hold it, to examine the fine thing.

"What is that? How did you get it? Why do you have it? Can I look at it?" My thoughts all tumbled out and William grinned, dropping the pendant into my outstretched hand.

"I couldn't decipher what it said, but I thought maybe you could."

I held it like the gold would crumble in my hands. It was still warm from William's body heat. I ran my fingers over the etchings, mentally scolding myself for just *touching* such an ancient relic but it was just in a pocket–it's not like it was being transported gently. The markings were faded and hard to make out, but they didn't look like any word that I had seen before. My mind filtered through every ancient language I ever studied, and nothing. It certainly *looked* like hieroglyphics, but it could be anything, or more likely: nothing.

"I don't recognize it," I said, and William's shoulders drooped. What had he been hoping this was?

"You're sure?"

"Reasonably, but I'd like to study it some more. Can I take some pictures of it?"

William gently took the necklace from my hands, searching my face. I wondered what William saw there as emotions flitted across his features. I wanted to ask what he was so afraid of, but I didn't.

"Sure, go ahead," William finally said, but too many moments had passed and I forgot what I asked to begin with. Anything to get William to keep looking at me like he didn't want this night to end.

"I'll, uh, I'll get my camera."

William slipped the necklace around my neck, letting the pendant lightly thud against my bare chest. The metal had lost its warmth and the chill seeped through my frame. It hung around my neck like a noose, heavy and solid.

The windows of the hotel rattled.

My glass of water wriggled across the little nightstand and crashed to the carpeted floor soundlessly.

William stumbled, and I grabbed onto his shoulders to stabilize us both.

Our eyes met, the nerves of whatever William felt before transformed into genuine fear as we held onto each other.

The rattling intensified, until we both crouched behind the bed, holding our ears and each other. William covered me with his body, shielding me from whatever was happening as his fingers dug into bare shoulders. I felt the thunderous beat of William's heart, and didn't let go, didn't look away from him.

The East Wind rises again, a storm without end, a lover in search of home.

"Did you hear that?" I whispered, but William didn't respond.

The East Wind rises again, a storm without end, a lover in search of home.

The East Wind rises again, a storm without end, a lover in search of home.

The East Wind rises again, a storm without end, a lover in search of home.

"William," I started, but didn't know what to say. The words chanted over and over in my mind, clanging through every thought, every pore and fiber of my brain until I heard nothing else, felt nothing else.

My lips moved on their own, repeating it again but not in English. The words flowed out of me in Egyptian, "*The East Wind rises again, a storm without end, a lover in search of home.*" I knew in my core that that's what came from my lips, but not *how*.

"A lover, lost and alone, feels the East Wind caress his face and knows he will never stop searching."

William replied in Egyptian, wide eyes as the rattling settled.

My hotel room was a mess; the window was broken, the frames came off the wall and shattered, all of my things had been swept away by some invisible wind scattering my things throughout the room.

"What the hell just happened?" I asked. In English.

"I don't know, but you saw that right? You saw the room shaking?"

"Was it an earthquake? Sandstorm?" William took a few long strides to the broken window, carefully stepping around the broken glass.

"Nothing changed outside," he said.

"Nothing? What do you mean? The whole building was shaking."

"Come look, be careful, here give me your hand–"

"I can walk on my own," I snapped. I wasn't sure why I was snapping. A few marvelous kisses shouldn't be enough for me to suddenly be fragile.

"Fine smart ass, come look. Nothing," William sniped back. The pendant heated as I searched for some sign of a storm.

Nothing.

"Ah, damn–" I said, trying to get the necklace off.

"Are you okay?" William asked.

"Yeah, it just felt red hot all of a sudden–"

"Arty, your chest!"

I looked down and saw that there was text scrawling over my pecs and down my left arm. The ink was black as night, unfurling down my arm and soaking into my skin.

I could read it immediately. *The East Wind rises again, a storm without end, a lover in search of home.*

"William–"

"What the hell is going on?" he muttered, his fingers trailing over the symbols as they appeared on me.

The touch left goosebumps in its wake, and I shivered. William didn't stop tracing each whorl and line and I leaned into his touch.

"The East Wind rises again, a storm without end, a lover in search of home," he said against my skin, his lips suddenly just hovering over the markings. When he hissed and leaned back, rubbing at his chest.

"A lover, lost and alone, feels the East Wind caress his face and knows he will never stop searching," I whispered and the text appeared across William's chest too. I watched as the symbols moved down his right arm.

In the center of our palms another symbol appeared: love. The lotus flower was perfectly formed on each of our palms, and I studied mine and William's together. The flowers were mirror images of each other, the stems and blossoms opening on opposite sides. I tugged William's hand closer and saw the recognition flash across his face too.

"You heard it too," William said. It wasn't a question, just simply a statement. William heard the voice too.

"I thought it was just in my head, and then you said the words aloud," I admitted.

"Yeah, you too. I wonder what it means?"

"The East Wind rises again, a storm without end, a lover in search of home. A lover, lost and alone, feels the East Wind caress his face and knows he will never stop searching," I repeated and the text glowed against our skin; the black symbols were harsh on my pale chest, but seemed to compliment the gold of William's.

"Do you think it's because of the necklace?" William asked. It was still around my neck, and I touched the pendant. Without looking, I knew it was glowing too. The heat it radiated seeped through my body, warming my insides while my skin felt like ice. The words echoed through me again.

"Yep, definitely related," I said, trying to remove the necklace. The clasp had vanished and the chain shortened so there was no way I could lift it over my head. William tugged at the chain, but yanked his fingers back when the contact burned us both.

"You think?" he said, sucking on the pad of his middle finger.

"Where did you get this damn thing?" I tugged on it too, and also burned my hand.

"Won it in a card game," William said, his eyebrows shooting up like he realized he said it out loud.

"I didn't know you still played cards," I said. He studied the black eye and swollen cheek. The dots connected themselves and I was touching the wound again.

"There's a lot you don't know about me, Arty."

"I'm starting to realize that."

"Tell me something about you that I don't know."

"How am I supposed to know what you don't know?" I quipped. I stood to put some distance between us–between the kiss and the wrecked room, I felt like everything around me was crashing and breaking. I wondered where I could step, where I could move, what to say before something cut too deep.

"Arthur–"

"I think you need to leave, William. I don't know what's happened, but I need to process this. And I need to try to wash this off of me," I said, rubbing at my bare shoulder. I felt completely bare, but didn't cover myself.

"They're tattoos, they aren't just going to wash off."

"How could you possibly know that?" I snapped, that familiar annoyance rising in me just like when we would spar in class. William stepped into my space, not letting me retreat. He cupped the back of my neck, making me tilt to look in his eyes.

"Watch," he said, and the word was thick on his tongue like it was still stuck in his throat. William released me, and licked my collar bone. I sucked in a breath at the contact as William ran his thumb across the mark. It didn't fade or move. The symbology was intact, still a stark contrast to my paleness.

"See?" he said, and I swatted at him.

"And you couldn't *possibly* j-just try to wipe it off!" I said. The place where William's mouth just was still tingled, like my body demanded another test just to be certain they wouldn't come off.

"Arthur, you were in my lap not twenty minutes ago–"

"Stop. We shouldn't have done... whatever it is that we did. We haven't seen each other in years and now–"

"And now you want to kiss me again?"

"Yes, exactly. What! No, I meant, now we have this situation! Look at the window!" We both did, but the window was no longer broken. I stumbled. Where had the glass gone? The room was still a wreck, my things strewn everywhere, but the glass was gone. I couldn't breathe; did I hallucinate this whole night? The kisses, William here in my arms, the window, the words?

"It was broken, right?" I asked, my voice so soft, that William tugged me into a hug from behind. The solid wall of muscle behind me, the weight of his arms on my shoulders–that was real. This was real.

"It was, yeah."

"Then how did–"

"I think it has something to do with these new tattoos of ours." Our hands fit together so perfectly, the tattoos lining up like words on a page. Or words carved in stone. I looked at the words on me and noticed that they flowed from my chest, down my arm, and across to William. The words on him wound up his arm and finished near his heart.

I flopped on my bed and William fell with me.

"Should I go, Arty?"

Our noses were so close, if he moved an inch, I would be touching him again. That would be a bad thing, wouldn't it? It should be, but I couldn't remember why now. His green eyes were soft and warm. William's breath hit my lips and instinctively, they parted. I couldn't stop staring at him, and I knew I was staring, but William—despite being a pain in the ass—was utterly stunning.

"Arty?"

I dreamt about this moment, hadn't I? So many times, I dreamt of William Ford in my bed looking at me like I was something special, and now here he was.

Tomorrow. Consequences would have to wait until tomorrow.

I threaded my tattooed hand through William's hair, memorizing the feel of him because surely tomorrow would wipe this night away, and I let our noses brush and our lips brush.

If I only had this night, I was going to fall asleep with William's scent on my skin and swollen lips from his kisses. I was tired of waiting for life to happen to me. *WWID.*

When William's sharp inhale broke my thoughts, I let go of any hesitation and deepened the kiss. With deft strokes, I claimed William's mouth, claiming a part of him that I secretly hoped no one had ever seen. This needy, desperate version of William where he was undone and yielding to every one of my wishes.

The tattoos lit up again and we broke apart. I watched how the words for *lover* shimmered and I paused. Lovers. Were we lovers now? Could we be if I took this further?

"It's glowing again," William said.

"Lovers," I breathed, watching the shine fade from our skin.

"I wonder what this means. It has to mean something. I mean, this whole thing is like a myth. Howling warnings, tattoos, shattered glass. It's weird," William said. I barely registered what he was saying because I was too busy watching his mouth move.

"No chance we just had a collective hallucination?" I asked and we both laughed.

"Afraid not. It's getting late, I should go before I end up staying the night," William said. He started to get up and I reached for him again. I couldn't stop myself and I knew I should just let William leave, but our fingers were laced together again.

"What are we going to do about these?" I asked, touching the tattoos. Did I imagine that buzz when we touched again?

"No idea, honestly, but maybe we can do some research tomorrow? I can't think straight anymore," William said, rubbing his eyes. He winced as he touched the bruising, and I simply nodded.

"So, I'll be seeing you tomorrow?"

"I think you're stuck with me for a while. Maybe we'll get to work together in the field. Wouldn't that be fun?" William smiled and I thought that seeing William covered in dirt would be enjoyable. Especially if I got to help him get cleaned up. I blinked *that* thought away and let William's hand drop.

"See you in the desert," William said, planting a kiss on my forehead. The tenderness of such an act hit us both, and William headed for the door before he even pulled his shirt back on.

I toyed with the necklace, letting my fingers roam over the worn etchings. Something stirred in the back of my mind, and then I knew exactly what was written there.

East wind.

VII

William

I TOSSED AND TURNED in bed until well into the middle of the night. Between the lust flooding my system, the new tattoos, watching the hotel shake like a leaf, and Arthur's dazed brown eyes every time I kissed him, there was no sleep to be had.

I tried to scrub the tattoos off. They threaded down my arm and even though it had been years since I studied, I could read every word.

A lover, lost and alone, feels the East Wind caress his face and knows he will never stop searching.

The lotus flower on my palm was stunning; it looked more modern than ancient, and I studied the petals. It wasn't a hieroglyph. The flower was just a lovely drawing etched into my palm. There'd be no covering that one; the rest I could cover under a long-sleeve shirt, but already knew I wouldn't. It was too damn hot and I could always just blame my *impulsive nature* for the new tattoos.

I rolled over on the couch, cursing myself for losing the necklace too. I was just supposed to show it to Arthur, and really, I shouldn't have even done that. But now Arthur had the necklace and it was stuck around his neck. Along with a little, tiny hickey on his collarbone.

A chill ran through me and I let my mind replay the rattling windows, how Arthur clung to me, how I saw something come straight for us at the window. I didn't think that Arthur noticed the face staring at us through the broken glass, and I chose not to bring it to his attention.

Enough weird shit had happened without adding to it.

But still. I saw that pained face. It looked human, mostly. I thought. It happened so fast that I could have just seen a twisted reflection, but there was something haunting in the eyes. Ancient and unseeing–like they searched for something beyond this world, finding nothing.

Sleep would not come easy tonight.

I rolled on my back with my hand in front of my face. There was enough light that I could see the tattoos. They were hieroglyphs, but there was something off about them too. Too stylized, too curled. It reminded me of cursive writing; formal and looping, like the curves on each marking were drawn with a flourish. Like a letter to a lover.

The thought struck me as I looked at the lotus flower. Arthur's looked just like this and when we threaded our fingers together, the petals brushed.

I wondered if Arthur was still awake; I could picture him pacing back and forth, back and forth, chewing on some old ass pen that he dug out of his bag. He'd run his hands through hair and rub his eyes from wearing his glasses too long. The image was so clear, so crisp I felt like he could have reached out to touch him. My phone dinged and I already knew it was Arthur.

I can't sleep. Tomorrow is gonna be a long day.

Were you pacing?

What? How could you know that?

Some habits never change

I keep looking at the tattoos. They make me itch

Highly doubt you're allergic to them, Lewis

Don't be an ass

Go to sleep

Why are you still awake too?

My tattoos itched

Asshole

***

Zahra shook me awake and I nearly headbutted her as I sat up. She leaned back, laughing.

"Easy tiger, we've gotta get up," she said. Zahra was already showered and dressed. The smell of her coconut shampoo was a familiar, comforting smell. I'd spent so much time with Zahra that her routines felt like my routines now. I also loved how my hair looked after I borrowed that shampoo.

"What time is it?"

"Like nine, I figured you needed the sleep. You never sleep in this late."

"Yeah, thanks," I said. I grabbed his phone with my right hand and nearly dropped it. The tattoos. They were gone. I examined my hand, and the lotus flower was gone too.

How?

I pulled my shirt off, looking at my chest and aside from the lovely purple bruise, it was totally clear. Not a single mark on me.

"Ugh, at least go to the bathroom before you start stripping. Rami will be here in about fifteen minutes. Go shower. You stink," Zahra said. She braided her thick mane of hair, but that did nothing to fully tame it. Shorter pieces escaped, framing her face in soft curls. She huffed at them, desperately trying to get them out of her face, but it was pointless. Zahra's hair had a mind of its own and didn't care about her feelings at all.

"You should have woken me up sooner," I said, but she waved me off with a handful of bobby pins in hand.

"Why'd you go back out last night?" she asked, innocently looking away.

"Ran into an old friend," I said. "We had a drink and hung out for a little while."

"An old friend? Please tell me you didn't get tangled up with the Spice Traders again."

"What? No, it was Arthur."

"Arthur, of course."

"What's your issue with him?" I asked and I didn't like the edge in my voice. Zahra was entitled to her opinions. Even if they were wrong.

"I just never liked him. He was a stuck-up prick to everyone, *especially* you, and yet you act like he's the best thing ever."

"Arthur was just–"

"Being a dick, yeah, but it's fine. Us plebeians are used to being looked down on," she said, rolling her eyes. The braid was as secure as she was going to get it. "Go shower, seriously, you reek. Whatever you got into last night, it didn't agree with you. You smell like a crypt."

"So sweet of you," I said as I headed into the bathroom.

"And don't use up all of my shampoo!" she shouted down the small hallway.

In the shower, I was able to look at myself closer. I took stock of the cuts and bruises. They looked better each day, but my ribs were still a mess. Another couple days, I won't look like I got into a bar fight.

But it was my chest and arm that held my attention. The tattoos were completely gone. I traced where the hieroglyphs should have been, and as I trailed my fingers on them, they reappeared.

I nearly slipped in the shower.

I ran my hand over my arm and they popped back up, like the water had activated them. I rubbed my arm again and they faded. I balled my fist, picturing the lotus and when I unfurled my fingers, it was back.

I needed to talk with Arthur. Immediately.

I washed at record speed, the soap likely still a sheen on my skin as I vaulted out of the shower. When I reached my phone, there were several messages from Arthur.

Did the tattoos disappear?

What the hell is going on

Okay seriously, what's going on, bc now they're back

JK.

Wait

They're back

I need to photograph them in case they change.

What direction is your lotus?

Dammit William, this is not the time to go MIA

I laughed, and rubbed my arm, the heat of my other hand making the tattoos bloom across my skin like a hidden message.

There! Happened again. So strange.

I stopped laughing. I applied pressure to my shoulder, lifting my hand to see more of the marks.

Now my shoulder

I called Arthur and he picked up on the first ring.

“I need to see you,” I said, pacing the small bathroom. I pressed a kiss to my palm and watched as the lotus flower unfurled. Arthur’s steady breathing hissed through the speaker of the phone.

“It’s activated by touch,” Arthur said.

“Yeah, I think so too.”

“Let’s test it. What did I touch?” Arthur asked, and I scanned my image in the steamed up mirror. I didn’t need to see it though, now that I was paying attention, I felt the barest touch ghost over my shoulder.

“My shoulder.”

“So, as long as we don't touch it, it should be fine?”

“Right.”

“There’s a logical explanation to this,” Arthur added, and I smiled. I knew the look on his face even without seeing him.

“Sure there is.”

“There’s a logical explanation to everything, William. You just have to look for it. I’ve got to go, I’m meeting Wes in a bit.” Arthur hung up and I was left in the bathroom with nothing but my thoughts.

VIII

Arthur

William Ford was in my bed last night and now there was a disappearing tattoo scrolling down my arm. It was a coincidence. It had to be. Everything could be explained with logic, with facts. And the facts state:

William kissed me.

A lot.

William handed me an illegally acquired artifact made out of gold.

The chain was new.

The pendant was not.

My window was smashed, a feral scream erupted through the room, and then everything was fine.

Except it wasn't.

"Arthur, you are fucked," I breathed out, plopping down on the couch in my room. Where William was last night, holding me in place as he kissed along my jaw–

Those thoughts were not going to help anything today. Wes was already waiting downstairs. God, I prayed that William didn't do anything stupid like leave his room or show up to meet Wes.

It shouldn't matter that I was completing my PhD and that I was the one invited here; deep, in the ugliest parts of my heart, I knew Wes would be elated to see William. Would he secretly wish that William was leading this expedition instead of me?

William was the better student, naturally gifted and charismatic. All of the professors loved having him in classes with his brilliant observations and easy smiles. I was awkward and worked my ass off, and it was finally paying off.

Except now he was here, about to crash into the first expedition that I was leading. Co-leading, technically, but it was a supervisory role and that was a big deal. As was the fact this would complete all of my fieldwork requirements and be enough to complete my thesis. The start of my career was in grasp and seeing William again made me realize how easily it could all slip through my fingers.

PhD or not, having William Ford on my dig site was going to be a pain in my ass.

I stuffed all of my things in my backpack, grabbed a wide brimmed hat to shield the Egyptian sun, and shuffled out into the hallway.

It had been years since school; William's life wasn't going the same direction as mine–wherever that might be, really–and I wasn't still the awkward kid that I was back then.

Wes was in the lobby as predicted with all of his gear ready to go. One day, I would have a pack like his, filled with dig tools with my initials on them and enough supplies to survive for weeks in the desert.

"Arthur! Good morning! Are you ready? I caved and ordered an American breakfast sandwich, got one for you too. Sometimes the little comforts of home are the best parts of the day!" Wes said, thrusting a bagel sandwich at me.

"Where did you find these?"

"Hotel kitchen, actually! Come now, let's get going. We've got a solid two hour drive to prep the site."

"When are the day-laborers coming to start work?"

"Not sure, we'll have to work all that out with the folks here. This is the less exciting part of being in the field: dealing with all the red tape and the people."

"You love dealing with people," I countered, taking a bite of the sandwich. The cheese was heaven.

"Dead ones, yes, love them. The living ones? I could take them or leave," Wes laughed and patted me hard on the shoulder. I felt the tattoo coming up under my shirt. A soft tingle that spread down to my forearm.

"Can't wait to get started," I said, meaning every word.

"I've done more research on the myths of the east wind, but coming up empty. I'd still like for you to take a look at this translation. It's just not sitting right in my head. Otherwise, nothing really concrete anywhere. Maybe we'll find something once we get out there."

"You think so?"

"There's always something to be found, Arthur. You just need to know what you're looking for."

With that tidbit of wisdom, Wes strode out of the lobby and headed for our car. I followed him and caught a glimpse of William out of the corner of my eye. At least, I thought I had; I turned, expecting him to be there, but I was alone in the lobby with only silence around me.

My skin itched, and I rubbed at the tattoos, watching them splay down my arm. I'd need to document them more thoroughly before I could start researching. My mind was in too much of a haze last night to do anything else. I did a few searches for the words that played on repeat in my mind, but nothing came up.

Nothing came up when I searched the words etched onto William either.

The SUV was abysmally hot at seven-thirty in the morning. So much so, that Wes turned the car on, rolled the windows down, and blasted the AC. I don't think I've seen the man sweat before, but there were little beads forming on his brow.

"I've been thinking about this dig," he said, and I sensed the tremble in his voice.

"Hm?"

"There's something just not sitting right with me about it. Nothing popped on aerial photography or even with LiDAR. The university was approached by a donor, which happens of course, but normally it's some pie in the sky. Some lost tomb of a pharaoh or other such nonsense. But we're going to be searching for what exactly? Maybe it's just my old bones not being thrilled to spend my days in the sun."

"You're hardly old, Wes," I said, but I noticed the lines around his eyes and the wisps of silver in his hair. He never seemed *old*, just wise, but watching him stare out into the distance, I saw the age creeping up on him.

"You're either very kind or blind, but I'll take it nonetheless. Let's hope we find something about this east wind. Grab my journal and take a look at my latest notes. That translation is going to drive me nuts."

The car cooled down enough that we could get in without boiling, and I immediately pulled out my phone and his journal to start searching again. Nothing popped from our library's databases, or even just on a regular search engine. Wes' notes were scrawled on yellowed paper with hieroglyphs I hadn't seen before. It also looked phonetic, but even that didn't seem right. He huffed when I said as much, but I kept staring at the text.

Wes drove and the silence was easy. My eyes ached from staying up too late thinking about what happened with William. Equal parts the tattoos and the way his lips felt against my skin. I closed them just for a moment to rest.

The East Wind rises again, a storm without end, a lover in search of home.

A lover, lost and alone, feels the East Wind caress his face and knows he will never stop searching.

The words echoed again through me and I startled awake. The radio told me that I'd been asleep for nearly two hours and we were pulling up to the site. It was already alive with energy; people buzzed back and forth that I worried we were late.

"Glad you got a little extra rest, you looked a little wilted this morning, Arthur."

"Yeah, stayed up too late," I said sheepishly. The tattoo peaked out from my lightweight, long sleeve shirt. I rubbed at it to get it to fade, but it only seemed to make it darker, standing out like a beacon on my too-fair skin.

"Arthur, come on! I have a few things for you," Wes called, and I jogged from the SUV to catch up to him. He was halfway across the site, waving me down like an air-traffic controller. *Heaven help me*, I thought to myself, pasting a grin on my face.

"Meet one of my favorite colleagues, Dr. Irina Romanova. She's been a dear friend for the last, what, thirty years?"

"God Wes, you age me!" she laughed, lightly smacking his arm. They embraced, hugging so tight I heard the air puff from Dr. Carrington.

"Nice to meet you, I'm Arthur Lewis. I'm a PhD student with Wes," I said, offering a hand. Dr. Romanova hugged me instead. Her braided blonde hair was tied in a crown around her head with little wisps of hair escaping around her ears. She had a lovely tattoo of lavender flowers on her arm, just near her elbow. It was small and delicate much like the rest of her. I wondered what she would think of the sprawling thing on me.

"I arrived last night and met with the local gov. They already had a crew ready to go, so I started gridding out the area. We've got a large section to work! I've got about seven squares outlined already and we should have another five to have a full twelve by twelve area. Let's get you guys set up," she said.

"You're an angel," Wes said. His eyes were practically twinkling as he looked at her.

"What's the story there?" I asked, careful to keep my voice low.

"Ah, that's a tale for later. Preferably with beer and a good fire. But while Irina gets the rest of the grids ready, there was something I wanted to give you. Here," he said, opening his large pack. He pulled out a crudely wrapped box. The paper was sand-colored as was the twine wrapped around it. It looked like a gift from the 1900s, but that somehow added to the charm. Of course Wes would wrap a gift in plain brown paper and twine.

"Thank you," I said, and he motioned for me to open it, waving his hands.

I tore at the paper carefully; I refused to let the trash slip away and become litter in this pristine desert. He took the crumpled paper as I opened the box. A brown hat sat on top of a smaller box.

"You hide it well, but I know how much you love the adventure of archaeology. It's why we all start, I think. You needed an adventurer hat." I took it out and swapped it for my sunhat. It fit perfectly, and for a split second, I imagined being inside a hidden temple encased in gold, surrounded by treasures the world had forgotten.

"How did you know?"

"Because we've all muttered *what would Indy do* at least once," he said, the smile on his face so loving it nearly knocked me over. I opened the next box and opened a pouch full of tools, just like his. The pouch felt like genuine leather, and the handles of each pick and brush were a lovely polished wood. The trowels had the shimmer of newness, and the rolled up packet of baggies and pencils was tucked neatly into the largest pocket.

"I don't know what to say," I replied honestly. It was my first, real set. I'd borrowed tool kits from other sites, but this was different. This was graduating from student to peer, and my eyes welled up.

"You have the head for this, Arthur. Never forget that. The days are long, but the years, they go by fast. Enjoy the ride. This set will last you for a while. I lost the first set I ever had and I've regretted that from the moment

I lost them. There's something special about your own kit."

"Thank you, Wes, truly."

He patted me on the back, and there was so much pride on his face that my chest felt like it would burst. I hugged the tool kit to my chest and thanked him again.

"Nice hat," a voice said from behind me, and I shot up, standing ramrod straight. No, absolutely not–

"My god, is that William Ford? Surely, it can't be. My eyes must be playing tricks on me." Wes shook his hand and pulled him into a hug, laughing. The moment between us seemed so far away now, watching him be giddy with William. I scanned him, looking for any flicker of last night, any evidence of the heat between us. The lotus flower opened on his palm and my cheeks flushed.

"Good to you see, Dr. Carrington," William said, his eyes sliding from Wes to me. And there it was–there was the heat, the intensity.

"I'll have you know, this hat is iconic," I said, letting the challenge roll off my tongue.

"Iconic? Looks a bit outdated, but it suits you, I guess." William's lips twitched up in an almost-smile.

"What are you doing out here?" Wes asked, stepping back so he was in line with me. The wind picked up, rustling William's hair and kicking sand up around us. I batted it away but William didn't even flinch. The ass.

"I got hired on for this dig site. Not as an archaeologist, just part of the labor crew."

"Well that's nonsense, you're a trained professional," Wes snapped and my spine stiffened. No, no, no, he wouldn't *possibly*–

"Hardly a professional," William cut in, but it wasn't a true objection. The smirk on his face was evidence of that.

"You'll just have to join us as a junior associate. Arthur here is leading this dig, and I'm just here to guide if needed. It's his show, so you'll be answering to him. I think it'll do him some good to have a familiar face! William Ford, as I live and breathe. I thought you were lost to the wind," Wes said, laughing as he waved us to follow him. The wind picked up again, like it was pushing William closer to me.

"You planned this," I hissed under my breath.

"I didn't. I was just going to say hi and then lay low–"

"Bullshit, Ford. If you wanted an in back into this world you could have just asked me," I snapped. That familiar goading sparked between us, and I watched the emotions play across his face before that damn competitive streak settled on his brow. I could read him like a book, and he knew it.

"I'm not here to make trouble for you, unless that's what you're looking for," he said. When did he step into my space? The wind shoved at his shoulder, the current sparkling and *visible*, until I braced to catch him.

"What was that?" I whispered, heart racing. The contact made my stomach flutter and I bit down a curse. This man was insufferable.

"Just the wind, Arthur. And you weren't complaining about me being so close last night."

"Oh no, noooo sir, we are *not* going to talk about what happened last night here. This dig means everything to me and we are not going to have a repeat of that. So just cool it," I said. I nearly tripped over all of my words and he just smirked. That infernal, fucking *smirk*.

"Whatever you say, but I think the wind has different plans." The tattoos reappeared on my hand, and when I pulled my sleeve up, there they were again. The dark, black lines appeared on William too as the wind caressed my cheek. No sand moved, not even William's hair rustled, but I felt the breeze against my cheek, soft like a lover's touch. Like William's touch.

A rumbling in the distance drew our attention, but no one else reacted. There were people everywhere–working to set up the grids, the tents, moving supplies–and not a single person turned toward the sound.

The East Wind rises again, a storm without end, a lover in search of home.

A lover, lost and alone, feels the East Wind caress his face and knows he will never stop searching.

He will never stop searching.

Never, never, never.

"William–"

"Yeah, I heard it too," he said.

"Meet me in my tent later, and we can talk about it. Right now I need to catch up with Wes and get the assignments scheduled."

William tapped the brim of my hat, pushing it down to my glasses, and said, "What's my assignment, boss? Should I follow you?"

"Doesn't seem like I have much of a choice," I muttered, and the wind blew through my hands, curling around my fingers.

"That's really weird," William said.

"You see it too right? The little shimmer?"

"Yep. Weird." He headed off in the same direction that Wes did, toward the only standing tent. It was a huge dome, designed to be our home base. It was sturdy despite being technically a tent; a solid wooden floor had been secured and the curved walls were reinforced with thick tent poles. Soon there would be several more set up over the grids and smaller ones for on-site residences. Most people would head back to their smaller towns, but for the main archaeological team, it was too far to commute daily. Wes promised periodic hotel stays for breaks, but I didn't care. This was what I was made for, what I dreamt of.

"You coming, Lewis? Wouldn't look great for the boss to be late."

"This is going to be a very long assignment if you're going to be this irritating."

"I'm a delight, and you know it."

"Debatable," I said, my tone as deadpan as I could make it.

"Guess I'll have to convince you." I jogged the short distance to catch up to him and push ahead, making it into the dome just ahead of William. He smelled so good despite the heat, clean and fresh. I didn't even want to catch a whiff of myself, knowing that would certainly *not* be the case.

"Are you sure that we don't have enough, Irina?" Wes asked. Dr. Romanova and Wes both huddled close, chatting over some documents at the folding table.

"We're going to have to double up; there's more folks that decided to stay on site. It'll just be until I can order more tents, but it might take a minute for them to arrive."

"Ah Arthur, come introduce William to Dr. Romanova. And I've got great news! Since we're a bit low on space, you two will need to share a tent! I figured since you were such good friends in college, this was just another smile from the universe!" Wes clapped his hands, clearly pleased. *You've got to be fucking kidding me.*

"And we will bunk together too, just like in the old days, huh Wesley?" Dr. Romanova said. His eyebrows nearly hit his hairline.

"I thought we would be bunking together, and William can just stay in his own tent," I said, and Wes smiled at me.

"This expedition isn't made of money, Arthur. So, we all have to bunk with someone, besides you'll have more fun with someone your own age instead of an old dodger like me." I saw how his eyes sparkled that he would be with Dr. Romanova, and knew the battle was lost.

"If you think that's best–"

"I do. Lovely to meet everyone. Arthur, I'm going to need you to get started on the grid assignments–" Wes elbowed her, and she stopped. "I mean, that's what I would recommend, if I were in charge," she said with a wink.

"Sounds good, would you like to go over it with me?" I said and she smiled wide.

"Smart man."

"William, since we're officially roomies, can you start getting the tent set up and moving our stuff into it?" I said, not looking at him. I couldn't stand to see that smirk again.

"Aye, aye captain."

VI

William

ARTHUR WAS TOTALLY IN his element, working side by side with Dr. Carrington. It stirred something in my chest to see him so engaged. Gone was the shy, timid guy from college. Arthur stood in the sunlight completely at ease with himself.

Mostly.

I shouldn't blow kisses or wink at him to see his cheeks redden, but I never claimed to be a saint.

Zahra would vouch for that; she hasn't spoken to me since we arrived. She set up her tent across the site from me, and has been busying herself with working on the grids. Currently, she was holding a tent pole in place so more domes could be erected.

"You get the tent up yet?" Arthur said. I didn't realize he had snuck up on me and I jumped. The shine in his eye told me he was pleased, so I licked my bottom lip, forcing Arthur's eyes down. The blush was my reward.

"Yep. Even rolled out the sleeping bags. There's not much room with all of our stuff inside, so the bags are close."

"How close?" he asked.

"Close."

"William–"

"Oh calm down, I'll behave if you do." I flashed him my best smile, and Arthur rolled his eyes, shoving me out of the way to go into our tent. Our shared tent. Our tiny, shared tent.

"I can't believe we're sharing," he muttered.

"Don't be too excited," I said, the sarcasm nearly dripping from my words.

"It's not that. It's just with the tattoos and this," Arthur gently pulled the pendant from his shirt and the gold made my breath hitch. There was something different about it. The gold shimmered in the sunlight and the tattoos bloomed down my arm so intensely that my skin felt like ice.

"Shit, what was that?" Arthur hissed, dropping the necklace to scrub at his shoulder. I zipped the tent and pulled up my shirt. My skin ached, like it was starting to blister. Arthur fumbled at the buttons on his shirt, but his hands trembled.

"Let me," I said, reaching to unbutton it for him. Arthur rubbed at his palm, and I noticed the lotus was gold now. I untucked his shirt, lifting it off of him, and when my hands rubbed over his bare skin, he shivered. Did I imagine that he was closer to me now? The tattoos were no longer in Egyptian, but a mix of English and Arabic. The words on Arthur were in English, but now they were in Arabic on me.

"They changed," I whispered, tracing the words from his shoulder down his arm. They repeated, wrapping around and around starting at his collarbone. I brushed my fingers over it, and our hands found each other.

"How did that happen?" he asked.

"I don't know," I said, baffled at the beautiful looping script across his body.

"I meant our hands," Arthur said, barely a whisper. I tried to pull my hand back but he squeezed it tighter. Arthur raised them to his heart, and the back of my hand touched his chilled chest. How was he chilled in this weather?

"You can let go whenever you want, Arthur."

"Smartass. I *can't.*" We both tugged and our hands wouldn't budge.

"Okay that's a little weird," I admitted.

"I didn't even reach for you, you were just *there*," Arthur protested, yanking on his arm. Nothing happened, except he jerked me around too.

"Okay, stop, let's be logical. You're good at logic," I said, trying to soothe myself. Arthur held my right hand, my dominant hand, and I struggled not to use it.

"We're past logic, William. Magical wind shattered my hotel window but then, just kidding? It's fine? Magical disappearing tattoos that also just change shape? And now I can't let go of you!"

Wind rattled the tent, blowing so hard that we tumbled onto the sleeping bags. Arthur landed right on top of me, his weight a solid blow, making the impact hurt my aching ribs. The air rushed out of me and I saw stars. Whatever healing had happened over the last couple of days was just reset from Arthur landing on me.

"Oh god, William, are you okay?" he said, checking my ribs, gently pressing to the bruised and tender places. It took every ounce of willpower not to groan. My ribs fucking *hurt*.

"Yep, great. This doesn't hurt at all," I said through gritted teeth. My vision had gone black, stars dancing at the edges as I breathed through the pain. If I didn't have a broken rib before, I sure as hell did now.

"I'm sorry," he said, cupping my face.

"Don't get all mushy on me now, Lewis."

"William, look at our hands," he said, and I realized then that he was cupping my face with both hands. His thumbs ran over the edges of my bearded cheeks, and he felt good settled against me. I twisted just a little so the pressure was off of me, and Arthur laid his hand on my shoulder.

"Don't get used to this. I'm just here because the wind pushed me."

"You can get up at any point."

"Not sure I trust the magical wind to not shove me into the floor," Arthur laughed. I laughed. My arm burned this time, the skin so hot I thought it was going to fall off of me, and watched as the tattoos shifted again.

"Why does that hurt so damn much?" I hissed, and Arthur lifted my arm, rotating it so he could examine the tattoos again. I sucked in a breath when he turned my arm a little too far, sending pain shooting down my ribs. Moving wasn't fun. Breathing wasn't fun. Arthur deciding I was his next research project? Also *not fun*.

"I don't recognize this language," he said.

I didn't either; was it even a language? The tattoos were all loops and swirls, cascading down my arm toward the unfurled lotus blossom on the palm of my hand.

"Do they change every time we feel that wind? Or is there another trigger?"

"Let me try something," I said, sitting up slowly so Arthur and I were side by side. Arthur raised an eyebrow, studying every movement. Shirt or no shirt, being pinned by that look from Arthur left me feeling completely exposed. My pulse raced, every beat of my heart and breath I took rippled through me. Just a kiss, just a chaste, simple kiss.

I brushed my lips against his collarbone, where the tattoo started and he sucked in a breath.

"Just a kiss, Arthur, relax."

The tattoo faded where my lips were.

"Fascinating," Arthur murmured, poking and prodding at the place I kissed. So I nudged his hand back and kissed his shoulder, his bicep, down to the crook of his elbow, and forearm, until my lips grazed the back of his hand.

The tattoo faded completely.

"It likes affection?" I said, and noticed how Arthur's pupils practically spanned his whole eye. The heat flush across his cheeks made that smattering of freckles stand out. I wanted to kiss them again, this time just to see how far that blush would spread.

"It isn't sentient. It's ink. Or something similar."

"Arty, I think it's magic."

"Nonsense, maybe it was just the temperature of y-your lips," he stuttered. This was the tipping point in the argument; once Arthur started to stutter, I knew I had him on the ropes, so I nuzzled against his ear. I sighed as softly as I could, watching him shiver. The lotus was still on his palm, so I flipped his hand up and pressed another kiss to it. The petals closed, and Arthur watched with wide-eyed attention. Either at me or the flower, I couldn't tell. So I kissed him again, and the petals grew lighter, fainter. One more kiss, lingering for just a second longer, and the lotus was gone too.

"Are you going to kiss away my tattoos, too?" I asked, and Arthur huffed.

"Insufferable. Absolutely, *insufferable–*"

"It might just be easier to admit that you're attracted to me, and we can move these little tiffs along faster." Arthur bolted upright, nearly colliding with the curved side of the tent, huffing and puffing as he pulled his shirt back on.

"We need to get ready for dinner. Wes and Irina and everyone is going to be looking for me, and probably you now too," he said.

"So no, to the kisses? Should I wear a sweater?" I leaned back, my ribs screaming for me to stop slouching.

"You always did look nice in a sweater," he said dryly and exited the tent before I could say another word. The light from my phone caught my attention, and I wondered how I even had signal out here. The number was unknown.

How's that payment plan coming along?

My heart froze. It came from a blocked number, but I knew it was Annatto. It had been just a few days, but the interest was piling on by the minute. It was easier not to think about it once we got out of the cities, but there was no escaping it. Him.

There had to be a treasure here, something valuable enough to pay back my debts.

Or I had to find a way to pry that necklace off of Arthur.

***

Zahra finally decided I had been punished enough for remembering Arthur existed and sat with me at dinner. There were some long picnic tables set up by the main dome. The makeshift kitchen had its own space, but everyone ate outside. With all of the lamps and the fire burning, it felt cozy.

"Still mad at me?"

"I'm not mad, I'm annoyed. Having connections is great but not when we're in the process of trying to steal shit."

"I still hate this plan."

"I hate that you have a gambling problem, and yet, *here we are*," she said, stabbing at her sausage. It was some form of kielbasa, but it tasted like ash. I choked down as much as I could, but there would be no compliments to the chef tonight.

"I never said this had to be your problem too."

"Yeah, well, two birds, one stone, and all that."

"So you're ready to talk to me about your own issues now? That you're doing a shit job at hiding?" I nudged her shoulder and she gave me a weak smile.

"Soon, yeah. But not tonight?"

"Soon works for me. I'm patient, it's one of my many virtues." I stuffed another piece of the over-done sausage in my mouth and forced a smile.

"This really is wretched," she laughed. Arthur caught the corner of my eye and I couldn't help but turn. He had ash smudged on his forehead and his glasses looked grimy. There were no visible tattoos, but I still itched to touch him to see if I could get them to respond.

"Yeah, terrible," I said, the words trailing off like my eyes trailing after Arthur. His soft brown hair was matted with sweat and I swallowed hard as he ran his hands through it, swearing under his breath at the tangles. He'd smell like burnt barbeque tonight if he didn't shower–and probably even if he did, that shower didn't inspire confidence–and I'd still want to run my fingers through his hair.

"You're practically drooling, honestly, William, what has gotten into you?"

"Scratching an old itch, I guess," I said, and wondered if that was all it was; a lingering attraction. Arthur was prickly. Annoying. A tad rude when pressed. A know-it-all, even though I outranked him in college. Ohh, how that killed him. I knew it did. My lips twitched up. Whatever it was, Arthur Lewis was *fun*, and that was something I was sorely lacking lately.

"Annatto texted me," I whispered and every muscle in Zahra's body went stiff.

"How do you know it was him?"

"Doubt there's many blocked numbers that text me about payment plans," I muttered. I couldn't force down the rest of the sausage. The rice wasn't fully cooked either, so I speared a piece of the veg and popped it into my mouth. No idea what it was; the vegetable lacked all semblance of what it once was and took on an unusual, crunchy, ash-like consistency. I took a large swig from my water bottle and swished it around my mouth.

"Could be a fluke," she said, but even Zahra didn't buy her own lie.

"Yeah," I said. We sat in silence for a minute before Zahra nudged me with her foot.

"Rami will be joining us in a few days. He said he got delayed, but he's going to join soon." Now it was my turn to go rigid. How much did she really know about her dear, ole cousin? I owed him a good punch to the jaw for the shit he dragged me into. The weight of my phone felt like a brick in my pocket, the threat of that text replaying. Rami was supposed to make things easier, but this was all turning out to be too much.

"What does he plan on doing here?"

"Helping us," she said, and just like that, Zahra stood to scrape the burnt remnants of our dinner from her tray. "I'm cleaning up tonight."

"Zahra, I think we should just stop–"

"This is happening, William. One way or the other." She headed off toward the kitchen tent. She didn't look back even when I called out to her. Dr. Carrington and Arthur chatted by the entrance of the dining hut, pausing as Zahra blazed past them. Arthur cocked his head, studying her; I wondered how much he remembered about Zahra from college. She wasn't in many of our classes, but she was always around. Arthur probably didn't even clock her presence.

Our eyes met and I saw the stain of heat on Arthur's cheeks. Dr. Carrington's broad smile waved me over and the intensity rolling off of Arthur could have cooked me like the sausages.

"How was dinner?" Dr. Carrington asked and I grimaced.

"Great, if you like shoe leather."

"It wasn't that bad," Arthur huffed.

"Ah, you'll get the hang of camp cooking soon enough, Arthur. We all botch our first few meals, but I'll help you tomorrow. I'm going to retire for the night. Irina wanted to review the grids and I had some papers to cover with her. Maybe she's heard of this east wind that kept popping up. Maybe she's seen the mythos before or has a better idea about that damn translation," Dr. Carrington said, muttering to himself as he headed off.

"You made dinner?" I laughed.

"You try cooking a hundred sausages over a tiny flame," he shot back, arms folded and ready for battle.

"Did you tell him about the tattoos?" I asked, and Arthur shook his head.

"This site is supposedly connected to the god of the east wind, but we've never seen anything about him before in any of the research we've read. And until this," Arthur fingered the pendant hanging around his neck through his shirt, "I didn't think anything of it. But now, it just feels too coincidental."

"Yeah," I said lamely. Arthur's mind was at work, the dots and pieces connecting in a way I could never keep up with. Sure, I could score higher on a test but there was something fascinating about the way his mind tore through information like ripping apart a threadbare cloth. He barreled through information until everything was laid before him, exposed and ready for examination.

When he leveled that calculating gaze at me, the hair on my arms rose.

"I don't believe in coincidence. We're going to talk through every detail of this," he said, and the tattoo bloomed at this collarbone.

"I've already told you everything," I said, and the lie felt thick in my throat.

"No, you haven't." Arthur left me standing there as he headed for our tent.

I'd already showered, put everything away, and walked the site twice. There wasn't much else I could do aside from head back to the tent.

But still, I didn't.

The moon was full tonight, and the light poured over the desert. I walked until I was alone under the moonlight. Silence hung in the air like a weight around me, and I felt it pushing me down into the sand.

God, there were so many stars.

The sky was illuminated with them. Between the moon and the stars, it was bright enough that I didn't need a flashlight to find my way around. The camp was behind me with the vast openness of the desert ahead. I sat down heavily, letting the coarse grains rub against my skin. I'd need another shower now–another way to put off going back to the tent.

It wasn't that I wanted to avoid Arthur; I just didn't need him ripping out all of my truths for him to examine and dissect. He'd come to some clinical diagnosis, forgetting that those little truths and facts were the fabric of myself.

I didn't know how much time passed as I watched the sky. The stars shifted slowly and the color of the sky slowly changed from an inky black to a softer, midnight blue. The breeze had me chilled even though it wasn't actually cold. Sand brushed against my arms and face, the grit a reminder of how raw everything still felt. My body still ached from Annatto's goons, and that text earlier sat heavily in my thoughts. How had he reached me?

"What are you doing out here?"

Arthur had found me already, coming to sit next to me. "Watching the sky," I said, and Arthur turned his attention upward. It was like he never realized to look *up* and see what was right in front of him.

"Stunning," he said more to himself than me.

"Yeah. We could spend all night counting stars and still never know how many there are," I said.

"Kind of like your freckles," Arthur replied. His eyes went wide like it dawned on him that the words came out.

"I doubt I have millions of freckles. Maybe a couple thousand. And you're one to talk, you have loads of freckles."

"You've never wanted to know how many freckles you have?" he asked, and I laughed. Arthur cocked his head again, cataloging this response for him to dissect later. Probably while we laid side by side tonight.

"Never crossed my mind, really. Same with the stars. I don't need a number to know that they're beautiful."

"That much I can understand," he said. My phone buzzed and it was another unknown number. I declined the call but Arthur noticed it and waited for me to explain.

"It's nothing," I said, and he raised an eyebrow.

"Nothing is usually something. I should head back, Tomorrow is going to be busy," he said, but I grabbed his hand.

"Just stay a bit longer."

"Why?"

"Because I'm asking you to stay."

"Why?"

"Because, because I just want you to!" The wind picked up then, a shimmer of gold fluttering to life around us, wrapping around my hand and Arthur's, curling up his shoulder until his eyes shone gold too. They were not Arthur's eyes: gold and full, they held no recognition, no warmth, no snark. The grip on my hand tightened enough to hurt, and Arthur's face was as impassive as stone.

Only an idiot would try to run from a predator, and right now, that's what Arthur was. That cold, assessing gaze grazed across the desert, through the tents before we finally stopped at the edge of camp. The wind rustled around us, Arthur's fingers dug into me and I flinched. His attention snapped to my face and I froze. Those sharp, unseeing eyes made the blood in my veins run cold. His smile was forced and wild, so different from the Arthur that laughed when he was uncomfortable, or when he knew I was winning the fight.

I had no idea how we got back to the site, but I stood at the front of the encampment with Arthur holding my hand so tight the bones felt like they ground together. I didn't dare breathe, because this version of Arthur was foreign, feral. The glint in those gold eyes sent fear dancing down my spine.

"I want you too," he said, and his voice had changed. Deeper, darker. *Ancient.* The words cracked on his tongue like they were of ash. Golden wind swirled around us, and he stared right through me.

"You want me? Like, in what way, because I like things to be perfectly clear–"

Gold-eyes Arthur surged toward me, releasing my hand but grabbing me, yanking our bodies together, until his lips brushed against the shell of my ear. His breath was icy, just like the rest of him.

"Beloved, I want all of you," he said in the cracking, darker voice.

"Arthur," I said, and his body rippled, the wind washing over us in a ferocious gust until Arthur collapsed in my arms. He was limp and clung to me. His breathing was labored with a sheen of sweat on his brow.

Sounds of people broke the spell between us and I helped Arthur stand on his own. He looked like he'd just been hit by a truck. His eyes were his normal brown and I could have fucking collapsed with relief at seeing them.

"Tent. Now," I said, and he just nodded.

The breeze picked up and we both stilled. It was a regular breeze; no golden wind, no golden eyes. I put space between us, stepping away to give Arthur a chance to breathe. His hands shook, and I wanted to comfort him, but not out in the open. Not where his mentor might see, or worse, Zahra.

Our tent was on the other side of camp and Arthur's feet shuffled along, kicking up sand everywhere.

"Are you okay?" I mumbled, and he nodded blearily.

"Just tired," he said as he stumbled. I caught him, my ribs protesting, but I didn't let go of Arthur. He was going to pass out. So I looped my arm around his waist, and pretended we were drunk. I wobbled, pain shooting up my side, plastering a shit-eating grin on my face. Arthur shuffled along, looking every bit the half-asleep drunk guy.

Workers and site staff glanced our way, but lost interest quickly. I hurried us across the site until our tent was just a few feet away when Arthur perked up, able to stand on his own.

"Thanks," he said, ducking back into our tent. He'd hung up some lights, and it made the small area feel a little larger. The fairy lights didn't help with actual lighting, but they were soft and with the glazed look on Arthur's face, a little romantic.

"Trying to seduce me? It'll work. I'm easy," I said, laying down on my bedroll. The cot shifted, adjusting to my weight. Arthur knelt next to me and the coldness was gone.

"What happened?" he asked. Arthur's voice was barely a whisper. I groaned, sitting up as carefully as I could manage.

"Your eyes changed. They turned gold, and you weren't... you."

"Did I hurt you?" he asked, picking up my hand. He examined every inch, touching me like it was broken.

"No," I lied; he did nearly crush my hand, but there was so much anxiety and fear etched into his face, I didn't want to add to it.

"What happened?" he asked again, and I didn't know what to tell him. I didn't know either; he was Arthur and then he wasn't.

"I–"

"It was the necklace," Arthur said, and it responded with a soft glow like it acknowledged the recognition.

"I think we're in deeper shit than we realize," I said, and Arthur simply nodded. Words felt so far away. What was there to say?

He peered out of the tent, watching as the rest of the camp had gone totally silent. The desert was silent like the world no longer existed. When Arthur zipped up our tent, it felt like he closed the door on the rest of the world.

"Tell me what's going on. With the calls. The bruises. Everything," he said, and I laughed.

"Just because we're in this shit doesn't mean you get auto-access to the rest of my shit. I got into some debt and that's all you need to know."

"That's why you're here? Just to work then?"

"Yep," I said, popping the p. Arthur took his shirt off, stretching. His lightly-muscled frame was so damn appealing to look at, but the attitude was less-so. I felt the snarl about to come from him, the readying for a verbal spar. His mind whirled and I watched the emotions, the thoughts, playing out across his face.

"You're a terrible fucking liar, Ford," he finally said. Arthur slipped an old, beat up college shirt over his head and got into his side of the bed. The cots were practically on top of each other; we had just enough room for them and Arthur's research. My bag was stuffed under the cot. It barely fit; I had to take out most of my clothes just to get it under the tiny bed and had them laid at the foot of the bedroll.

"And you're a space hog. Did you really need all that shit?" I said, gesturing to his table with the laptop. We didn't have power strips, so how was he powering the damn thing anyway?

"I wasn't expecting to have a roommate."

"Aren't you lucky?"

"Oh yeah, super lucky. Sharing a tent with William-fucking-Ford with a curse hanging around my neck. Absolutely *peachy.*"

"You weren't complaining last night," I spat and he rolled over to face me. Arthur had taken his glasses off and he looked utterly kissable. The nosepiece had left little indentations on the bridge of his nose, and I smiled.

"That was a mistake–"

"It wasn't."

"You're unbelievable."

"Sorry, *why* exactly are you upset? Because I got the impression that you didn't hate me, at least not when I had my tongue down your throat."

He poked me in the chest, his finger stabbing at the muscle of my pec. "Because this is the biggest opportunity of my career and you just waltz right in and end up in my tent. You're not even in school and yet *here you are.*" He scrubbed a hand through his hair, breath shuttering.

The tattoo was so black on his fair skin. This was probably tan for Arthur; I remembered how pale he was in school with his nose always in a book.

"This shit doesn't just come naturally to me like it did for you. I have to research and study and *work.* And I do it because I fucking love it, and I get that doesn't mean shit to you, but this," he said waving his hand toward the excavation site, "this means everything to me."

"Despite your glaring ego, I'm not here to get in your way, Arty. I'll keep my mouth shut and follow your orders." His shoulders softened a bit, and I decided to press my luck. My fingers moved on their own, trailing over his cheek bones. "*All* of your orders."

"For chrissakes Will," he laughed.

"I like it when you call me Will."

"Yeah?"

"Better than *William-fucking-Ford*," I said, doing my best to imitate his voice.

"I don't sound like that."

"Yeah you do."

"Do you try to be this annoying or does it just come naturally?"

"Another gift, I suppose." We were facing each other now, our knees practically on top of each other. His oversized shirt dipped low and I saw the patch of skin where the tattoo started. It was just images now–no text.

"It's changed again," he said, nodding to me. I rolled up my sleeve and he was right. Flower petals cascaded down my arm. Pretty, but not really the vibe I'd choose for myself.

"I wonder why it changes," I said, twisting my arm to look at all of the flowers. Lotus blossoms unfurled and shed their petals everywhere.

"No clue. I'd still like to know how to get this thing off of me. Then we can figure out the dancing ink."

"What's your tattoo now?"

"Not sure. It looks like a temple, but not one I've seen before." I tugged at the hem of his shirt and Arthur stilled.

"Take your shirt off, let me see it."

"Will–"

"I'll behave, god." Arthur lifted it over his head and I studied the tattoo without touching him. Touching felt like a step too far right now with this fragile peace. Arthur was all thorns, and I didn't want to get stabbed. Again.

The tattoo was a monument for sure; there were tall pillars that didn't look Egyptian to me. It looked more Greco-Roman, but the hieroglyphs that stacked and weaved across his arm were definitely Egyptian. The same familiar words repeated over and over again on his arm, forming like a path to the lotus on his palm. The flower was sealed up now, and I thought that was fitting for him right now: Arthur curled in on himself, trying to protect whatever it was that he felt the need to keep hidden.

"This temple doesn't look Egyptian to me."

"It does, see the shaft? That's clearly Egyptian. And the capital looks like–"

"A lotus," I said and Arthur nodded. "Do you remember what you said to me? When you were... not you?"

"No, I don't remember anything. I felt like I was trapped in a tiny box. I could hear you, but I couldn't see you. Or anything, really," he said, with his voice trailing off.

"You called me 'beloved,'" I said. A creeping blush rose up Arthur's chest and warm satisfaction built in mine. He was so damn cute when he was flustered.

"Beloved? You're sure?"

"Yeah Arty, you were inches from my face. Not like I could have missed it."

"Ah. Well, I'm sorry."

"Don't be too nice, it's weird," I said. Arthur reached for his shirt but I stopped his hand. His fingers were cold despite the heat, and the blush intensified as he watched me with careful eyes.

"What're you doing?"

"You're the one in charge, Arty."

"And you're just going to do whatever I say?" his voice deepened, and I watched as his eyes dipped to my lips. His nipples peaked and there were goosebumps all over his chest. I wanted to plant a kiss right on those sensitive little buds, but I didn't move. Would he jump if I licked his collarbone? That thought made me smile, and Arthur leaned forward. It had to be subconscious; Arthur would never give me the satisfaction of admitting he wanted to be closer.

"Whatever you say," I echoed and he swallowed hard. I watched his throat bob, begging for attention.

"So if I asked you to take your shirt off?" I tugged it over my head and tossed it on his laptop. That earned me a glare. He scanned my torso with savage efficiency.

"Done."

"And if I said that you should come closer?" I started to scoot over to him, Arthur leaning back on his arms, letting me climb into his space. His breath was against my lips again and I smiled.

"I'd accommodate."

"And if I said I wanted you to kiss me again?"

"Oh, that's an easy one," I said, already threading my hands in his hair. Arthur's mouth was already parted, already waiting but I teased him with little kisses. Gentle, barely there flutters against his mouth until he made an annoyed noise. His breaths were shorter, tickling my lips. I pressed another kiss to him, a gentle, playful tug on his bottom lip.

"Like that?" I asked, wanting him to tell me what he wanted. Demanding it. Our foreheads touched and his skin was so flushed that the heat from him had my heart racing. My arm behind his back cradled him close to me, pinning him.

"Well–"

"Have to be clear with your orders, Arty." I nuzzled against his ear, nibbling on his earlobe until the tension in him started to melt away. Until Arthur's arms snaked around my neck.

"Kiss me," he said.

"Where?"

"Anywhere, everywhere," he breathed, nudging me to his lips, but I didn't follow. I kissed along the column of his throat until I got to lick the hollow of his collarbone. He gasped, and that urged me on, sucking softly until a tiny moan escaped.

"Here?" I asked, rolling my teeth against the tender spot. He'd have a hickey tomorrow, and I grinned thinking about it. The wind rustling his shirt just enough for Dr. Carrington to catch a glimpse of what Arthur had been up to.

"Yes," he sighed, and I moved to the base of his throat, letting myself explore every inch of him. How many times had I dreamt of him while we spent the nights leaning over the books in college? *Too many, you idiot*, I scolded myself. Now wasn't the time for memories; it was time to make them, and damn did I want to memorize every moment.

"Maybe here?" I said, rocking back so I could trail my lips and hands down his body. He was hard, and shit, how far would Arthur let this little game go? There was a wildness to him now that I didn't know; this needy, demanding Arthur was so different than the man always in control. Well, at least pretended to be. Arthur was a controlled trainwreck.

"Will–"

"Gotta be precise, Arty. I'm not good at following directions." He laughed, his voice so rough it went straight to my cock. "You should always call me Will."

"I think you should take your pants off," he said. The words came out so fast, so hurried, I nearly didn't hear him. He sat up on his elbows, breathing hard. Those luscious brown eyes were all pupils. After I unbuttoned my cargo pants, Arthur's eyes were glued to me. His attention was always so unsettling. I was naked before him even with my pants still on. A breeze picked up between us, and that's when I noticed his arm.

The tattoo changed again; the buildings were gone and now there were lotuses just like mine. The patterns matched, and I wondered what that meant, if we were in sync with each other. Our minds certainly seemed to be.

"You think? Or are you sure?"

"I–"

"Arthur, are you still awake? Something's happened at the site," Dr. Carrington called from the outside of our tent. "Arthur?" He tried to knock on the tent flap, but it made no sound. I rolled off of Arthur and he grabbed his shirt, tossing it over his head so fast I wondered how many times Dr. Carrington had nearly walked in on him.

"Yeah, I'm awake. I was getting ready for bed," he said and that smirk nearly knocked the wind out of me. *Oh, two can play this game.* I palmed myself through my pants; a long, slow stroke that made Arthur's eyes go wide. I blew him a kiss and his glare was so sharp it could have cut me.

"Well, put some pants on, man. I think we've already had a break in," Dr. Carrington said. His voice was already fading, and Arthur froze. He looked at me, and I got up too, head bumping on the top of the tent.

"A break in?" I asked, but Arthur was already on his professor's heels.

"That didn't take long," he said, as I raced to get my clothes straightened to follow. My phone rang again, and I checked the message. The night air felt like I had stepped out barefoot in the middle of winter. The site was alive with activity, people chatting and bustling around. The message was only two words but that was enough.

Found you

The Spice Traders knew where I was. They knew about the site which meant something even worse: they knew about Arthur. And Zahra. Every face that passed by, heading for the main building was a blur. I wondered which one of them worked for Annatto.

Dr. Carrington was about ten feet ahead of me, shuffling and kicking up sand. Arthur was just behind him, and I wished I hadn't left the tent. There was too much commotion so late at night–it was past midnight but the site was lit up like it was morning. People buzzed around, and I tried my best to look as nonchalant as possible. I didn't want to draw any more attention, but I knew this was because of me.

The main building where Arthur and his professors were chatting had large slashes in the tent walls. Some had crisscross slashes, opening the panels of the tent completely. The research table that had the map of the grids was gone; what would they want with that? Nothing had even been found yet.

"What the hell happened?" Arthur said, his voice carrying. The workers, the staffers all hurried away from him. Arthur raked his hands through his hair, and I felt so powerless watching him.

The dome was trashed; it would have to be completely rebuilt, and I doubted there was extra funding for that. Considering Arthur was bunking with me instead of having his own space as the lead researcher spoke to how dry that funding well was.

"Ghouls," Dr. Romanova spat. Her hair was a mess but still somehow lovely; the blonde braid was mussed and she had hair sticking out but her rosy cheeks and fierce blue eyes scanned over the tent the same way that Arthur scanned over me. Ruthless efficiency; it had to be a trait of the job.

"Grave robbers? We don't even have any artifacts yet," Arthur said. His tattoo had faded again and it felt like a stab in the heart. Not that it should matter. Not that it *did* matter.

"Just means we need to be extra careful with anything we do find; somehow this site is already on the radar of at least one group of scumbags. We need to secure all of the research and anything we find. I don't care if we only find a piece of pottery the size of my thumb nail, I'll be damned before I lose anything from this site," she declared and the warning clanged through me. Zahra's idea was quickly going to shit.

"Agreed, Irina. It looks like the grid map is missing, but we can make another one. Everything needs to have a backup. No one wanders alone. Stay with your tentmate. We'll announce the new rules first thing in the morning," Dr. Carrington said as he took a small step closer to Dr. Romanova. There was so much tension between them, that if they didn't have sex to get it out of their system, I was going to need to jack off just to function. Arthur's eye caught mine as Dr. Carrington spoke, and I wondered if everyone around us felt the same way. Could they see the tension between us? If the wind caressed Arthur, that lovely little hickey would be visible, and was it wrong that I wanted everyone to see it?

"How can we fix the tent?" Arthur asked.

"Duct tape, of course. It fixes damn near anything, and it'll have to do until we can make it back to town this weekend. I'm not wasting a tank of gas to have a nice looking tent," Dr. Carrington said.

"Well, let's get to work," I said, and their attention all snapped to me. I was good at not taking up space when the occasion called for it. Arthur noticed me though; his gaze was locked on mine.

"Tonight?" Dr. Carrington asked me, and Arthur's brown eyes glittered in the overly-bright dome.

"Just tell me what to do, Arty. I'm good at following directions," I said, my lips twisting up in a smirk.

"Catch," he said, tossing a roll of duct tape towards me. "Do you need me to spell out how to tape the pieces together so the tent isn't flapping?" That sharp, delicious tongue of his has heat flooding my belly, racing right to my cock.

"I'm a quick learner, but I know where to find you." When the Drs. were turned away, I blew him a kiss and he gave me the finger.

X

Arthur

THE DOME HAD BEEN repaired by the time I woke up. William and a few others worked through the night, trying to get everything back to normal. He crawled back into our tent around three in the morning.

Not that I was waiting for him.

Or even still awake.

William just filled the space around him, and his oppressive presence filled the tent, waking me.

It had nothing to do with William stripping down to his well-fitted boxers.

He was still asleep, no blankets covering his mostly-naked form. William's body was a work of art; chiseled muscle and washboard abs, William Ford looked like he could have stepped out of an underwear model catalog, except for the bruising. All he was missing was the tiny smug grin–

"You should just take a few pictures so you can stare at me whenever you want. What's that saying? Take a picture, it'll last longer?" he said, stretching and sitting up in our shared tent. What kind of fucked up karma had us sharing a tent?

"You really are an insufferable ass," I said, but I was staring. A picture wasn't a bad idea, really. Maybe I'd stop acting like a teenager with a crush if I could just stare when the whim struck. Not that it struck often, of course.

"And I can see you thinking about taking a picture. At least get my good side," he laughed. I tossed his balled up shirt at him. William left his clothes strewn about the tent like he had done some strip-tease before bed. My cheeks warmed when I realized he sort of *had* stripped before the commotion last night.

"Get dressed," I said, trying and failing for my words to have any heat behind them.

"Here," he said as he grabbed my phone from my bed. William flicked open the camera, tucked an arm behind his head and snapped a few pictures of himself biting his lips. It was disgustingly hot, and I had no time for it this morning.

"Gimme that!"

"What's the plan today?" he asked. William tossed my phone back, and I caught it with William's half-lidded expression still on my screen. I closed it before I could study the edges of his jawline or how his beard seemed thicker this morning than yesterday.

"Working, you know that thing you're pretending to do here. I've got the grid assignments up."

"Are we working together, roomie?"

"Why don't you go check?" I said. For once I'd have the last laugh with William.

***

William huffed and puffed under the sun while I stayed in the relatively cool research dome. It looked like shit; the walls were duct taped together and light filtered through the canvas casting odd shadows everywhere.

I wanted to be in the field too, digging and searching through the grids. After not sleeping most of the night, I read through all of the mythology I could find on the east winds. There admittedly wasn't a lot.

With the attack on the site, and then the necklace hanging around my neck like an anchor, I needed to do something. The words from the pendant tumbled around in my mind like a spell I couldn't break.

"The East Wind rises again, a storm without end, a lover in search of home. A lover, lost and alone, feels the East Wind caress his face and knows he will never stop searching."

Nothing turned up on a search engine, and nothing matching that description fit any of the mythos around the east wind. Aside from being a destructive force, it was just that: wind. I rubbed at an ache in my shoulder, kneading the muscle, and felt the shifting tattoo again.

Closing my eyes, I focused on the sensation. The ink moved under my skin, like it buried deep into the tissue, before it resurfaced. I felt each letter, each twist and edge, of the text reemerging on my arm. This time it was in English. The lotus bloomed and I pressed my thumb into my palm hard, but the lotus didn't react.

William popped his head into the tent, jarring me from my thoughts.

"Hey," he said. He was sweaty and his hair stuck to his face. Why was he so beautiful even when he should be disgusting? My heart pounded so much that it felt like the pendant shook. Wind stirred all of the papers on my desk; I wrote everything down, because writing gave my thoughts and ideas a physical being that I could hold and look at. The story was easier to see once I could hold it and piece the scenes and the research together.

But the wind in the tent didn't care. It shimmered gold and my blood turned to ice. It settled across me and for a second it felt like William ran his fingers through my hair, like he had me pinned to the bed again, his weight a calming, welcome presence against me.

"Hey," I said back, but William was already next to me. His green eyes were wide and luscious. He watched me like I was something precious and my heart—dear god my *heart*—raced so hard, it thundered. It beat so hard my ribs rattled around, shaking me through my core.

The wind swept around us, tucking us into a corner of the tent, and my hands were on William's chest, dipping under his shirt.

"Hey, woah, Arthur, what's going on–"

His words were too far away for me to care about. I needed to see him. All of him. I needed William to be laid bare, his heart open and beating, pulsing with warm, warm blood that meant he was here and alive–

"Arthur! Snap out of it, what the hell–"

William's brow was furrowed; what was he so concerned about? There was nothing to worry about here, not when the wind held us close, not when there was no one else in the world that would dare take him from me.

Not when William Ford was no longer a lover lost and alone.

The wind swelled and I felt the power of it; it buzzed through me, filling my head with energy. I was alive, alive, *alive*.

"Arthur, look at me, stop. You're destroying the tent. Your research. Can you hear me? Come on, Arty, you're the one in charge remember? How're you gonna boss me around if you can't even hear me?" William's voice broke and I watched his lips moving. Why did the words sound like I'd never heard him speak before? His voice was so distant, so small.

"Will?" I said, but my voice was not my own. It was deep and gravelly, so different from my normal voice.

I clawed at my throat–tried to–but my arms weren't moving. They didn't budge.

I couldn't move.

"Beloved, you are no longer lost. You are no longer alone. I'm coming home now. You can rest, the search is done."

Fear sizzled at the base of my spine, and I saw it reflected on William's face. I stroked the side of his face and William froze. He didn't dare move and I couldn't stop. He knew this wasn't me right? He could feel the shift in the air between us? He felt the wind.

The wind!

"I'm not lost," he said. William's soft tenor voice wrapped around me in a hug, and I felt the tension fading. "I'm not alone."

"You are not alone any longer, Beloved." My mouth moved on its own and the words tumbled out.

"I'm not alone, Arty," he said, and the wind rushed out of me. The tent expanded and stretched before the wind slipped out too, and I nearly collapsed. William's arms encircled my waist, and my weight sagged. The heaviness that hung in my chest was suddenly gone, and I felt like the last moments were some distorted dream. William was here, and I was here, and I was me again.

"William–"

"Yep, got it, you're back to normal. The tent is trashed again. We need to at least make it look like we didn't do this before someone sees. Then we need to talk."

"I thought I was giving the orders," I said, trying for a joke, but his face had hardened. William let go of me so fast I almost stumbled. He was right; it was trashed. What had I done? I knew in my gut that this mess was my doing.

"We can play that little game later. Right now, we need answers before we get any more fucked than we already are."

"What do you suggest?"

"I was hoping you'd have the ideas, Arty," he said. William prodded at his ribs again, and my hand was on his side before I could stop myself. He winced, but didn't back away.

"You really should have seen a doctor," I said. William stood statue still, letting me poke and prod. The tent could wait; this need to make sure he was okay overwhelmed all of my senses.

"Arty, I'm fine. It'll heal. Let's get this cleaned up before you lose your job. I've been digging all day and haven't found a damn thing."

"That's generally how it goes, yes. It's not a race, Will. You don't just make a life-altering discovery every day."

"This is why I could never be a real archaeologist. Too impatient. I need that instant gratification," he said, flashing that killer smile that made my knees weak while setting off an ire only he could muster. Why was everything about this man so irritatingly attractive?

"You start on that side, I'll get my research sorted. Wes's stuff is always a mess, so I doubt he will notice anything." We worked to tidy the tent, letting silence fill the space between us. I liked that; the need for constant chatter, constant input was so utterly tiring. But William didn't shy away from the silence; his over the top charisma was more of an act than anything, and watching him rest was more comforting than any words could be.

"I think between the commotion last night and the rush of starting the dig, he wouldn't notice if a sandstorm swallowed us whole." William ran a hand through his hair, shaking out whatever tension gathered between his brows. It was like watching him mentally reset: I saw how the stress smoothed over his shoulders, softening and releasing his jaw, eyes that fluttered closed with a breath so deep it dragged him back down to earth from wherever his mind had been floating.

When William opened those green, green eyes again, his attention was laser focused on me. I refused to squirm under his scrutiny, but my cheeks heated. "The people that I owe money to, I think they know I'm here."

He wasn't resetting so much as he was covering himself in a mask; William's face was icy cold, none of the warmth or charm I was getting used to. "What aren't you saying?" I asked.

"I think they trashed this place looking for me."

"But why–"

"Because money is a helluva motivator, and working on a dig site means access to potentially high dollar stuff."

"One problem at a time," I said, and I tried to get myself to believe it too. It was only three in the afternoon, and there was still time to work. I could join his grid to dig–this was my site, and I could technically work anywhere I wanted. Our hands were casually linked, like this was something friends did. Colleagues. College buddies. Nothing more, nothing at all. When did our fingers reach for each other? The pads of his fingertips were calloused and the touch skin tickled. I pulled my hand away, and William didn't react. Of course he wouldn't. There wasn't anything to react to.

"I'm joining your grid. I'm just going to grab my tool set and then I'll join you in a few?" William nodded and headed out of the tent. All at once, I felt the weight of the afternoon pressed on me and I wanted nothing more than to crawl in my bedroll and pass out. Before I could escape from the dome, Dr. Carrington popped in. The dark circles under his eyes worried me, but I didn't say anything.

"Arthur," Wes said.

"Hey," I replied.

"Are you alright, son?" he asked and I paused. Was I alright? No, not particularly, but how do you say that you might be haunted, going crazy, or in over your head without seeming unfit to run this dig?

"Yeah, just a lot on my mind," I said. It wasn't a lie, and that was something. Having to lie to Wes didn't sit well with me, but whatever was happening with the necklace wasn't something I could share yet.

"I saw William coming from the tent and he looked... well, upset, I suppose. Did you two fight?"

"What? No?"

"Something is bothering him. I think you should check on him."

"I'm not his keeper, Wes."

He held his hands up in surrender, that irritating smile that said "*but son, I know more than you do,*" firmly in place and said, "Never said you were, but you are his friend. He looks like he needs a friend, Arthur."

He needs a swift kick in the ass, I thought.

"I'm going to join his grid in a bit," I said instead, and Wes patted me on the shoulder. That bout of familiarity brought me back to my college years again, when it was the three of us having spirited debates, but now it was just the two of us, with William off living a life that didn't involve the history we all so loved. How did he walk away from all of this so easily?

"Good lad," he said, and went over to his research. The pile of papers and notebooks was haphazard at best, but just as I suspected, he didn't notice the mess. Wes's office was a constant state of chaos, regardless of location.

"How's Dr. Romanova?" I asked, not sure why I was pushing it.

"She's great. I needed to get out of the sun for a bit, but Irina won't take a break until someone carries her off the site. She's still digging."

I hesitated, but wanted to get his opinion on the words that kept playing in my head–and in William's. But this felt like it wasn't just my secret, my burden, to share so instead I smiled, and headed for my tent. This would be the first time I used the tools that Wes had given me, and even though there was so much I didn't understand happening, I wanted to break in those tools. I wanted to claim this set as my own, using them on the dig that would be the official start of my career.

My tools were just where I left them in our tent, sitting on the small desk I had tucked into the corner. Not that there was much else it could be, but still, seeing the desk with the two bed rolls made the tent feel like a home.

Arthur, stop that thought train before it derails, I chided myself. The heat had to be getting to my head. I was already exhausted when I reached his assigned grid, and now I was cursing myself for putting William in a grid without any shade.

William was sweating, his white tee clinging to his chest, as he brushed layer after layer of sand and dirt away. The workers had removed a lot of the top sand early this morning, and now we were closer to the soil where we'd start the stratigraphy process. Soil sampling was absolutely necessary but it was about as interesting as, well, dirt.

His focus was wholly on his work, and that might have been sexier than the way his shirt clung to the edges of his biceps, or stuck to his shoulders. The tool set was a comfortable weight in my hands, and when I dropped down in the excavated grid, William smiled at me. Not the boisterous grin or the smirk with charm practically dripping off of him, but the soft smile he so rarely seemed to give to anyone.

This man would be the death of me, or at the very least, an exasperating heartache.

"Have you been taking samples?"

"I did actually go to school with you, remember," William said.

"Are they labeled–"

"By location, time of sample taken, soil characteristics, and nomenclature I made up for the hell of it." William wagged a vial of sand in front of me and his neat, tiny handwriting on the label reminded me of the summer we did some field work on the northeast coast of Maine. He was bronzed and lean, evidence of too much partying written on his face with the deep bruise under his eyes. William covered his grassy green eyes with heavy shades back then, but now the bruises on him weren't from late nights and too many shots. Now it was too many hits–someone attacked him and he was smirking like the same asshole he always had been.

"Glad you remembered something from school," I said, knowing damn well his mind was a steel trap.

"I was the valedictorian, after all–"

"Alright, give me the samples. Maybe we can start dating them."

"A few kisses and you're already talking about dating? Arthur, Arthur, Arthur, you're going to make me blush."

"Just keep digging," I snapped, knowing that I was the one blushing. I couldn't hide my emotions with my fair complexion, and he knew it. William raked his knuckles across my cheek bone, and I froze–we were out in the open, anyone could see us.

"We can have that dating conversation later, maybe once I've showered and have you pinned to the bed again. You're a lot more agreeable then."

"Whatever the hell I did in a past life to deserve this must have been truly terrible," I deadpanned. William's bark of laughter sent little sparks of electricity and joy through me.

"We've got like at least four more hours of daylight, so if you're done lecturing, start digging," he said. I handed him a water bottle and to my absolute dismay, he didn't drink it. William opened the cap and splashed the water on his face, letting it *drip all over him* and more importantly *the spot he was digging*.

"What the hell are you doing!"

"It's water. I'm hot. I know you aren't getting a math degree, but this should be obvious."

"You're getting water on where you're working!"

"Water isn't going to hurt the dirt, Arty." I was going to strangle that gorgeously long neck. He seemed to sense my ire fading and crossed the small grid until we were nearly touching again. Why were we always so close? How did William enter my personal bubble so easily, like he had just decided that's where he belonged? His hand skirted the hem of my shirt and just the slightest brush of his fingertips across my skin lit a fire in me. I never should have kissed him–this was crossing a line we couldn't walk back from, that we couldn't pretend never happened. The kiss was too good, felt too fucking good, for either of us to turn away.

He was so close now. William was only a few inches taller than me, but when he shifted his weight, leaning heavily it seemed like more.

"We're going to talk about that little incident in the tent, right? Because we can either do it like adults, or I can just," he said, lowering his voice and getting right next to my ear, "pry it out of you."

"Why are you like this?" I said, shoving him back a bit. My heart fluttered, but William only grinned.

"Because fucking with you is nearly as fun as kissing you."

"Aside from some dirt, have you found anything?" I asked, putting distance between us again. Why did I work in this grid? There were two others that were being excavated at the same time. I could have been learning with Dr. Romanova, but I chose to hang out with this idiot. It's not like we wouldn't be stuck together all night. There were plenty of other opportunities to talk about what happened in the research tent, and yet, here I was, digging myself deeper in this mess.

"Nothing," he said, and knelt back in the dirt to start brushing away more layers of the sand. The sand composition hadn't really changed, and I wondered if we needed to go deeper into the sand. My mind started cataloging all of the varying known soil types in the Egyptian desert. This grid was about six feet deep. The walls of the grid were packed tight; wooden beams supported the area and the sand oddly cooperated. There were physics and other things at play, but watching the grids stay together always felt like a feat of magic–this was why I studied history, not anything related to math.

I unfurled the tool kit, and the smooth wooden handles were sculpted beautifully. Wes gave me a kit that would last, and I marveled at the craftsmanship. The brush handles were stained a dark red, and had Arthur Lewis engraved in them. The picks were a brushed nickel, and I smiled at how the matte finish made it seem aged. They would lose the patina over time. It would be fun to see how the finishes faded and changed, how use and choice would tell the tale of my career, and what my hands favored while working. One day, would this kit be something a historian would be excited about? Would they see these tools and feel a kindred spirit?

I grabbed a trowel and brush and started on the northwestern corner of the grid. My knees would ache in a couple of hours of kneeling, but this was the part I loved: chipping away at the dirt to see what was there.

That golden wind surged back and wrapped around my fingers. Soft and gentle, it curled through my fingers, up my arm.

“Will!” I hissed, trying not to shout, not to alarm anyone.

“What–”The wind fluttered across my face, smoothing the hair out of my eyes. It was warm and it played with the edges of my shirt, the tips of my glasses so they shifted on my face, twisting around me like an embrace.

“Arthur, what is that?” William asked and the wind was gone. It died out so fast–too fast–for me to process that it was gone. I didn’t know what he was asking about, the wind or something else. Surely he had seen it too?

He wasn’t looking at me though. He looked *through* me. I followed his line of sight and turned to see part of the gridwall exposed. The tightly packed sand crumbled, and the image of a lotus flower was etched into stone.

Stone?

I reached for it without thinking, without grabbing any gloves or something other than my fucking fingers, and traced the delicate etchings. The lotus flower hieroglyph was perfectly preserved in the stone, like it had been placed there earlier today instead of thousands of years ago. I studied how the tool marks picked at the lines to engrave the lotus. They were etched so deeply in the stone that it wasn't like a regular piece of script.

"It's a marker," I said, mumbling.

"What do you mean?" William asked.

"Look at the rest of the stone, there's no other script. No other etchings. It's a marker of some sort. What else could it be?"

"A name," he said, and the wind rewarded him. A gentle tendril scooped a lock of hair from his face and tucked it behind his ear. "Beloved," he breathed and the wind sighed around us. The recognition of being seen, being noticed, filled the air.

"Beloved," I said, and the necklace warmed against my skin. I fished it from my shirt, and studied the markings on it again. It was one symbol–a lotus. The etchings here were not as well preserved, and I could hardly make it out, but now that I saw it on the stone before me, there was no denying the meaning. "Beloved," I said again.

William lifted the pendant, bringing it closer. I had to move into his space, the chain refusing to come undone still.

"It's the same," he said.

"Yeah."

"No, I mean, it's the same, look Arty. Look how the petal curves here," he pointed to the stone, then a faded curved line. "I think the same person made both of these."

"There's no possible way to know that," I said, but it seemed right. It felt right. Between the way the wind behaved, and how it seemed to bring us right to this stone, something was happening. Something was brewing and we were in the middle of it.

"Let's take some pictures so we can compare. I can't see the necklace this close," I said, but really, in my gut, I knew he was right. They were the same. They called to us–pulled us over here, somehow.

"We need to talk," he said, and there was a softness to him that I didn't like. Where was the cocky bastard talking about pinning me to the bed? Where was the arrogant swagger that he thought made him bullet proof?

"I don't like when you get like this," I said.

"Like what?"

"Serious. It's weird."

"How much longer until we can call it a day?"

I glanced at my watch and it was close to five o'clock. Technically, we could stop any time. Especially if there was something worth stopping over, but I didn't want to show this to Wes just yet. I didn't want him to see it and tell me it was nothing. He'd never say that, but I didn't want to hear that we stumbled upon someone's forgotten love note. On any other day, I'd kill for that little scrap of insight into the past, but tonight I needed something more.

William took out his phone and snapped several pictures of the stone and the necklace. He opened the top buttons of my shirt, so he could get a photo of the entire thing. His fingers were so gentle, so precise. There was none of the heat or the flirting now; he was strictly business, zooming in and snapping so many pictures it was likely overkill.

Then he lifted his phone up and smiled, and I stupidly grinned back. He snapped another picture.

"What the hell?"

"That one's just for me," he said, winking. "Let's go get ready for dinner. I think Zahra is on kitchen duty tonight so at least the food will be edible. Whoever cooked last night shouldn't quit his day job."

"It wasn't that bad," I spat, knowing full-well the sausages I made could have been throwing weapons.

"Don't quit being a historian, Arty. Cooking will ruin your hands," he said. The heat was back, and I wanted to ask him *why, what do you like about my hands?* "Meet back in the tent in twenty minutes. Dinner won't be until six, and we need to hide this."

"Hide?"

"Yeah, if anyone else sees this, they're gonna try to dig it out. I wanna know what shit we're digging out before we start."

"How exactly are we going to hide part of the wall?" I asked, but William was already moving, grabbing a tarp to drape over it. He smeared some dirt and sand on it, splashed a bit of his water and really made a mess of the tarp.

"Would you look at that? Silly me, got the tarp all messy. I'll just hang it here to dry overnight."

"Your creativity is astounding," I said, but we were already back to packing up our tools and closing the site for the evening. William moved the small ladder and laid it next to the entrance into the site.

He brushed the dirt off of his shirt sleeves, and then grabbed me by the elbow and hoisted me up. Evening approached in the desert, and the sky blanched to a soft pink. Haunting and beautiful, my attention was drawn to the sky. William turned to watch the sunset too, and our knuckles brushed against each other. I took a step forward, a step away, but he followed. The clouds passed by so slowly like they moved in time with every breath we took. Barely inching through the sky but they glowed with the sunlight peeking through them. The color shifted from a cornflower blue to pink to a deep gold, like the sand was reflected above. It took my breath away every time I watched a sunset in Egypt. With the pendant around my neck, and the wind at my back, how could I not believe in the magic of this land?

First our pinkies linked, and we stood like that without saying anything. One smug word would ruin this soft moment, and we both knew it. After another moment our hands were joined, and something settled in my chest. Comfort and affection–every instinct told me to flee before something happened, but my feet were planted. The breeze picked up and I wondered if it was real or–

"I'll never get over seeing this," I said. The silence was suddenly too heavy to bear.

"Me neither. It's nothing like the pictures, you know?"

"Yeah, there's just something so..."

"Surreal?" William finished my sentence, and he was right. The desert was surreal. This was surreal; him standing next to me, our hands clasped together. That was surreal. Wind curled around our hands and I felt William smiling at me.

"That happens every time I want to touch you," he said, just barely over a whisper.

"And you want to touch me now?"

"Arty, I've been thinking about touching you all damn day." His words raced straight down my spine as he tugged me toward our tent.

"I thought you were gonna shower?"

"I will later," he said. William dropped my hand and I kept pace beside him. The tent was about ten yards away, and we walked in silence until he unzipped it and got inside. I couldn't read the expression on his face: was that desire? Did he need to talk about something else? Trapped gas, maybe?

"Stop thinking so hard, Arty, I can see the wheels grinding in your head. We need to talk about how you went all Dr. Jekyll-Mr. Hyde on me earlier. In the dome. What do you remember?"

"I remember feeling... like I was just a spectator in my mind. I could see you, but I couldn't do anything. It was like nothing I'd ever experienced before, well, aside from the first time I checked out, I guess," I confessed. I'd spent the afternoon dissociating from the experience with little luck. The wind skimmed across me throughout the day, demanding attention like a needy pup. It stirred in my blood, and I knew the wind would be back soon. I sucked in a breath, knowing it would follow.

The gold, barely there glitter came back and William went so still, he could have blended into the wall.

"I remember that gold shit, then your eyes turned gold, and you were calling me 'beloved,' again. Not that I mind a pet name, but I'd rather you be in control of giving it to me," he said.

"You want a pet name?"

"That's really the only part of what I said that you heard, huh?" William scrubbed his hands through his hair, stretching out a day's worth of labor. He cracked his back, hissing at his ribs. The wind had dissipated, but the air still felt charged between us.

"It scared me," I said softly. Was it pathetic to admit my fears? If it was, then William would see me for who I really was: unafraid to be afraid. I'd lost the false bravado after years of debating in school. Now I was just me, comfortable with the man I saw in the mirror. Mostly, anyway.

"Me too," he said, sighing and plopping down on the bedroll next to me.

"Why do I feel like we never leave this tent?" I said, laying back to be next to him.

"Because it's where you want to be, maybe? Admit it, I'm growing on you, Lewis."

"Like a fungus, yes. Oh, maybe that should be your pet name. Fungus. Mold. Mushroom–"

"You'd think your creativity would have gotten better after all of that college," he huffed.

"Do you know anything about the east wind?" I asked.

"Not really? In what context? It's a directional wind and it's etched on our arms sometimes, but that's it," William said. He placed a hat on his face, arms tucked behind his head and ankles crossed. Ten minutes like this and he would be unconscious.

"There is an Egyptian god of the east wind. Wes mentioned it, but we don't have any information about him or what he did."

"So like, a lesser known deity? That's not that weird," he said.

"No, but I think we need to try to find something about this east wind. I think it could start pointing us in the right direction, at least."

"Okay, what can I do to help?" I rolled over and grabbed my satellite phone and turned on my hotspot. Signal out here was spotty even with the sat-phone, but it was better than nothing at all.

"Help me research. There's gotta be something about the east wind out there," I said, taking his phone. I punched in his code–9455, his name, the same code he's used for everything–and the screen unlocked.

"How do you know my password?"

"Because aside from being insufferable, you're also completely predictable. Now, I've added you to my hotspot. Start searching."

"It's kinda hot that you could just unlock my phone without even trying," he said, voice dropping. The sound of his voice stirred something deep in me, and the wind came rushing back into the tent, whipping around us–

"Okay! Message received! No flirting!" he said, swatting at the wind.

"For the record, I'm fine with flirting," I blurted out and that wolfish grin spread across his face. He needed a shave; his beard was coming in thicker and it made him irresponsibly, ruggedly attractive. "But maybe after we figure this out. You know, because the weird wind thing keeps trying to possess me."

"Let me see your tattoo," he said, leaning on an elbow to get closer to me. His hand snaked its way under my shirt, already searching for it. This closeness still alarmed me; was this too fast? Not fast enough? Depending on which head was doing the thinking decided the speed of things.

"It's in English now," he said, the words that were so familiar to us appearing like a brand on me. He read them, tracing a finger down the text, "The East Wind rises again, a storm without end, a lover in search of home. A lover, lost and alone, feels the East Wind caress his face and knows he will never stop searching."

"It doesn't feel like a prophecy or some spectacular text," I said.

"No, it feels like love notes between two people that couldn't stay together."

Rumbling behind rattled around the tent like there was an earthquake about to swallow us whole. My arms flew open to reach for William, but he was already reaching for me. We stumbled out of the tent, searching for the sound.

It didn't take long to find.

A sandstorm had blown in around us, and I felt like I was stumbling blind. William's grip tightened, and we stayed close, fumbling our way through camp. I'd seen small sandstorms before, but nothing like this. The wind whipped sand everywhere, and it bit against my skin. I struggled to keep my eyes open, much less see anything. It was dark, but not as dark as it should be; the sun had set, but there was too much light. A chill shot through me–there was too much light.

The wind.

"Will–"

He nodded, seemingly understanding my thoughts all at once. He pressed me against him, tucked tight to his chest as we inched our way around the camp. The stone with the lotus on it had to be protected; it was so perfectly preserved that it couldn't get ruined now after surviving for so many years. I wanted to race off toward the grids, but William paused, before he tackled us to the ground.

"Shh!" he hissed in my ear, before a blast rang out in my ears. The sound was absorbed in the sandstorm, but I saw the flash of muzzle fire, and heard angry shouting in the distance.

"Who's that?"

"I have a guess," he said through gritted teeth. We crawled toward the showers and opened the door to get out of the storm. Sand and wind raged around us, and we stayed quiet as we listened.

Two men spoke in Arabic right next to us.

"This has to be the place. William Ford should be here."

"I can't see shit in this storm."

"You shouldn't have fired, what if you hit someone else?"

"Who cares? We just need to find Ford and leave."

Their voices were muffled and my Arabic wasn't flawless, but I understood every word. I stared at William, waiting for a reaction. He screwed his eyes shut, took a shuddering breath before he looked at me.

"Spice Traders," he mumbled, so quietly it was nearly lost to the storm.

"Who are they?"

"Remember I said I was in debt? It's to them," he said as he peeked through the door. The shower doors were not exactly private, but it was secluded enough. He glanced through the hinges, through a tiny sliver of space, searching.

"And now they're here. How do they know you're here?" I asked, then thought of a better question, "Why are they here?"

"Not everyone showing up at a dig has honorable intentions, Arty. They're definitely on the less honorable side of things. I'm guessing they're looking for something to steal."

My throat closed up; thieves? Here? There wasn't anything to even steal yet, there might never be anything to take, but yet they were here, poking around our site during the perfect guise of the sandstorm.

"Why were they shooting?" I asked, and William pulled back quickly, a finger shooting up to his mouth to shush me.

A beat passed. Then another. Another, before William sighed and said, "Probably hoping to hit me so they can just sell my liver or something."

"That's... horrible," I said, not able to think of another word.

"They're gonna get their money from me one way or another," he sighed.

"Is that why you're here?" I asked, the truth unfurling in my mind. He was here for money–not the honest wage of the laborers, but for some serious cash. He was looking for an easy way out and my stomach churned at the prospect.

"No. Yes, no–"

"Who are you?" I spat, stepping away from, out of his arms. I hated that my body was chilled from being away from him. Pressed against the shower wall, there was no place for me to go.

"I'm me, you idiot," he spat back.

"The William I knew would never be a fucking grave robber."

"The William you knew wasn't in enough debt to a butcher to ever have to think about shit like this."

"What happened after we graduated? You just fell off the face of the earth," I said, anger rising in my chest. How could he have brought this shit to my site? Willingly, knowingly endangered how many people with his stupidity?

"Not now," he said, and I felt like he had slammed a door in my face.

"What do you mean *not now?* You don't get to call all of the shots here–"

"I *mean*, those guys are still here and arguing with you in a shower stall wasn't on my bingo card, so please *shut up*."

"Stop! Someone help!" Dr. Romanova screamed. Her voice carried through the storm and I shoved William out of the way. I was going to help her, sandstorm and thugs be damned. He tried to grab my arm but I yanked out of his grip, until I was back in the storm.

He didn't follow.

Dr. Romanova was a few feet away, on her knees with her blonde hair whipping around her face. I ran over to her as fast as I could, but the storm raged on. By the time I finally got to her, she was trying to get up, but the wind pelted her.

"Irina! What happened?"

"Someone was here! They tried to break into my office and I chased after them, but then got turned around–"

"I think they have guns, we need to get out of the storm." She nodded, trying to keep her scarf around her face to shield from the sand. God it was *everywhere*. My glasses were coated in dust, and I could barely see out of them. We walked with our arms around each other, stumbling through the storm in the direction of the main dome. I hoped no one else was out in this mess.

The wind roared again, shaking the ground behind my feet, and Irina paled. Wild eyes scanned the horizon, but I wasn't sure what she was looking for. I searched for William, knowing damn well that he was still hiding out in the showers.

Coward. That absolute, idiotic *coward*. How did he even fall into people like that? I'd heard the name Spice Traders before: anyone working with historical, valuable artifacts knew that name. Bounty hunters, treasure hunters, thieves. All of the above; they stole and robbed and maybe even killed for what they wanted.

Would they kill William? Or just exact their pound of flesh? He could survive without a kidney, maybe a spleen. Stupid, arrogant *prick*.

"Why are they here?" she asked, and I shrugged.

"Thieves are my guess," I said, angry at myself for deflecting blame off of William. I should have served up his lies on a silver platter and gotten him kicked out of the dig, once and for all. But I didn't want his blood on my hands, and I couldn't live with myself knowing William Ford was out in the world without a spleen because I was angry.

Dr. Romanova took a deep breath, coughing up all the sand in her mouth and nose. I moved to get her a water bottle from the small fridge, but she waved me off.

"We have more problems if there's thieves here already. Did you see anything about them to be able to identify them?" she asked.

"No, I could barely see my hand in front of my face." It wasn't a lie; I didn't *see* anything to know who they were, and going off of William's word was never a great plan.

"I have a few ideas. I've dealt with thugs before. I'm concerned because they were armed. I heard the gunshot and poked my head out. That's when they grabbed me, and shoved me out into the storm. I don't know what they're looking for in my office. We just started, it's not like we've found a damn thing. I wonder what tipped them off about this site though. It's pretty low key. It's not like we're digging next to the Great Pyramids."

"Yeah, I wonder too," I said, knowing damn well what drew them here. William Ford. My blood simmered, boiling me from the inside as anger crept up my spine. The storm slowed, and I could see my hands in front of my face now. Dr. Romanova and I moved slowly through the camp, heading for the main tent. If the thieves were still here, that would be the target.

This was the second attack on the camp in as many days; the duct tape was still fresh from getting it patched up. The white walls of the dome were like a beacon in the storm, and we crept along slowly until we made it inside. My lungs burned from all the sand, and I felt it covering me everywhere. Still, I needed to go check on the lotus stone and make sure it was still alright. I needed to find William too, and make sure he was still in one piece too, but the stone was more important.

"It looks like they didn't make it in here," she said, glancing from desk to desk. The main dome was set up as a research center, but there were desks and tables everywhere, making the large space feel cramped. Even more so with all of the mess from the clean up. Research was piled high on every desk and it was in such a state that I wanted to organize it. I needed something to do that would make a difference, and the only thing I could comprehend now was cleaning. Staying in here made me think of William though and how the necklace seemed to take over my mind. Luckily, there was no sign of that force now.

"You don't need to start on that now, Arthur–"

"I just need to do something," I said, and I hated the desperation in my tone. When did that come about? I was so good at keeping my feelings, even my thoughts and opinions, on lockdown that seeing them spill out everywhere unnerved me. I could verbally spar, bring an academic opponent to their knees without breaking a sweat, but lately I couldn't speak three words without my voice wobbling.

"It's been a rough start to this dig. No one will blame you for being flustered," she said gently. Irina touched my elbow so softly it made my skin itch. The tattoo started to appear and I hastily rubbed at it, trying to get it to fade before she noticed the swirling marks on my skin. Who knew what it was going to look like this time; I wanted to inspect every variation, photo and document them to study at a later date. I wanted to document William's too, but that would mean being close to him and I couldn't stomach that at the moment.

"It's more that I'm worried about the security of the site," I said.

"I am too. We might need to shut it down for a week, then return with some security in place."

"Who has the budget for that?" I asked, knowing who absolutely didn't: us.

She let out a long sigh, pinching the bridge of her nose. "Good point. What do you want to do?"

"Keep going, if we can. I think we need to just make sure we're as secure as we can be, and if we do happen upon something to get it locked up in storage ASAP. Who all has keys to the safe?"

"Just you, me, and Wes. I wasn't going to give copies to anyone else."

"Good, I don't think we should."

"The storm is finally over, so I'm going to get cleaned up and go to bed. I should have gone to bed already, but I got caught up. What do you know about the tales of the east wind?" she asked and I froze.

"The east wind?"

The words played over and over in my head and I swallowed down my panic, praying that the golden wind didn't come back.

"There was a god of the east wind named Henkhisesui. I can't find much about him, but he was said to be aggressive, destructive. That plays into the common narratives about eastern winds, so that's nothing really new. Wes mentioned that he saw some iconography referencing east winds in the initial project notes for this site. I've been looking into local mythology, and all I've found is Henkhisesui, who apparently was rather beloved by his followers. So beloved in fact, there was a human man that was said to be his actual lover. Which would be incredible to find evidence of, but this is all just common folklore. Who knows how much of it is true or has been warped over the years? I never like starting my research on some fireside tale, but that's all we've got. Wes is convinced this site is some sort of temple, but I don't see anything to mark it as such yet."

My mind took a moment to process this knowledge. Henkhisesui. East wind god. Loved a human *man*. Beloved. Beloved. *Beloved*.

My pulse raced so hard that it hurt to breathe, hurt to feel each beat of my heart. This was it, and I knew it in a way I couldn't explain or define. I knew it like I knew the golden wind was tied to him, and how William was approaching the tent. It was instinctual, and I heard the words echo through me again.

The East Wind rises again, a storm without end, a lover in search of home. A lover, lost and alone, feels the East Wind caress his face and knows he will never stop searching.

The East Wind was Henkhisesui.

William didn't enter the tent, but sat right outside, waiting. Was he trying to give me space? Respect that I was livid for him not telling me the truth? Or was he being a coward again, not wanting to face me?

"I'm going to see what else I can find on Henkhisesui. There has to be something," I said, and she nodded.

"I think if we can put those pieces together, we're going to be able to find something more than just sand out here."

She waved goodbye and left me in the disaster of an office. I picked up the stack of papers next to me and flipped through them. It was Wes's shit handwriting but I could decipher it in my sleep. He had terrible sketches of the hieroglyphs for wind, and the more I studied it, the more I realized it wasn't the east wind. It was Henkhisesui spelled out.

I flipped through, looking at the rest of his notes, scanning quickly. Bits and pieces of the saying we heard were scattered through the notes, like he was piecing it together from somewhere else. His field journal was on another desk and I snatched it up, searching through it. He had a lotus drawn in the corner of one of the last pages and my heart nearly stopped. He had all of it, but didn't know it.

"Can we talk?" William's voice said, filtering in from outside.

"Come in," I said, my eyes not leaving the journal. William lumbered into the dome, his footsteps echoing in the quiet. The sandstorm had been so loud, and now that everyone was tucked away for the night, the world felt silent. Had no one else seen or heard those thugs? They came and left so quickly that maybe they hadn't; wouldn't that be a blessing. I never thought I'd be so grateful for the cover a sandstorm brought to hide our secrets. Like the one standing just a mere few feet behind me, waiting for a tongue lashing.

"You're in one piece I see, so that means they didn't kill you," I said. He flinched. "I want you to tell me the truth, unabridged, and now."

A muscle ticked in his jaw, and I shifted my weight to cross my arms. The journal laid on the desk behind me, open and ready to spill its secrets to him too, so I moved in front of it. William wasn't learning a damn thing until he came clean with me.

"You know, just because we have some history together doesn't mean you're just entitled to every facet of my life."

"I am when you bring it to *my dig* and then someone shoots at me."

"They weren't shooting at you, they were shooting at me. They probably don't even know you exist, and for that much you should be thankful."

"Thankful! You dragged a host of thieves and shitbags to my dig! Why should I be *thankful*?"

"Because I could have just cut that necklace off you and given it to them, or I could have just handed you over to them if you were too much of a pain in the ass. Like always," he snarled. I stepped into his space.

"You think I'd just let that happen?"

"I think you'd be outgunned," he said and his breath was against my ear. He always did this–he moved so he was lumbering over me even though we were nearly the same height. I stood a little straighter, squared my shoulders.

"I think you underestimate me, and I'm really fucking tired of that," I said, shoving against his chest so he staggered back half a step. Heart thundering, wild and joyous, I smirked at him. I stood up for myself, shocking us both, but I'd never admit that. William always felt like a wild creature, but tonight he was something more. He was itching for a fight, and so was I.

"Arty, we both know you're not made for the world outside of academia."

"Because I'm smart enough not to get caught up in this bullshit or because I can actually count cards and wouldn't lose to begin with?"

Recognition flickered on his face, and I wondered if he remembered how I'd always beat him when we'd play cards after a study session, or how I'd gently coach him when he played with friends. So many nights I'd played and thrown games just to preserve his pride; I should have eviscerated him in cards and maybe this notion of him being a decent player would have never developed.

"You're such an ass," he said, and I knew the argument was won. I didn't want to share what I had found about the east wind when he was in a mood like this. There was too much to be said and I had no words left in me for anything civil. But God, he smelled good even coming through a sandstorm. There was something so alluring about William that set my senses on fire, and I needed space.

I hated that part of me wanted to kiss him.

"I'm going to shower and then head to bed."

"Correction, *I'm* going to shower and then go to bed," he said, already turning for the tent flap. I scooped up Wes' journal while his back was turned and tucked it into my jacket pocket. The cool air of the desert hit my face as we stepped out into the night. All of the lights we had were gone. The lanterns were scattered around the camp, or blown away completely. So much for securing them. The camp was desolate and eerie, but it didn't deter me from making a beeline for the shower. William thought I'd just give in but those days were done.

"I'm not fighting you for the shower," I said, and he gave me that stupid grin that made my knees weak. He had to know that.

"Neither am I."

The shower was near the edge of the camp for the sake of privacy. Water only stayed warm for a handful of minutes before turning to ice, and it took forever for the tank to reheat. I was not about to stand out here waiting for half an hour to get a trickle of luke-warm water because William had blasted through all of it.

We power walked to the shower, edging in front of each, back and forth, back and forth, until we crashed through the door at the same time. His hand pressed to the top of the door while mine went for the door handle.

I turned the handle and we both shoved into the stall, the space too small for two grown men.

"I was here first," I said, crossing my arms.

He pulled his shirt off and even in the very low light of the shower, I saw the tattoo on his arm. Lotus blossoms bloomed over his skin; realistic and hieroglyphic depictions. In any other circumstance, I'd want to admire the beauty. "Maybe, but I'm gonna be naked first."

I'd never taken my shirt off so fast in my life.

William fumbled with the buckle on his pants, with his arms bumping into my stomach, my hips.

"Not if I am first," I said, the challenge leaving my lips before I could stop it. That damnable grin came back, and he pulled his belt off, flinging it over the shower wall. The metal hit the sand in a soft hiss. I watched as his thumbs hooked into the belt loops of his pants and yanked down. His feet still in shoes got stuck in the pants, and I took that fraction of a second to look at him. To *really* look at him.

I was done for.

The dark trail of hair leading south from his navel was like a guiding light to his cock, and my eyes were glued. To all the gods in every pantheon, why was he *hard*? I swallowed and the noise brought William's attention to me. He stared at my lips, eyes tracing down my smoother, lither body.

I unbuttoned my pants and pulled them down too, stepping out of them and my shoes in a much smoother motion. We stood naked except for our socks in this very tiny shower stall. I flicked the water on, and it was so cold that I took a step closer to him. Wet socks be damned, I was officially showering *first*.

William wrapped an arm around my waist, and I felt how aroused he was. He rubbed himself against me, and I suppressed a moan, biting my lip. The tension and the anger faded from me, William's hands moved to my hip and up my chest until he lightly–too damn lightly, really–flicked a nipple.

"Why were we fighting?" he asked.

"Fuck if I know," I said. The water warmed and he twisted so I was the one under the meager spray. The heat from the water and the cool air made everything heightened. William tipped my chin up and as the water hit my face, he brushed his thumb over my lips.

"Truce?" he breathed. He was so close, I'd be kissing him if I just moved an inch.

"Truce," I said, and he nodded. It was the only thing he needed to hear because then William had his hands in my hair, kissing me like I was the air he needed to breathe. I opened my mouth for him, inviting him in, closer, more, more, more.

When his hand wrapped around my cock, I bit his lip.

"This okay?" he said, tugging enough to make me buck into his hand. I nodded. What were words? How did he still have words?

"Good," he said. He grabbed a couple pumps of soap, lathering me up as he worked my cock. One hand massaging the sand and dirt and grit from my skin, the other pulling me closer to the edge. Our foreheads pressed together, I placed kisses along his jaw, his earlobe, his lips–anything I could reach. As the soap ran over my body, I sudsed up my hands and wrapped a tentative hand around him too. He groaned, low and throaty; it nearly made me break.

"This okay?" I repeated, and he laughed.

"More than okay." The water was nearly scalding now, but only in the places it could reach; William's body heat warmed me more than the water could. His thumb rubbed over my sensitive head, and I felt my toes curling, sensation building along my spine, ready to break. I worked him harder, and he bucked into my hand, his hips jerking. William kissed just under my ear, the low rumble of his pleasure rising the hair on the back of my neck.

"You feel good," he gritted out, and his admission, his desire sent me over the edge as I spilled into his hand. He worked me through it, soft kisses and hands holding me steady as I came.

My body was spent, but I didn't let go of William, until he was ready to break too. His forehead knitted together like he was concentrating on something difficult and I scratched at the base of his skull. Our eyes met through the spray of the shower and I smiled, real and true, and so did he as he came in my hand. The water washed away the sand and the evidence of this moment, but we stayed in the shower, holding each other.

I let the water rinse me, let it seep into my pores, and take away the day's stress with me. William took most of the tension away, but there was something especially cleansing being in water after a long day. He worked the shampoo in my hair, another excuse for us to touch, and I said nothing. Leaning into his touch, he turned me so my back was to his chest as he lathered my body from head to toe.

"I think I won," he said as the water rinsed away the remaining soap.

"You won?" I said.

"You came first."

"You touched me first!"

"Was that against the rules, boss?" he said, rolling his teeth over my ear. I leaned into him again, quietly savoring the feel of his damp skin against me.

"No, but–"

"Ah, shit!" he said, laughter lighting up the night. The water turned suddenly frigid, and we bolted out of the shower.

"Did you happen to grab a towel?" I asked, shivering and laughing.

"Nooope," he said, and we both cackled. I swatted at him, trying and failing to shush him.

"Race you back to the tent," he said, the challenge back in his eyes.

"But we're naked–"

"Better run fast then," he said, already scooping his clothes up and running into the night. I grabbed mine and the journal and followed him, naked and wild, back to our tent.

XI

William

OUR TENT WAS QUIET, and the truce seemed to extend through the rest of the night. Arthur laid on his side, his ass pressed firmly against my side. But this wasn't cuddling. I couldn't cross that barrier yet, and I wasn't sure I even wanted to.

He was a dick, really.

Had a really nice one, too, but that's beside the point.

We ran naked through the camp and I grinned the whole way. When was the last time I'd done something like that? Arthur sighed in his sleep, the exhaustion from being in the heat and the stress of the day weighing on him. His shoulders were finally relaxed, and I leaned a bit toward him, just to watch his even breathing.

He opted not to put a shirt on, and it made me want to touch him. The planes of his torso were smooth and toned; the smattering of chest hair made him seem younger than he was, along with the freckles on the tops of his shoulders. He slept so deeply, so pressed against my side that there wasn't a lot of room left for me on the bed roll.

His ass was nice and firm as he didn't cuddle with me.

Holding Arthur Lewis wasn't on my game plan, but I rolled over anyway, my arm around his middle. I spooned him, laying my head against the top of his back. He didn't stir or wake, and I knew there'd be hell to pay in the morning, but what was one more debt?

The Spice Traders clearly knew I was here; they trashed the dome, then came back looking for me. What a fucking mess. I needed to check in with Zahra. She'd stayed out of the way the whole night, and I was thankful for it. Dealing with her rage wouldn't help me at all, and trying to keep her from getting into trouble with them would have taken an act of God. It didn't seem like they searched the tents for me; most people stayed in their tents, quiet and comfortable, ignorant to what was happening. Maybe I lucked out and the sound of the shot fired was swallowed fully by the storm.

When had I ever been lucky, though?

Arthur wriggled, trying to borrow even closer to me. The thin blanket was just enough to chase away the chill, especially with Arthur's added body heat. His skin was overheated, but I didn't let go of him. He'd had to roll away before I let go—best to tuck *that* thought away for later.

Absent-mindedly, I ran my hand through his hair. He didn't react, so I did it again, savoring the feel of his silky soft hair. It was short, but the strands still slipped through my fingers with ease.

The rhythmic sounds of his breathing and comforting silence of the desert finally lulled me to sleep.

***

When I woke up, Arthur was already gone. He left a note on his desk that read, *see you at the lotus.* The sun was up, and I stretched out the kinks in my back and neck. After a couple of splashes of water on my face and some fresh clothes, I needed to grab a quick breakfast before heading down to the grid I'd been working. Zahra waited for me at the breakfast line, her face a mask of cool indifference. I was sick of her being a bitch to me too, but I felt my own frosty expression falling into place.

"You're alive," she said with a raised eyebrow.

"Were you hoping I wasn't?" I retorted and got a smile from her.

"I heard the shot last night, but I stayed in my tent. I don't know if they know who I am or not," she said, and I nodded. Smart girl. No need for her to disappear with a bunch of thugs.

"They found me here," I said quietly. She nodded.

"We need to leave soon."

"We haven't found anything yet."

"It doesn't matter. They found you. How much are you up to now? Thirty thousand with the interest?"

"I don't even know," I admitted and the crushing weight of doom hit me so hard I nearly stumbled. They were going to kill me, and it was only a matter of time.

"Maybe Rami can help–"

"Rami has his own shit to deal with, and he's not exactly their favorite person either."

Zahra's beautiful, sun-kissed face drained of all color. Her lips went white and I grabbed her elbow to steady her. We walked away from the others waiting for their meal, and sat by a campfire. "Tell me he's not in bed with them too," she pleaded. Zahra's brown eyes shone with unshed tears.

"You already know he is," I said, trying to soften the blow. She knew; she had to have known. Zahra was anything but stupid.

"Why didn't he tell me?"

"Because he said you have your own shit too. What did you do, Zahra? You can't possibly owe them money–"

"I work for them," she blurted out and the look on her face was like she just swallowed a knife.

"You... *work* for them?" I asked.

"In... a sense, yes." She couldn't look at me and my stomach sank. Not her too.

"What do you do for them, Zahra?"

She grabbed a couple pieces of fruit and stood, trying to flee. "Zahra!"

"It's better if you don't know," she said before she pushed away from me, and headed toward the grids. I wanted to follow her, but she picked up the pace, nearly jogging now and I didn't want to look like a creep chasing her through the camp. I sat on one of the log benches alone with my thoughts until I heard someone approach.

"Why are you sitting here alone?" Arthur said, sitting down next to me. He took a sip of his coffee and made a face. I took a sip of my own coffee and made the same face. This wasn't even hot bean water; it was brown goop. How the hell was the coffee *lumpy*?

"I was talking to Zahra, but she headed off."

"You mean she ran off. I saw her bolting through the camp. What did you say to piss her off too?"

"Believe it or not, most people find me charming."

"Most people are idiots, so that does track." He bit into his apple and I watched him chew. The attention made his cheeks turn pink and I turned away, satisfied. Arthur continued to eat his apple, and my thoughts went back to last night in the shower. Did I imagine it? Arthur's lean, naked body was a sight to take in, and I already wanted to drag him back to the tent to see him again.

"Such snark from those pretty lips," I said, letting my voice drop an octave. Arthur choked on a bite of apple, coughing with his cheeks growing brighter. My bark of laughter was cut short when he threw the apple at me. Probably deserved that.

"You are ridiculous–"

Zahra's scream cut through the camp and we both bolted upright. I scanned, searching for her. Sound in the desert felt omnidirectional. I couldn't place where it was coming from, and the panic in my chest surged like nothing ever had before. Zahra didn't *scream*. I'd seen her slice her finger with a knife chopping veggies and she barely flinched. My mind whirled, and everything blended together. I couldn't tell where anything was in the endless tawny landscape. Even the tents seemed to blend in with the panic consuming me.

"There, let's go," Arthur said but he was already off and running toward the entrance of the site. There were people gathering there and it had to mean something. My legs burned; I hadn't run in so long that my body forgot what it felt like. I caught up to Arthur fairly quickly and his labored breathing sent the panic into overdrive.

"What's wrong?" I asked. Arthur leaned with his hands on his knees, struggling to breathe deep.

"Asthma," he wheezed, fishing for something in his pocket. His hands seemed to move too slowly, so I reached in his pocket, then moved to the next one. His cargo pants were perfect for the dig, but he couldn't fucking breathe and he needed an inhaler, something–

When I finally pulled it out and took the cap off, Arthur brought it to his mouth and administered the medicine. After a couple of beats, the color in his cheeks returned to his normal hue, and his eyes didn't look so sallow.

"Now isn't the time to try to feel me up, Ford. Maybe tonight if you play your cards right."

"Unbelievable. You were dying!"

"Then again, you not playing your cards right is what got you into this mess, huh? And I wasn't dying. I can't run, and I should know better. Relax." I wanted to punch him. I wanted to kiss him.

"Zahra," I said, and he nodded, pointing to the crowd. It didn't take long to see what was going on, and then I was the one that went pale.

There was a splatter of blood in the sand. Bright and fresh and so fucking red.

A lock of beautiful black hair tied to a small dagger, sticking out of the sand with an ace of hearts stabbed through it. The words tick-tock were written in shitty handwriting, and I knew that was a message for me. I knew it in my bones.

I knew it because those assholes grabbed Zahra, and they knew that would light a fire under my ass like nothing else could.

Nothing else that they knew about, at least. Arthur knelt down next to the dagger and pulled it out. Zahra's hair fell and the wind picked it up, scattering the strands. His piercing, assessing brown eyes shot right through me. Every secret I ever had would have been laid bare before him, and Arthur would still want more information.

"Nothing to see here, get back to work," he shouted, and the day laborers all startled and hurried off. Arthur's normally friendly tone had vanished. His voice lacked any warmth at all, and I wanted to turn away but my feet were rooted in place.

"You're going to tell me every fucking detail, and you're not going to skip a damn thing. Do you understand me, William?" he said, and I felt like a boy being scolded in school again. I held my chin up, ready for a fight, but that sharp, brutal laugh he had split the silence. "Don't even try to worm your way out or lie. I know all of your tells, and I know whatever it was that Zahra just told you this morning is involved. Tent. Now."

Arthur kicked sand over the blood, and I stopped him.

"Stop it!"

"That's not enough blood for her to be dead or even severely wounded. It is however plenty to spook the entire crew and cause them to walk off. So like I said. Tent. Now." He punctuated every word. I watched as he buried the evidence of Zahra's—what? Injury? Kidnapping?

"I want to go by her tent."

"Then you're coming to ours."

"Aye, aye boss." I gave him a mock salute and he grabbed my wrist, his fingers digging into the flesh there.

"Stop being flippant. I'm worried about her too, but you've got to realize that you've seriously fucked up, right?" Arthur let go of me with such force that I staggered as he pushed by me, not bothering to move enough so he checked my shoulder as he moved past.

"I–"

"Save it. Whatever you have to say, save it. It's bad enough that the Spice Traders have been here *three times* and have escalated like this. I don't want to make this any worse."

Arthur was gone before I could say anything else. He slammed into my injured side, and though the bruises were getting better, my ribs burned. Asshole.

Zahra's tent was on the other side of the camp; she only showed me where it was once, but that was enough. Hopefully the woman she was sharing with wasn't there, and I could just slip in and out before anyone saw me creeping around the women's' tents. I did my best to move through the camp calmly, not engaging with anyone that I passed. People whispered in Arabic though about what had happened. Of course they did. This dig was turning out to be a clusterfuck that no one wanted to be involved in.

I slipped into her tent and it was thankfully empty. Her bed roll was neatly made with her small leather bag resting on it. I didn't even know what I was looking for, but seeing her things made her absence feel more real. The blood replayed in my mind, and I prayed she was okay.

"I work for them," she had said. Doing what, though? I couldn't imagine Zahra doing anything like that, but she said the same thing about me with the gambling.

Except Zahra found the game for me.

Except Zahra came up with this whole plan to join the dig.

Except Zahra was the only one here that knew how to contact me, other than Arthur.

And Rami.

He was supposed to join the dig too, but I hadn't seen that weasel since we arrived. A chilling thought struck me–maybe we *had* seen him but couldn't recognize him because he was in a mask. I tried to think back to the sound of their voices, but I couldn't be sure. The sandstorm raged and everything sounded distorted, but it certainly could have been him.

I needed to find Rami.

Arthur was back in our tent, reading something in a notebook I didn't recognize. Dr. Carrington was in our tent too, hovering over Arthur's shoulder. Creased brows and hunched shoulders sent me spiraling. What were they reading?

"Arthur–" I started but the words died on my tongue. What was there to say? I'd ruined this dig, his final research field work. Dr. Carrington studied me and I realized that he was staring at the tattoos. His eyes shifted from me to Arthur, taking in all of the details. The tattoos transformed back to the original hieroglyphics.

"I told Wes about the necklace," Arthur said and my stomach bottomed out.

"This is possibly the most significant find in modern history," he said, now lifting my arm to study the symbols up close.

"The necklace?" I asked.

"No, the magic part, with the golden wind and the tattoos that cover your arms," Dr. Carrington deadpanned.

"Ah, yeah, that."

"Wes thinks the attacks on the camp have something to do with the necklace," Arthur said.

I swallowed my pride, stamped down my shame, and said, "No, I'm pretty sure that's because of me. Professor, have you heard of a group called the Spice Traders?"

Dr. Carrington blanched and nodded.

"Well, I owe them some money. A lot of money, and I think they tracked me down to collect it."

"How would they even find you here? Cell signal is spotty at best, even with my sat-phone," Arthur said. His glasses had slipped down his nose, it made him seem much older than we were. He looked bone weary, and I wondered how much of that was reflected on my face.

"Zahra," I said. Her name felt like a betrayal on my lips, but she had made her bed and now I was lying in the shit.

"She works for them," Arthur said. "Of course. She led them right to our doorstep."

"I'm sorry," I said, and I realized then just how sorry I was. This whole mess was my fault and as the sun caught the light on the pendant around Arthur's neck, it felt like I had tied a noose around him. He stood still, waiting for me to say something else, but what else was there to say?

"We need a plan," Arthur finally said. He didn't acknowledge the apology, and honestly, why would he? Dr. Carrington picked up the notebook and compared our tattoos to the notes.

"Arthur, you're right, they are exactly the same," he mumbled, completely oblivious to the turmoil between us. "I think we need to document the tattoos–"

"Arthur did that already, and every variation that we've seen so far," I snapped. Dr. Carrington looked up at me then, as if he realized that I was a person standing here instead of an object to examine.

"Variations?"

"They change," Arthur said, "but that isn't important right now. Zahra is missing, the Spice Traders have broken into the camp, and I can't get this damn thing off." He yanked on the necklace and the golden wind shot through the tent, knocking his hand away.

"Do you think the sandstorm was related to the necklace?" I asked. I wanted to bring up Arthur's little personality swap too, but he didn't seem eager to talk about that just yet.

"Considering the wind responds to us, I'd say it was a good chance," Arthur said. He met my eyes then and the chill had faded. Arthur looked so tired, and I hated that I wanted to just comfort the asshole. He turned to Dr. Carrington and asked, "Wes, what drew you to this sight, specifically?"

"I saw some aerial photography of the area and it matched a description of an ancient temple. The topography seemed promising, but we haven't seen anything to support that now, have we?" He sighed, and I wondered if Arthur had mentioned the column that we found. The thought must have crossed his mind at the same time as our eyes locked.

"Actually, there's something you should probably see," I said, and Arthur nodded.

"Oh?"

"Yeah, maybe we should get Dr. Romanova too," I said and his eyes lit up. The old guy needed to make a move on her before he missed his chance again. Arthur pocketed the notebook and headed out of the tent.

"I'm no expert, William, but I think you need to make things right with him. I haven't seen him this upset in years," Dr. Carrington said.

"When was the last time he was torn up like this?"

"After graduation. He thinks I'm oblivious, but I knew he was heartbroken that you didn't join the program with him. I was too, to be honest. Watching you two spar was an art form," his voice was full of nostalgia, and it choked me up too.

"Well, I doubt he wants to hear anything I have to say now."

"Quite the contrary, William. He wants to hear everything. Arthur doesn't make a move until he's analyzed every piece on the board. You hiding the truth from him will only make it worse when he figures things out."

"When did you become an expert in Arthur Lewis?" I joked, trying to smile.

"Because I see myself in him, and I know just how badly he wants you to talk to him." Dr. Carrington patted my arm, and followed after Arthur. Getting lectured by both of them today wasn't on my to-do list, but after Zahra went missing, I'd accept any tongue lashing. I deserved every punishment and then some for what happened with Zahra.

The grid that we worked in was uncovered when we got there. There were no workers in sight and something felt off. Silence slid across the desert and I stilled. Cornered in the open air, I moved like someone was watching my every movement. Dr. Romanova stood at the edge of the grid with a frown deeply set on her usually pleasant face. It made her age show, with the etched lines of her forehead creasing. Arthur was already in the grid, his head and shoulders seemingly sticking up from the ground. By the time we all climbed into the grid, Arthur had uncovered the lotus. The professors ooh-ed and aah-ed over it while Arthur hung back with me. His tattoo was uncovered and it had shifted back to English words.

"The workers have fled," he said under his breath.

"What do you mean fled?"

"I mean, there's only four people left at this site, and we're all standing in this grid. Word of Zahra's kidnapping spread like wildfire, and everyone bolted."

"You're sure–"

"Irina told me. She tried to talk people into staying, but it didn't work. We didn't have a huge crew, and between the sandstorm and the camp being invaded at least twice, people weren't willing to stay around to see what happened next."

"Arthur, you have to know that I never meant for any of this to happen," I said, but he leveled me with that cool, icy stare. Did the wind pick up or was that my imagination?

"Just because you didn't intend for this to happen, doesn't change the fact that it did. Now we have to deal with the consequences. *Your* consequences," he said.

The wind blew through his hair, and not for the first time, I was struck by just how beautiful he was. Arthur's fine nose and full lips. The color of his skin and how his cheeks heated at the change of his emotions. He paused, the wheels turning in his mind as if he was calculating what to say to twist the knife even more.

It wasn't my imagination, and this time the wind swelled. Arthur felt it, turning just in time for it to sweep across his face.

Those golden eyes reflected back at me, and I couldn't breathe.

"Beloved, it is time," he said in that voice that wasn't his own. Dr. Carrington and Dr. Romanova popped their heads out of the grid, trying to identify the voice. I tried to signal to them to go, to hide, but they didn't. Not in time for Not-Arthur to turn toward them, wrath gathering around in a bitter storm.

A sandstorm.

It clicked into place–last night–that wasn't just a freak storm. It was this, it was whatever was in Arthur's mind and controlling his limbs.

"You are not welcome here," he hissed and the Drs. dove out of the way, trying to avoid the gusts that Arthur hurled at them.

"Stop!" I shouted, grabbing his arm. Not-Arthur stared at me like I was a bug beneath his feet.

"Do not stand in my way, Beloved."

"Arthur–"

"That is not my name!" he thundered–truly thundered as the sky roared and cracked with lightning above. The ground shook beneath me and Arthur was *floating*. Wind swirled around him, golden and wild, and I was drawn to him. Every inch of me wanted to move closer, nearer, and I knew that was a horrible idea but I couldn't help it. Something tugged me forward as I shuffled closer to him. The professors held each other, cowering in the corner of the grid, trying to get out of the way before they were noticed again.

They had nowhere to go: the grid was crumbling and they were trapped.

"Call me by my name, Beloved." He spoke to me and that pull—that energy, that magic—made me shuffle closer to him. It drew me in, forcing my steps closer and closer to him.

"Your name is Arthur Lewis, you're a pain in the ass but you're brilliant and—"

A roar escaped from Not-Arthur and his lip curled up in an awful but weirdly hot snarl. Golden wind wrapped around me and I couldn't move at all. I was encased in a tornado, the funnel spinning furiously to keep me there.

"You will remember my name. You found our home, you'll remember the rest. You never stopped searching," he said and this time his demeanor flipped from this raging creature to almost gentle. Not-Arthur stroked my cheek, gazing at me with a tenderness that I'd never seen from actual Arthur. Was this how it would look if he actually wanted me?

The words of the tattoo glowed the same color as the golden wind, my body heating as if I'd touched a live wire. The words flowed across my skin, replaying in English, Arabic, in hieroglyphics, over and over.

"My tongue, your tongue," he said, showing the tattoos to me. Arthur's swirled and flowed too, the lotus slowly taking over the entirety of his arm. The ground kept shaking and the sand slowly parted.

This was something out of a campy adventure movie, except I didn't feel like I was playing the hero. I was the damsel in distress, trapped in the swirling, raging vortex of a tornado. Not-Arthur raised a hand and golden, shimmering energy danced at his fingertips. It was like looking at the sun and I couldn't tear my eyes away.

A cleft the size of a mid-sized sedan opened up and sand poured through it. For a tiny, brief second, I thought it was a black hole. The opening went on forever, black except for the sand that poured into it.

But even in all the darkness, I saw an image appearing in the sand. I might have stopped breathing.

A lotus. Life and rebirth. The cycle continuing on and on, like a love song that was heard throughout the ages, forever and ever.

The East Wind rises again, a storm without end, a lover in search of home. A lover, lost and alone, feels the East Wind caress his face and knows he will never stop searching.

It came back to me like a memory, like I was looking at an old photo album. The images flashed in my mind so quickly that they didn't make sense. I tried to slow it down just to understand what I was seeing, but I couldn't.

The winds around me slowed as the lotus appeared in more detail. Mandrakes and lotuses popped up everywhere, blooming in earnest in the middle of the desert. Not-Arthur turned to me again, the smile on his face so serene it made my chest ache.

"I know you will never stop searching," he said, echoing the words that were etched on us, and then collapsed. The force that held me in place collapsed, and I landed in the sand, sliding down to where Arthur was, unconscious and being consumed by the opening. It took me until just then to realize that the lotus that was drawn by the sand was actually *very* far away. My legs sank into the sand and I lost my balance, tumbling with speed until I got close enough to Arthur to grab him.

"Arty, hey, wake up," I said as we fell together. I hugged him tight, bringing his face to my chest to try to shield him from the fall.

"William!" Dr. Carrington screamed and he leapt after me; he fell in slow motion with Dr. Romanova right behind him. They tried to stay together, but the light faded and I didn't know where Arthur and I were headed. Ground still seemed very far away until I crashed with Arthur's weight on me.

Sand everywhere, but I could breathe, and I felt the shallow breaths from Arthur against my neck. His hands were balled in my shirt, and I knew he was awake, or close to it. But everything was black around us. Black in a way that wasn't darkness, but the absence of light. Terror tried to claw its way through me, but I stamped it down. I'd never had a panic attack and wasn't about to start now.

Although being in absolute darkness, well underground, with a likely concussed friend seemed like legit reasons to lose my shit.

Arthur stirred, struggling to sit up, and he pressed hard against my injured side for balance. It took everything in me not to scream.

"Glad you're awake, please move before I pass out," I gritted out. If my ribs weren't cracked before, they damn well were now. Arthur had a knack for plowing into them. Pain pulsed in time with my heart.

"William, what happened?" he said. His voice cracked and was so groggy I couldn't bring myself to joke him. The pain in my side made thinking harder too. He leaned all of his weight against me, trying to maneuver off of my injured side.

"Magic wind, you went all creepy and golden and opened a portal or some shit, and we fell through. That's the cliff notes. Also, you called me Beloved again."

"Why is that the highlight of the story?"

"Because magical-pissed off you was not thrilled that I didn't *know your name*, even though I know who you are." I tried to gesture with my hands, but he wouldn't see it, because again, *pitch-fucking-black*.

"Where are we?"

"In the grid. Like, below it maybe? I don't know what you did, because I was stuck in a tornado trying not to piss my pants."

"I don't remember anything once we got to the grid," Arthur said, and he felt around, reaching for me and grabbing at the darkness. He touched my thigh, my hip, until I realized he wanted my hand. When our fingers touched, a spark of light came from Arthur. I held his hand, our palms fully touching, and the glow intensified. In the wane light, I felt the knots in my chest release. Arthur was here, and he was alive, and so was I.

That was enough for this moment.

"Neat party trick," I said, and he chuckled. It was that "I'm annoyed but you're still cute" laugh. I knew the different laughs from Arthur. When had I started noticing those?

"At least we can see," he said. When Arthur moved to let go of me, the glow dimmed. Of course I wasn't panicked though; the pitch black nothingness that went on forever in every direction was nothing to be afraid of. My heart raced and my mouth was dry, but that likely had nothing to do with being terrified. Very unrelated.

I grabbed Arthur's hand simply because I wanted to, not because I needed that little hint of light.

"We should stick together," I said and Arthur nodded. Was he pale or was it the lighting? He rubbed the back of his head, and another worry hit me. Was he injured?

"Relax Ford, I'm fine. You look like you're about to cry. Don't get dehydrated on my account."

"Wasn't I the sexy, snarky one?"

"Not sure if you hit either of those, but whatever makes you feel better. Can we stand? I can't tell if there's a ceiling here." Arthur lifted out hands, the glow around them failing to illuminate the darkness. There was no ceiling that we could see. There weren't any walls either; the dark was so crushing that we wandered blindly, holding onto each other as the only anchor in the blackness.

"I'm both, actually, but let's not fight when I can't see you getting pouty. I have no idea where we are. The not-you-you waved your hand around and then something like a sinkhole opened. I fell through and then so did Dr. Carrington–"

"Wes is here?"

"Dr. Romanova too, but I couldn't see where they landed. I don't know what happened after I fell."

"There has to be a way out. This is just like–never mind." Arthur cut himself off, trying to flee from me but I held him firmly. There was no way in hell I was going to let go of that glimmer of light that came from us.

"Like what? Have you seen a place like this before somewhere?"

"Just from a movie. It's silly–"

"Movies have slivers of truth. What happened?"

"Indiana just kept going and eventually he found a tomb. But this isn't a templar knight, it's Egypt, and the construction systems are vastly different–"

"Indiana Jones," I said, waiting for him to respond. "Your mind went to Indiana Jones."

"Dr. Jones was a brilliant character," Arthur sniffed and a belly laugh erupted from me. Oh, we were going to die for sure, but at least I had one good laugh before the end.

"No arguments, but I was hoping for maybe a Mummy reference. Something a little closer, geographically."

"Another cinematic masterpiece," Arthur said, and there were sparks of joy coming from him instead of the glare I usually got.

"Okay here's my offer. We get out of here, and I'll buy enough pizza and beer for a weekend long movie marathon. All the greatest archaeologists in the world."

"Let's throw in Sherlock Holmes too and I'm sold."

"Done deal. Now, *Dr. Lewis*, if you'd be so kind," I said, gesturing with our hands to keep going. His soft laugh made the orb of light from our hands pulse. He stopped, and we examined our joined hands.

"Does it react to you too?" he asked. Arthur turned toward me and he was so close again. We kept finding reasons to be close, for our lips to brush if we just leaned in.

"Dunno, it came from you."

"Laugh," he said, and I smiled.

"Most people can't actually laugh on command, Arty."

"Your existence is a joke, so there has to be something you can laugh about."

"Ouch! When did you get so sharp-tongued?" I asked. The orb grew a little brighter. I saw the faintest hint of blush on his face. "Although, from what I can tell, it's not that sharp. Not when you're kissing me, anyway."

"Is this so? Should I be sharper? I don't think you appreciate just how much of an asshole I can be too, you know."

"I think you just called me an asshole, but I stopped listening," I said, brushing my nose against his. Arty instinctively tilted his head, ready for a kiss. Even in the dark, we knew how to do this dance. The soft, timid glow from our hands grew brighter as I pressed my lips to his before he could change his mind, before the walls came back up, and he wanted to pick another fight. There would be plenty to squabble over soon enough, and arguments for Arthur to dream up. But he wasn't fighting now, not as he leaned into me, letting go of my hand to wrap his arms around my neck. The light went out but I didn't mind because there was a small light in my chest coming straight from Arthur.

I was getting in too deep with him, but that didn't matter now because he was Arthur and for this moment, he was mine. The consequences of my feelings would be for another day if we ever made it out of this place.

The kiss deepened, Arthur sighed against my mouth and he opened to let me in. His tongue wasn't sharp at all now, but warm, sending heat straight down to my cock. His hands tangled in my hair, but even in the dark I knew what he was feeling. I could tell that he wanted me closer, and I wanted to be closer too–god, I wanted to be a *lot* closer to him, but not here where all of the nuances of his face were swallowed in the dark. I wanted to memorize each gasp and each sound he made. I wanted to watch how his eyes darkened and his need made him cling to me.

My hands snaked down to his waist, lower until I cupped his ass just like that night back in college that we never talked about. Arthur sucked in a breath, raking his teeth across my bottom lip. He nodded, and I squeezed, his body responding to me. It was easier somehow in the dark; easier to reach for the things we wanted without having to speak them.

The pressure in his pants, straining against my thigh, sent electricity through my nerves. Arthur made a little noise, a huff, as he kissed back more assertively. My hands went to his belt, fumbling without any light, and he stilled.

"What–?"

"Do you trust me?"

"Is that a rhetorical question?" I undid the buckle, unzipped his pants, and they sagged against the slim bones of his hips. It was a shame that I couldn't see the blush on his face because I could feel how his skin heated. I pushed them down, and the gentle shoosh of fabric as they landed at his feet filled the silence. His boxers were tight and fitted, and I palmed him.

Sinking to my knees, Arthur tucked his hands in my hair, tugging and scratching his nails at the base of my skull.

"Trust me, Arty," I said, pulling his boxers down and down.

"I don't want any sand on me–"

"Trust me, Arty," I said again before licking the tip of his cock. He shuddered, but didn't pull away. I licked him again, and Arthur seemed to stop breathing. When I took him all in my mouth, his hips bucked and I held him still.

"William–"

I didn't respond, instead I licked the base of dick, swirling my tongue around the sensitive skin, and his grip in my hair tightened. It urged me further, as I let my hands roam across his thighs, to his balls, before cupping his ass.

Arthur liked it deep and slow, maddening strokes of my tongue until his body tightened. My ribs ached, but I didn't stop. Arthur whispered my name like it was some kind of prayer, and I relished this. His walls were down and he was this raw, primal version of himself where he wasn't fighting just to fight. He was giving to give, and I wanted every fucking ounce of him. His release was building as his groans grew, he grabbed and tugged me, trying to buck his hips as I held him steady.

When Arthur finally came, it was a hot rush of release, and I sucked him through it. I used my strength to hold him up, massaging his legs and ass while he rode the last waves of his climax. Arthur's strained voice rumbled in his chest, his skin blissfully overheated, as he started to sink to me. I held him firm and he tensed.

"What–?"

"You said no sand," I said, standing and bringing him with me. Arthur leaned against my chest and I had my hands on his bare ass.

"I should pull my pants up," he said, and I laughed.

"I wouldn't mind you exploring whatever this is naked. Sounds like a good time."

"You are–"

"The best? Yes, I know. We need to do this again, but with the lights on. Next time I wanna see your face when you come." Arthur had to be beet red, and I grabbed his hand so the light would return. The faint glow illuminated his red cheeks. I knew it. He was fucking adorable.

"Ah, um, we should get going," he said, trying to pull away but I squeezed his hand.

"What, no cuddle sesh? Our magical hand holding is the only light we've got, so stop trying to run off."

"What is causing this? I mean, I'm grateful for the light, but it's strange isn't it?"

"Arthur, are we still pretending that this isn't some ancient curse or magic? Because you can't take the necklace off, you went all possessed with golden eyes and opened a secret tunnel to an underground... something under the sand. And then the glowing hand thing."

"I'm willing to admit that the evidence suggests there's something beyond our comprehension causing this," Arthur said like he was conceding an argument. He waved our arms around, looking for a direction to go. With his unbuckled pants askew and glow making him look so utterly adorable, all I could do was grin at him. I knew it got on his nerves, which made it even better.

"You don't believe in aliens, do you?" I asked.

"I believe in the possibility but no, not until I have proof."

"You've gotta have faith in the unknown, Arty. That's what Indiana Jones would do."

"He wouldn't actually, he also wanted proof."

"You're ridiculous," I laughed and he laughed too. The tension between us seemed to be at a cease fire for now, and I'd take it. Arthur's hand in mine felt nice, and I'd take that too. We stumbled along in the semi-dark, moving slowly. My eyes started to adjust and I could make out more shapes. The walls were more defined now, like we had moved into a stone building instead of packed sand. Arthur held our hands close to the wall, trying to read the inscription. I felt his shiver as his fingers traced over the ancient words.

I watched him with awe. Arthur was so engrossed in it, his hand squeezing mine so tight my fingers hurt, but I said nothing.

"Henkhisesui," he whispered, and the air felt so stale that I could choke on it. It was as if the world remembered that we were stuck in this forgotten hole and the air needed to match the vibe. He touched the hieroglyphics with such care, such reverence. Arthur mouthed the words as he translated, speaking in what sounded like perfect ancient Egyptian. Assuming anyone actually knew what it was truly like; but if anyone ever got it right, it would be Arthur Lewis. He spoke a little louder, and I recognized the words that had become the silent mantra in my head.

"*The East Wind rises again, a storm without end, a lover in search of home. A lover, lost and alone, feels the East Wind caress his face and knows he will never stop searching,*" he said in ancient Egyptian. It wasn't Arabic, and it wasn't English, but the words rolled off his tongue and I understood them nonetheless.

"Still don't believe in coincidences?" I asked and Arthur shushed me.

"There's more to it this time," he said.

"More? What does it say?"

"It says, *one day we will rise again and there will be no storm, no force that will stand between the East Wind and his lover.*"

"Rise again? Like... reincarnation?"

"Most likely, reincarnation was widely believed in, you know that. If Henkhisesui was here, then his lover was likely here too. Maybe they were buried together, assuming you can bury a god."

"Wait, a god? Henkhisesui is a god?"

"I was going to tell you about it but then you were an ass, and Zahra got captured. The right moment to talk about all of this didn't really come up."

"So you didn't tell me something *crucial* about our situation because you were in a bad mood?"

"Basically yes. Doesn't it feel great to be left in the dark?"

"You're about to find out," I seethed and let go of his hand. Arthur groped around reaching for me but I stepped just out of his reach.

"William, stop it–"

"Oh *shit–*" I said, my words swallowed as I fell. I didn't see a ledge there. I couldn't see shit, really, but I fell hard, tumbling across the hard, stone floor. My knees cracked as they hit the rocky ground. The skin split and they were bleeding; I felt the tearing and the sand getting into the cuts. Hissing, I rolled to my side, cradling my ribs, and tried to breathe.

"William!" Arthur screamed, and for the first time, I heard fear choking his voice.

"There's a ledge," I said and he screamed again, but I couldn't help him as the walls shifted, groaning and scraping together. I couldn't *see* anything, but I threw my hands out in front of me, desperate not to get caught between the shifting.

"Will–" he yelled but his voice was cut off, drowned out by the creaking of the walls.

When it finally stopped, I was covered in sand and dust and utterly, completely alone in the dark.

XII

Arthur

THE WALLS WERE CAVING in. This old structure wasn't stable and somehow it destabilized even more and collapsed. We were trapped here, in the dark, in different parts of wherever the hell we were. I called for William again, but there was no answer. Dust rained down on me, coating my skin and hair. My glasses were filthy and cracked, but that didn't matter when I couldn't see anyway. There was nothing but darkness and sand all around me.

Panic threatened to eat me alive, but I tried my best to stamp it down. Breathing in and out with slow, controlled breaths. Shaking hands and knocking knees made thinking impossible so I just kept breathing.

I had no idea how much time passed.

William didn't answer no matter how many times I called for him, and my voice was going hoarse. With no food or water, shouting wasn't going to help at this point. The lack of water made me dizzy, and I tried to breathe through that too.

There was no choice but to continue forward; the way we came was blocked by stones and sand. Without any tools or light, it was impassible.

Dropping to my hands and knees, I crawled through the dark, slowly feeling my way around until I could find *something*. We found evidence of civilization and life, so there had to be a way out.

Unless we fell into a cript, designed to seal them away for eternity.

I chased the thought away, crawling close to the wall I bumped into, and feeling for more hieroglyphics. It would be hard to read without seeing them, but I knew enough of the language that I could figure them out by touch.

I hoped.

The first wall I came to was smooth and empty. Why would it be empty? Especially if this was the tomb of two lovers, trying to stay together. They should have written their story on the walls, craving out their tale for the world to know. Maybe that's what reincarnation was; living on through the memories and knowledge of generations to come. Did Henkhisesui and his lover write their story here, hoping someone would read it one day?

I'd give their story life, if I ever got out of here.

The wall gave me no clues, no hints. Tears welled up in my eyes, but Indiana Jones never cried, and I wouldn't either. Not now, not when my body needed every drop of water to stay hydrated.

Blinking back the tears, an idea came to me.

It was stupid. It was illogical.

It could work.

I touched the necklace, and whispered, "Henkhisesui, can you hear me?"

I waited for a beat, then another. Nothing.

"Henkhisesui, tell me your story. Help me understand what happened to your lover. Who was he? What was his name?" I asked the darkness.

Still nothing.

I tried again, this time holding my hands together, trying to recreate the glow that came from holding onto William. If he was still alive, I was going to be furious with him.

Not if, I chided; he couldn't just die. William Ford was like a fungus, he didn't just go away.

"Please, Henkhisesui, if you can hear me, answer me. Send the wind," I pleaded, noting just how dangerously close I was to sobbing.

The slightest, smallest hint of air brushed against my cheek. I stopped breathing; did I imagine that? No, no, no, I thought, before I felt it again but stronger.

"Henkhisesui?"

"I am the East Wind, Henkhisesui," a voice said. My heart nearly stopped. *"You wear my emblem, you will help me rise."*

"Rise? What do you mean?"

"Rise to live again. Rise to bring him home. To me."

Every cell in my body forgot to function. I was frozen in fear, so bone deep that I'd never move again, that this was it. I'd die right here and this... being would kill me again for dying on him.

"Speak human."

"Help me out of here," I whimpered and I tried to hide all of my fear.

"Do not fear me. I will not hurt the one who bears my emblem. You will help me. I will help you."

"I need light," I said, and this time my voice didn't sound so weak.

"You need to find my altar."

"An altar? Is this a temple?"

"Yes, it is my temple. The people of the East Wind lived here. They worshipped me and I protected them. That was a long time ago. Long before the people of this land forgot themselves."

"Who was your lover?" I asked. My heart raced, because I had to be hallucinating in the darkness. I felt the walls, searching for anything to help me.

"Kheti," the god sighed and the wind brushed against my face like the softest caress. It reminded me of William, of the night he broke into my hotel room. His hands were soft then, touching me like I was something special.

"You know what it is to love," he said, and I panicked.

"You can hear my thoughts?" I asked Henkhisesui. I still couldn't see anything, but I sat back against the wall. The cool stone helped to clear my cloudy thoughts.

"You bear my emblem. I am with you. I am you."

I didn't have time to unpack that last sentence, so I asked him another question: "Where is William?"

"He will reach my altar before you. Find my altar and you will find your lover."

Was it rude to tell a god–or whatever–to slow their roll? William wasn't my lover. He wasn't anything. He was just William, and right now he was missing. And that was it. I wasn't *missing* him.

"How do I find your altar?"

"Listen to the wind," he said, and then he was gone. Air rushed around me, whispering in ancient Egyptian again. *This way,* it sang. Henkhisesui wasn't in my head anymore but he didn't let me down with the light.

Small sconces lined the walls and they glowed bright enough to illuminate the hall. I stood in a hall that seemed to go on forever. The carved stone walls were perfectly preserved; the hieroglyphics were still fully colored. I traced over a symbol for Horus, and goose-bumps covered my arm.

How many years had it been since a human walked this hall?

Tears welled up and this time I didn't stop them, or will them away. The enormity of what we'd found hit all at once: this was the best preserved temple in the world. I studied the story that scrolled across the hallway. When I turned back, I saw only the darkness and sand, the start of the hallway.

A huge, sprawling lotus was on the tiled floor beneath my feet. The dark lines of the lotus with the oddly bright yellow paint took my breath away. It was massive, at least a three foot span, and I tried to think if I'd ever seen something similar before but nothing came to mind.

I saw Kheti's name engraved on the stem of the lotus and my heart swelled. I wondered what he was like, that he was special enough to capture the attention of a god. Was he roguish or pious? Did Kheti make the god of the east wind laugh until the skies crackled with storms?

The stone tile floor was decorated in alternating patterns: a lotus and the wind. They swirled together and it was like even the floor was an homage to their love story. But for as beautiful as the floor was, the walls captured me more. It was the rest of their story, told in paintings.

This way, the wind whispered again, but I couldn't leave this place. I couldn't leave when there was still so much to learn.

This way, it said, pushing against my back.

I followed only once it was too much to resist, as the wind shoved me forward.

"Alright, I'm going," I said, and the wind eased. My footsteps now echoed through the empty hall, and the sound broke something in my heart. The emptiness here was too much to bear. I tried to take in the story of Henkhisesui and Kheti, but I needed more time to really capture the nuisance. Each clanking step on the tile echoed, and I tried to step as lightly as I could so I didn't damage anything. The walls were bright enough with the wall sconces for me to see more of their story.

Kheti was a jeweler. I touched the necklace and wondered if Kheti was the one that forged this piece. The pendant warmed to my touch and a light breeze fluttered across my hand. Was that Henkhisesui telling me I was right?

This way, the wind sighed again.

I watched as the murals unfolded before me. The god of the east wind with his ram-like head and the hieroglyphs for sails surrounded him as he stood before the man who had to be Kheti. Kheti didn't seem to be anyone special; there were no adornments to mark him as part of a higher class. He was a jeweler, but nothing more exciting than that.

They met and traveled together. This art was unlike anything I'd ever seen before; the style didn't fit the same time period as the necklace. I watched the art evolve and change, the murals becoming more and more modern.

Henkhisesui and Kheti sat together with easy smiles with a picnic before them. The abundance spoke to their joy, an over pouring of happiness and health. I could study these images for years if I had the tools to document it. There was so much to study–where did this style come from? Who did this? Was it Henkhisesui and Kheti? I loved imagining that: two lovers creating a whole new style of art to represent their unique love story.

They held hands and picked flowers. They shared embraces. Kheti now appeared with a feather in his headdress–a symbol for the wind. Was this Henkhisesui claiming him? Lotuses bloomed everywhere along with mandrakes. Life and love–the murals overflowed with them.

My heart was so full that I thought I might burst. I imagined what their days were like, walking through the desert towns, laying by the water of the Nile. Did they watch the stars and make up their own stories about them? I stopped walking to trace over a particularly detailed lotus. It was large, the stem going down between Henkhisesui and Kheti. The lotus was made from colorful tiles like a mosaic instead of paints.

Kheti, the wind sighed.

Kheti made this lotus. Was it his artistry in this temple?

This way, it guided and I followed. The wall sconces cast the entire temple in a soft, golden light. I hadn't taken a moment to fully appreciate the size and how grandiose it was. The ceilings were sky high and arched. I missed a step, stumbling at the height of the ceiling. How was it that high? Surely we would have seen it from above?

How far down did we fall? The thought made me shiver, as I let my eyes scan. It was too dark and too high to see the details, but I saw painted stars and swirling blues. It was so unlike any other Egyptian art that I questioned whose hands created it. There was a myriad of colors, like the sun setting into the darkest parts of the night. My feet followed with my eyes upward, as I watched the sky change. A large, crystal clear portrait of the full moon nearly knocked me over. There was a shine on the surface of the moon, like it was made of diamond.

This temple felt holy.

The air–or was it Henkhisesui–was charged around me. I'd never felt the energy of a space before, but something was different. The temperature dropped. My breath froze in my lungs, and my body felt sluggish. I watched the sky above me twinkle and shine like the stars were actually real. The golden wind that I knew came back and wrapped around my arms and chest. It was warm and soft, cradling me against the sudden cold.

It sighed again and this time when the wind brushed my cheek, it felt more solid. It felt like a hand caressed me, and some tiny part of my heart wished that William was here.

Only so I wouldn't be alone, imagining that the wind was rubbing my face like some kind of delusional idiot. He'd make a joke about this whole situation; something childish and probably involving his cock.

I didn't need to think about William's cock right now. Or ever. Well, maybe not *ever*, but certainly not right now.

The wind seemed to laugh at my inner monologue as it curled around me, shimmering and iridescent. I tried to get it to curl around my fingers, and eventually it did. Toying with the wind, I found myself walking without realizing or caring where I was going. The night sky painted on the ceiling shifted to morning. The startling, brilliant pinks and orange took over until the whole temple was bathed in warm light again.

At the center of the hall, a room opened up. Light from way up above filtered down and my knees went weak realizing that this was daylight. Sunlight. It wasn't the soft, atmospheric glow from the sconces, but *light*, pouring in from the sun.

There was a way out!

I ran, my chest heaving and protesting, but I didn't care. There was a way out, and I had to find it before Henkhisesui decided to get rid of it. The center of the room revealed a huge fountain.

The statue in the middle was obscenely large; so large I really should have noticed it immediately. I was so fixated on the light, I didn't notice the statue of a man with a ram's head. It was solid gold. The light glinted off of it and made it hard to stare at directly. The wings were coated in jewels extending straight out. Each feather of the wings was etched in gold. I stumbled. It was Henkhisesui.

The body of the statue was a large, glittering scarab. The black stones had to be some kind of onyx, anchoring Henkhisesui to a pedestal. He was kneeling, his human legs visible from the side. The pedestal was in the center of a large fountain with crystal clear water. My mouth was so dry that the water seemed like something out of a dream. The water rippled gently and I looked for the source of the movement; there were feathers around the base of the statue that had water coming from them.

It was clear and cool against my hands, and I rinsed them off, savoring the feeling of clean skin. I saw no signs of the water being anything other than clean, so I cupped my hands and drank. My lips and throat practically burned from thirst, but I forced myself to drink slowly. Last thing I needed was to choke and throw up in a pristinely preserved temple. The water trailed down my chin and it was the crispest, cleanest tasting water I'd ever had. I scooped handful after handful to my mouth until my belly was full of water. My body needed the water so badly and I sat at the edge of the fountain trying to catch my breath. Light filtered down from the ceiling and I was suddenly so exhausted that I couldn't move.

The pendant around my necklace felt so heavy that my body started to droop.

You're here, the wind whispered in my ear, and I wondered what here was. The altar? There were no traditional signs of an altar here, but what was traditional about this temple? Henkhisesui loomed over me until I felt like I was the size of an ant. The statue was brilliant with all of the gems tucked into it, but there was something else.

The wind.

Wind blew through here, rustling my hair softly, brushing against me. I swallowed hard; every touch of the wind made me think of William, and the tattoos on my arm rippled in response. The words changed from Egyptian to English, each symbol slowly shifting into the words of my native tongue. It was beautiful; watching how the past melted away to be the language in my mind.

The East Wind rises again, a storm without end, a lover in search of home. A lover, lost and alone, feels the East Wind caress his face and knows he will never stop searching, I heard the wind sigh. It filled my ears until the wind roared through me, whipping up the sand into a frenzy.

Another tornado–smaller and confined to just me again. It tightened its grip on me until I couldn't draw a breath.

"You found me, good work Arthur Lewis," Henkhisesui said.

The wind twisted between me and the statue. It held me in place until I was eye level with the ram's head. First the wings flexed and I thought I was hallucinating. The gold in them cracked and broke, showering the fountain with gold and jewels. The scarab's body popped more jewels off and the wings and legs broke free.

My heart might have stopped completely when the ram's head twisted, stretching its neck, intelligent, living eyes staring right through me.

Then it blinked.

"Very good, Arthur Lewis," the ram said as it smiled at me. Human hands and legs stretched and moved, the golden wind wrapping around them until he stood to his full height.

Henkhisesui had to be close to ten feet tall. If I had any food at all in my system, I might have shit myself. I regretted every gulp of water now as it roiled in my stomach, fear and adrenaline coursing through me with such force that I felt my heart beating in every nerve and muscle.

"It's time to raise Kheti, he has been sleeping for too long." Henkhisesui's words were in Egyptian, just like the tattoos down his arm. They matched mine. His golden skin had the blistering, harsh lines of the tattoo inked into him so deeply that it could have been carved out of his flesh.

And he was flesh now. Henkhisesui had shaken off every jewel and gold until he stood in his true form, radiant and terrifying. The fur on his head was bright white with the huge, curled ram's horns.

Watching him speak made my brain feel funny, like I was watching an optical illusion.

The wind holding me in place gently released me and I fell back on the floor of the temple. Light and magic–that's all it could be–scrawled across the floor, lighting up the tiles of the lotus.

"Find Kheti. Find the one called William Ford," Henkhisesui said and I looked to see who he was speaking to. Each tile of the lotuses popped up and I jumped, trying to get out of the way as little scarab beetles flexed their bodies and skittered to life. I wracked my brain trying to remember if they actually ate meat but my thoughts were too scrambled to remember anything.

What would Indy do, I asked myself, and all I could think of was *get out of the fucking way*. I climbed into the fountain; the water had mostly splashed out from all the gems hitting the water. My shoes and pants were soaked, as was the rest of me really, but I didn't care. Logically bugs didn't like water, so this was the safest move. The scarabs didn't even notice me as they fled through the hallways of the tunnel. Thousands of them moved as one wave of sparkling hell, sweeping through every crevice of the temple.

"Find them, and bring them to me. Do not harm Kheti, your master."

Henkhisesui didn't mention anything about not harming William so I shouted, "And William! Don't hurt him!"

Henkhisesui glanced down at me, that strange smile on his face. "*You have no power here, Arthur Lewis. They will not answer you.*"

"I thought–"

"*You thought wrong. Give me Kheti's necklace.*" I wrapped my hand around the necklace, the damn thing that started this all, and shook my head no.

Wind picked me up and tossed me clear across the temple. I crashed into a wall and prayed that I didn't damage it. Henkhisesui screamed in rage, so loud my eardrums felt like they were about to burst. The scarabs didn't notice or care as they continued on their path, back through the hallway and toward the darkness.

"*Give it to me!*" he bellowed and I scrambled to my feet. My back ached and my knee felt twisted, but I didn't stop. I ran. I ran so hard that my body felt like it was burning up, lungs aching. My inhaler was back at the campsite so I'd have to power through without it and pray that my lungs could keep up.

I limped as I ran, trying to find a place to hide to catch my breath.

"*You will not leave this temple alive, Arthur Lewis,*" he raged and I clapped a hand over my mouth to quiet the sounds of my breathing. God, what I'd give for William to be here now. Anyone, really, but especially William. His quick thinking would be useful, even if part of me hated to admit that. I wanted him to have some snappy one-liner to bring me back to myself, ready to fight and set him straight.

"Yes, I will," I said to myself and got up to run again.

"No, you won't," Henkhisesui appeared in front of me, nearly twice my height and I froze. He touched my forehead and I felt myself being forced into a corner of my mind, further and further until I couldn't see anything by darkness. My body moved on its own again, but this time I knew it was happening. I watched as Henkhisesui used me as a puppet, moving my arms and legs, turning this way and that.

"You will stay in that cage until I release you. No mortal man will defy the will of a god," Henkhisesui said and he closed the door to consciousness in my mind.

Everything went dark until I couldn't see, couldn't feel, couldn't *move*. I collapsed into myself, the crushing weight of his presence in my head shutting down my brain. *"William,"* I whispered but no one heard me.

XIII

William

I'D BEEN IN SHITTY situations before. Beaten up. Running from guys that wanted to beat me up. Losing a small fortune to a bunch of blood-thirsty loan sharks. But this, this took the cake.

No light, no way to know which way to go, no food, no water. I was fucked, and it was becoming more and more apparent with every passing moment that it was very likely I was going to die alone in this pitch black tomb.

So I sat in the sand, letting it run through my fingers, trying to ground myself enough to plan my next move. There was always another move to take, even if it wasn't great. The sand ran between my fingers, slipping through them as all of my plans and plots slipped away.

This wasn't how I imagined dying, but now it seemed fitting. I wondered what my mom would think; would she know on some instinctive level that I was gone?

Would that make her feel better or worse? Zahra might miss me, but that was up in the air at this point too. I wanted to ask if she led me to the Spice Traders on purpose, but for what? To fuck over her best friend?

Then there was Arty, of course.

He'd miss me. Probably.

He'd miss having someone to fight with at least; someone that would go toe to toe with him without backing down or giving in. God, it was fun to get the better of him. The only reason I tried so hard in school was just because it was so fun to piss him off. Wonder what he'd say if he knew I blew a professor for a final grade so I'd just edge him out of the valedictorian spot. Of course he was the brilliant one, but since I didn't take him to bed back then, I had to blow off the steam somehow. Watching him fume was a close second now; after seeing the way his cheeks grew red and how he bucked when I touched him, nothing would compare to that.

It figured that I'd die with blue balls.

I didn't know how long I sat in the sand, but I needed to move. Giving up and dying was too dramatic, even for me. I crawled–fucking embarrassing–through the sand. Wherever I fell from was blocked now, so there was only one way forward. That I could tell anyway. I couldn't see my hand in front of my face, so I crawled along until I bumped into a wall. My knees ached, but then I thought I saw a light.

It had to be my eyes playing a trick on me, but I crawled toward it. Any glimmer of hope at this point. I ventured up to my feet, stretching out my back and legs, as I walked with my hands out in front of me.

When I found Arthur, I was going to give him so much shit for this. When, not if. Maybe changing my mindset would help the crushing weight of death looming over me.

The light grew stronger and I rubbed my eyes. After blinking a few times, the light didn't vanish.

Was it real? I couldn't trust my perception of reality any more. The darkness clung to me like a second skin, and leaving it seemed impossible. My feet moved on their own, powering through until the light became so bright that I saw what looked like stone.

I didn't believe it was real until my shoes squeaked against the stone floor, and I sank down to touch it.

Stone. Real stone. The light came from a small torch on the wall–what was that called? I couldn't remember. The walls were also made of stone, and I noticed all of the art. Huge depictions of people were painted on the walls and it looked fresh. It looked like someone had painted this last week instead of thousands of years ago. I touched the wall expecting my hand to be wet from the colors, but it was dry.

But there were *colors*. There was something other than darkness and I took a few shaky breaths.

"See, not dying today. Progress," I muttered to myself. The murals were so unusual, but I couldn't put my finger on what gave me the chills. The obvious signs of war: horses rearing up, people holding bows and spears, or how there was a giant deity with a ram's head and wings. The body looked sort of like a bug, but I couldn't tell. I'd never seen that kind of creature before, and something about it gave me the creeps. It looked... cruel. The way it was depicted, reigning over the battlefield with glee, made my heart sink.

This place was a hall to memorialize the battles fought here and the red staining the walls and floor couldn't be mistaken for anything other than blood. My feet were rooted to the stone floor as I stared. The ram-like man had a hand extended to another man, and his face was less cruel. He looked afraid, but not of the ram-headed guy. His eyes were cast down at all the blood, and I wondered what it was he saw. The realities of war? Was this a place he knew?

I sent a prayer to whoever was listening that this wasn't his home, or that he wasn't in danger. A feather on his head made me think that he was connected to the ram-headed man, but maybe that was wishful thinking. Maybe the bloody scene wasn't the spoils of war but *he* was the prize to be won. Was that fear on his lovely face from something far worse?

Forcing myself to turn away, I tried to remember my college days and wished that I wasn't such a great test taker and better at actually remembering shit. The language felt so far away in my memory that I could have forgotten everything. Maybe Arabic replaced it in my mind; Arthur always said I was good with languages, but really I was good at talking.

The walls weren't great company to talk with.

The scenes unfolded with the man following the ram-guy around. They walked together, sat together, prayed together. Hordes of food and jewels surrounded them and with each mural, the man changed from the plain clothes villager to something more. His robes grew more elaborate, the jewels on his hands and wrists grew.

But then I saw the next mural with the ram-guy handing him a green-jeweled necklace with a pendant the size of my fist. An emerald that large would be worth a fortune, not to mention all of the other jewels. I stopped at the entrance of a room and understood the words above the doorway.

The East Wind rises again, a storm without end, a lover in search of home. A lover, lost and alone, feels the East Wind caress his face and knows he will never stop searching.

The words were haunting, filling my head like I was drowning in them. It played over and over again, until I wanted to claw my ears off to get it to stop. A thousand voices spoke at once and it roared through my head. I stumbled through the doorway and into a very large room. Landing on my hands and knees, I took a minute to sort myself out. The roaring had stopped but my stomach protested and I wanted to puke my guts out. Was this what Arthur felt when his eyes went all golden? No wonder he couldn't remember anything.

It was brighter here, but where did the light come from? The ceiling was covered. The little fires on the walls to light the way were the same.

Must be the giant mound of gold in the middle reflecting the light in every direction. I pushed up to my feet very slowly. This could easily be a fever dream, or whatever the darkness driven equivalent would be. Arthur would know if there was a precise term. I did my best not to think about him too much because it made the darkness heavier. It already felt like a second skin, like it clung to my pores and my hair and my shoes. Darkness had a weight–I don't think most people realized that. I sure as hell didn't until I was chewed up and swallowed by it.

But the darkness waned here, and some strange part of me missed it. I could hide all of my failures in the darkness and the inky blackness would welcome it. A force so powerful it could have swept away all of my mistakes until I was just a forgotten speck in the wind.

Tempting. So very tempting to throw in the towel and just disappear.

Don't be an idiot, William, I imagined Arthur saying, and it pushed me forward. Unfortunately his made-up warning wasn't enough for me to keep my hands to myself and not touch the gold.

The darkness could hide my problems, but a couple handfuls of this would solve all of them. I could pay off my debts to Annatto and the Spice Traders before they realized I had a mother back in America. I could buy her a house on the beach somewhere where she could walk barefoot in the sand and smell the salt air.

How easily life could change with just a few pieces of gold.

There was so much I didn't even know where to start or what to look at first. I picked up a small golden coin, and flipped it over in my hand. The symbol for air was etched on one side with a lotus on the other. My arm tingled and I'd bet all of the gold in this room that it was because the tattoo was changing. My shirt was torn from the fall, and I saw the outlines rippling under the fabric, changing again. Lotuses covered my arm with a few smaller mandrakes tucked between them.

When I opened my palm, the lotus there was fully opened again. I smiled at it; regardless of how I got them, I sort of loved the tattoos. They were beautiful and intricate, and some selfish part of me loved that I shared it with Arthur. I loved that he had the same markings on his skin, and it was a secret that we shared.

I heard a skittering sound and I froze. What the hell was that? The room was empty and that only served to ratchet my heart rate up even more. I scanned and scanned, but nothing. No one was here, and that was almost worse than knowing where the sound came from.

I didn't have time to look over everything here, so I scooped as much gold as I could up and tucked into my pants pockets, tossing necklace after necklace around my neck. I wrapped a few around my wrist for a makeshift bracelet when the skittering noise came back.

That awful, sinking feeling of being watched prickled all across my skin and I turned around very, very slowly.

The entire entryway of the room was black.

And moving.

There were hundreds of bugs, maybe even thousands.

They moved as one as if they shared the same mind.

"Oh, *fuck*, scarabs," I breathed before I took off in a run. I climbed over the mound of gold, not caring if I crushed something precious when those bugs were about to *eat* something precious: me.

Movement seemed to bring them to life, and they surged toward me. The tentative searching became a whirlwind of wings and legs. If I thought about it too much I'd make myself sick. The bugs plowed into the treasure, sending priceless artifacts flying like they meant nothing. Several pieces of gold peppered my back, soaring through the air like projectiles right at me. I tried to duck, but the swarm was too fast and hit the treasure too hard.

Gold exploded around me and they kept coming. I sprinted down through the room and down into another hall. The little lights on the wall had faded and I was quickly running back into the darkness.

Could a scarab see in the dark? I had no idea.

I didn't want to test that theory.

Hands out, I ran–I just had to keep going. Stopping meant death. Stopping meant being eaten and chewed up by thousands of tiny jaws.

So I didn't stop. I heard the swarm at my back and it was closing in on me. The darkness was far less terrifying than the bugs. What could possibly be worse than scarabs?

The universe was waiting for me to think of that; I ran smack into a wall, and my nose ached. Feeling around in the dark, there was nowhere to go. I'd hit a dead end in this fucking maze of a place and now I was stuck. Alone except for a hungry swarm of bugs. When was the last time they ate? I hoped the little fuckers choked on me.

"William!" a voice called and I tried to figure out where it was coming from. Hallucinating right at the end–cute, fitting. Of course I'd dream something up as I was about to die.

"William!" a woman's voice hissed, and it snapped me out of my haze.

"Dr. Romanova?" I said, trying not to make too much sound. Where were the bugs? They sounded like they were in the walls, above me, next to me–

"Yes, come on!" she said as a pair of strong hands grabbed me and half-dragged me along. The flashlight was nearly blinding, but I saw Dr. Carrington and Dr.

Romanova together, holding hands and holding onto me.

"Move!" he said, and I picked up the pace. The swarm was deafening, and disorientating. How could it sound like they were everywhere at once? Maybe I was losing it. Dr. Romanova led the way with Dr. Carrington just a couple steps behind her. She ran without hesitation, moving through the halls with alarming speed.

"Where's–" I started to say but they hushed me.

"Not now," Dr. Carrington said as he shouldered a wall. I didn't see anything unusual on the wall, but he felt along the edge of a mural until something hissed and clicked. "Help me."

He threw himself against the wall, but nothing happened. Dr. Romanova swung the flashlight around wildly, switching between us and the rest of the hall.

"Irina!" he said with his winded voice. Dr. Carrington rubbed at his shoulder before he threw himself at the wall again. I added my weight, pressing against the wall, but I felt nothing. It was solid stone, and it was not budging.

"It has to be here somewhere," she said as she dropped the flashlight on the stone floor. It echoed in the darkness, and for a second the chittering of the scarabs stopped. The lack of sound stopped me in my tracks.

Why had the bugs stopped? Why weren't they still following us? There was light and sound for them to follow; we were easy prey.

Unless there was something else that saw them as easy prey.

Footsteps pounded in the hall, shaking the walls, shaking me to my bones. Dust and sand fell in my face, and the Drs. stayed very still. Dr. Carrington pulled Dr. Romanova into a hug, cradling her face against his chest. She clapped a hand over her mouth, trying to slow her breathing, and the tear rolling down her face was too much for me.

I tried the wall again. Whatever the hell could scare off an entire horde of scarabs was not something I wanted to hang around to meet.

They said there was something here, so I got to work, shining the flashlight on the murals for any kind of clue.

The man with the jewels was here, but he was alone. No ram-headed guy in sight. Strange; he had always been depicted *with* the ram-guy. He looked down toward the corner of the painting where a lotus sat with open petals.

I smacked each petal, waiting for something to happen.

When I hit the last one, the wall trembled as it slid open. The mural disappeared and all that was left was the jeweled man smiling at the opening in the wall. He held a small cane that was twisted like a braid, and I remembered what it meant: magic.

"Holy shit, come on!" I yelled. I couldn't control the volume of my voice, but it spurned them into action. The professors stumbled through the opening and we ran down the narrow hall. This wasn't meant for everyday use; this hallway was a secret, a getaway. We powered through, moving as fast as we could.

Dr. Carrington slowed first, and then Dr. Romanova slowed to be with him.

"We can't stop now–"

"We have to, I can't keep up with this pace," he said between heaving breaths.

"How did you get in here?" I asked and they smiled at each other.

"It was actually marvelous. Whatever Arthur did, we got caught up in the storm, instead of fighting it, well–"

"We jumped right in," Dr. Romanova said, holding his hand.

"You both are nuts," I said, and they laughed quietly. Dr. Carrington started coughing as he tried to catch his breath.

"You saw what happened with Arthur?" I asked.

"I was rather hoping you'd explain. I've known Arthur for quite a while now. I'm assuming this has something to do with the matching tattoos," Dr. Carrington asked. "Something has been going on with him since we got here. Rather, since we met back up with you."

I felt the attack and the question, but I didn't take the bait. Arthur had shown him the tattoos, but did it even matter at this point who knew about it?

"Yep, we got matching tattoos in Fayoum. Surprise," I said, holding up my hand to show them. I wiggled my fingers for effect.

"Yes, ones that seem to change with your mood, or disappear. Tattoos that have words incorporated that sound like a love poem between a god and a man. Very standard stuff," Dr. Carrington deadpanned.

"Look, if Arthur didn't say anything–"

"Arthur isn't here. We are. Wesley said that he told him about the tattoos and a necklace. And we're stuck here unless we can figure out how the hell we got here to begin with. I've yet to see anything close to daylight," Dr. Romanova added.

I worked through the next words very carefully–mostly so I didn't sound like a complete asshole. "Can you read this?" I asked, showing them my arm. The tattoos were back to hieroglyphs, and I watched as their annoyed faces melted away to fascination.

The lotus on my palm was fully opened, like it was in bloom. I rubbed at it, trying to see if the lotus would respond. The petals ruffled and fluffed back out. Was that Arthur getting annoyed with me?

God I hoped he was still alive. How dull life would be without teasing the hell out of him for discovering a long lost temple because he died down here somewhere?

"This is the same phrasing that Arthur had on his arm. The East Wind rises again, a storm without end, a lover in search of home. A lover, lost and alone, feels the East Wind caress his face and knows he will never stop searching," he said.

"Yeah, that's what the tattoos say. They change between Egyptian, English, Arabic, and just art work. Arthur's were just lotuses and mandrakes once. I don't know why they change."

"Fascinating," Dr. Romanova said, turning my arm over in her hands. She had taken the flashlight back and it pointed to my arm.

"I promise to be your guinea pig once we get out of here. Have you been this way before?" I asked, gesturing to the small hallway. It felt claustrophobic and I did my damnest not to focus on just how small the walls were getting.

"No, we heard you and then followed the sound. Were those actually scarabs?" Dr. Carrington asked. I nodded. I'd never seen one in person, but seeing a few thousand of them swarming had me convinced that even if they weren't scarabs they were decidedly *not great*. The skittering sounded so far away now that I let myself relax for a moment and breathe. Everything hurt, and this was becoming my norm far too often.

"There has to be a way out," I muttered, looking around. I reached for the flashlight and Dr. Romanova handed it over. We were in a very narrow tunnel. The stone had given way to just sand, and as we trucked through it, my calves burned. If I ever got out of this mess, I was going to take a very long, very hot bath until every knot in my body came loose.

"We can't go back that way," she said, pointing behind us. Dr. Carrington nodded.

"Why would the tunnel narrow this much?"

"Servants. This wasn't decided for anyone important to see, assuming whoever owned this temple employed servants," he responded.

"Who wouldn't have them?"

"Good point. Maybe this was an active place of worship. The art has been most unusual," he added, rubbing the bridge of his nose. His glasses had a crack in them.

"Dr. Carrington–"

"For heaven's sake William, call me Wes. We're buried under the dunes, there's no need for any formalities at this point," he snapped. Wes took a breath before he apologized for snapping.

"Please call me Irina too. 'Dr. Romanova' is quite the mouthful," Irina said. I tried to flash them the best smile I could muster, but I didn't give a damn about their names at this point. When we got to the end of the tunnel and there was no obvious doorway, I felt all of my energy just leave my body. I was exhausted. Beyond exhausted. With every step further into this labyrinth, I was sure that death was going to come to greet me. I'd never been so thirsty in my life. My lips were chapped and ached.

Probably shouldn't have used so much spit on Arthur's dick, I thought.

Irina pointed at the wall and I shined the light.

A giant lotus was there, and I felt a chill. Wind crept through the cracks in the wall, and I saw the golden shimmer that I associated with Arthur now. Anything gold made me think of him. The lotus moved on the wall, the petals swaying like the wind moved them. We were close to something.

Was it Arthur?

Pressing my tattooed hand against the stone, praying that I was actually reaching for Arthur, the lotus bloomed and the petals opened until the rock of the wall began to crumble.

"Get back!" I shouted, shoving us all away while the largest pieces of the wall came crashing down. The rocks crashed against each other in a loud bang.

Wes groaned, and when I shined the light on him, his leg was under a very large chunk of the wall.

"Wesley!" Irina screamed, and whatever hope of stealth we had was gone. The wall left us exposed to another open room, and this time we weren't alone. God, how I wished that we were alone.

Rami stood in the room with a gun drawn, pointed right at Arthur.

Sunlight filtered down and it illuminated Arthur's drawn face. He wasn't afraid; there was anger shining in those beautiful brown eyes. Arthur was *livid*, and I was so fucking relieved to see that his eyes were his own. This rage was his alone.

The crashing of the wall tore everyone's attention to us: including the host of men with Rami. I didn't recognize their faces, but I knew the look. Arrogant pricks with more brawn than brains. They looted the temple as they moved, kicking at the walls and the statues, digging through the small mound of gold next to a throne. I wondered if they'd found the treasure that I had. The coins in my pocket felt so dirty now; I took the necklaces off and threw them on the ground. The clattering of the gold and gems felt like a weight lifted from me. Debt or no debt, there were lines I couldn't cross.

Arthur's eyes met mine and I watched as the smirk turned up on his lips.

My heart raced, and I knew he was trying to tell me something. His eyes shifted from me to Rami then to the left. There was an opening there.

"*Run,*" he mouthed while Rami stared at me. His goons finally caught on that something was happening and suddenly there were a lot of guns pointed at me. Why did they have guns? It's not like there was anything else down here–

I needed to stop talking.

Footsteps crunched through the temple, shaking more dust free. The guns went down as everyone tried to find what was causing that sound. It was hollow and horrible, like it was about to shake the entire temple into rubble. A low, dark growl shook the walls of the temple.

"Gotta move, come on Wes, let's get that leg out," I said, my words all tumbling out in a rush. Irina's tear streaked cheeks felt like a gut punch, as we both worked to get him free. The rock moved slightly and Wes screamed out.

The footsteps were closer.

Then came the skittering.

"Fuck me," I muttered, hoisting Wes up under his arms while Irina dug his leg out. The largest boulder moved and I was able to wrench him free. Wes's leg was bleeding and his boot looked crushed, but I didn't look too closely.

"Can you put any weight on your leg?" I asked and he shook his head no. His leg looked shredded. His tan cargo pants were soaked with blood, so I wrapped his arm around my neck and Irina looped his other arm around hers.

"We've got to move," she said, but *where*. Bugs behind us. Guys with guns in front of us. Mystery footsteps that promised nothing good. We were trapped.

"Arthur," I said as he came running toward us.

Rami fired his gun at Arthur but the wind knocked it from its path. The bullet lodged somewhere in the wall and Arthur was safe. He was alive and barreling toward me, faster than I'd ever seen him run before.

"Rami, stop!" I screamed.

Instinctively, I opened my arms for him, letting go of Wes to take Arthur in my arms.

"We've got to go," he breathed, and I heard how much his lungs struggled. There was a rattle to each of his breaths, and it made my heart ache. Didn't he have his inhaler? He had it this morning when we tried to run after Zahra. God, this endless fucking day. Just this morning Zahra was taken–

"Where's Zahra?" I asked, and Arthur's brows knitted together.

"I haven't seen her," he said as he knelt to look at Wes. His leg looked rough.

But none of that mattered now, because Rami was charging for us with his crew behind him. Every one of them looked meaner than the last; their faces were harshly sun-tanned and scarred. The wild look in Rami's eye made me freeze. He was wild, moving like a man possessed by some frenzied demon.

I'd seen that look before at the tables when I played cards. A man on the edge. A man betting his last dime on the next flip of a card.

What was Rami betting on?

He raised the gun to my chest and fired.

XIV

Arthur

ANOTHER GUNSHOT RANG OUT and I didn't have time to process it as William crumpled. He collapsed in a heap, his body rolling into me and knocking me down with him.

"No!" I screamed. Raw and guttural, it tore through me as we went down together. His body was so limp and heavy, laying heavily on me.

"Don't say a word," he whispered and then I felt the tension in him. I felt how taunt his muscles were, how poised he was. William fell with all the grace of a sack of flour, but his body was ready to leap into action.

There was no blood coming from him. I wanted to look to see where the bullet had hit, but I couldn't move.

"What are you doing?" I whispered back.

"Something stupid, probably," he said, pressing his lips to my forehead. I wanted to cling to him, but now wasn't the time. Rami–the man with the gun, isn't that what William called him?–and his idiots grew closer to us, and William said, "Can't go back that way, we've gotta break through them."

"That is stupid–"

He exploded upright, moving with a speed that shocked me. He was still injured, but it didn't stop him at the moment. William was up on his feet and spinning, his hand raised in a fist and launching at Rami.

The hit made my teeth clatter. William pulled back and punched him again, another savage hit that sent Rami to his knees, spitting blood. I jumped up to help, but William kicked Rami while he was down. He doubled over even more, until he let go of the gun.

Rami's friends stopped moving as he yelled something in Arabic. I didn't catch it; there was too much adrenaline in my system to translate. William had the gun in his hand and pointed it at Rami.

"William, no," I said, and he didn't respond.

"Where's Zahra?" he growled, and Rami laughed. William kicked him again, and Rami spat another glob at him. He asked again, this time in Arabic.

"William, we need to go, let's go."

"He's got Zahra, I know he does."

"Later, Will, later. Think about Wes, he needs help–"

He took aim at Rami again, and spoke with such venom, I nearly recoiled. "So does Zahra."

Irina and Wes limped over to us, and I got a better look at his leg. Bleeding, likely fractured. The twisted ankle was a concern, but the bleeding was slowing. Wes looked like hell, but he would live. He had to live.

I felt the wind at my back and my stomach dropped and my knees shook. Henkhisesui was back, and he was ready to take control again.

I whispered William's name before I felt the snap, the connection to myself, as he shoved me back into that little box inside myself. The noise, the movement, caught William's attention and he turned to me. His face went from rage to horror as he saw what happened. I knew he could see what was happening, even if he didn't understand. I knew he'd find a way to help. He was a pain in the ass, but he was brilliant when the chips were down. And I was out of moves, out of plays. My body surrendered itself to Henkhisesui and everything went black again.

***

Arthur was a strong man, despite his size. He was tall and lean; nothing like the human body I inhabited before. There was so little muscle on this form that I worried–just for a moment–that it wouldn't support my magic, support me.

I was Henkhisesui, god of the east wind, and I would not be contained again.

Not without Kheti. Not again.

My temple was still beautiful despite the years that had taken its toll on it. The humans with their weapons pulled stirred the rage of the east wind, and I let it consume me.

Destruction. Creation. The cycle would continue on and on, as it always had, as it always will.

My wind surged forth, wrapping itself tightly around my arms until they were long, biting whips. I cracked them at the ground, sending the humans fleeing. They were such fragile creatures, but some of them were born with the hearts of gods. Like Kheti.

His loss, his absence was still so visceral. Kheti's necklace around my neck calmed the storm in my belly, but it wouldn't be the same until Kheti walked once more.

Arthur's beloved stood in disbelief, watching again with wide, fearful eyes. I needed to find Kheti's other necklace. The set that bound our souls together; with only one piece, he would not get to fully enter the afterlife.

But first the humans.

They fled like the bugs they were; I called the swarm to me and heard their joyous shrieks, the permission to feed and to eat.

The humans with their little weapons died faster than their bullets could take them. The swarm consumed them, leaving piles of blood and bones in their wake. They crawled with speed, moving as one as they stopped before me, buzzing and humming with energy.

"Find the rest of those humans and eat," I commanded and the scarab swarm flew as one dark cloud through my temple halls. Kheti would be appalled; he hated scarabs. He hated all bugs, but especially the scarabs.

A hint of green caught my eye and I turned back to William Ford. Arthur's thoughts screamed in my mind, but they were easy enough to ignore.

Did William already have what I wanted? How fortunate. The winds carried me to him and William didn't flinch, didn't move away.

"You have something that's mine," I said, and he didn't so much as flinch. Yes, Kheti would like this one.

"So do you," he said, throwing his weight at me, trying to strike me. William grabbed my hand and the lotuses touched. He squeezed, and I felt it then–the shift of Arthur surging to come back, to regain control. I stamped it down until William brought our lips together, and I remember just how good the kiss of my lover felt. "Come back, Arty."

A tear formed and I let it fall. For Arthur, for Kheti. William cupped my face–Arthur's face–and I let go.

***

Henkhisesui let go and consciousness slammed back into me. William held me, gentling cupping my face, and his eyes warmed as he searched for evidence that I was me again. God I wanted to kiss him. What the hell was going on with me?

The room was oddly empty; what had Henkhisesui done? I tried to remember, but his presence made thinking hard, and the little box he shoved me in was too small for all of my thoughts. Was this why I could never turn my thoughts off? There were just too many to contain, too many for me to ever have a hope of sifting through?

My thoughts were a tangle of want and desire, pleading for sunlight and William's lips against my skin.

He ran his fingers through my hair, holding my head still. He wanted to kiss me, I knew he did, and we stood there in this lingering moment for what felt like years. We were frozen in time, forever stuck in these precious seconds.

"Hi," he said.

"Hi," I said.

"I'm going to kiss you until you can't breathe once we get out of here."

"Is that a challenge?"

"Not much of one, considering your asthma."

"You're an absolute twot."

"And you love it."

"I can think of loads of things, I love–"

He opened his mouth and I saw the words forming but instead he flashed a smile. That killer, wicked smile that meant he could do no wrong. I hated how true that was now; once that smile was a warning but now it was my siren song. Would he cross a line? Admitting this dance we were doing was growing more involved, more dangerous?

There was so much more on the line now than just his debts. How much more was William willing to gamble with?

I was the better player, after all.

I counted all of his cards, all of his moves, and time was running out before we both fell off this ledge of silence.

"Ahem," Wes said, his voice laced with pain as he leaned on Irina. "Not to break up... whatever is happening here, but we need to figure out how to get the hell out of here before we can't."

"There's light that way–" Irina said but she stopped short and we turned to see what caught her attention.

Rami.

He shook like a leaf, terror etched in him that he didn't seem to know where to go. William still had the gun in his hand, and I tried to take it from him but he refused to release it. I tugged it out of his hand and he hit me with a raised eyebrow and a smirk. I'd never held a gun before; never wanted to. It was heavier than I expected and I was paranoid it would suddenly explode, but I knew that didn't actually happen.

"Wh-what was that?" Rami said in heavily accented English. His face was a mess of bruises, and I was sure William's knuckles were too.

"Nothing you need to know about," William said, and he wrapped his arm around the small of my back. The gesture was sweet but annoying; I was the one with the gun after all, even if I had no idea how to use it.

"The wind–"

"Angry god, yes. Maybe you shouldn't push it, just in case he decides to come back," William said and Rami's hands shot up in surrender. I almost felt bad for the guy, but the way William looked at him with pure venom, any empathy shrank away.

"Zahra should be back in Fayoum by now. You know where to find her," he said, and turned to run.

"Wait, how did you get in here?" I asked.

"I followed the winding stairs," he said and Rami took off running. There was no way to catch up to him with Wes being injured, but we had at least some semblance of directions now. I tried to see where Rami went as he disappeared around a corner, but William was already stepping away to help Wes. Irina was drooping, struggling to hold his weight, and it would take both of us to get him out here.

A glimmer of green caught my attention, and I saw something around William's neck. There were other golden items on him too, but the green gem captured me. I knew what it was; I knew in my heart that it was Kheti's and that's why Henkhisesui surged back.

I felt his presence in my bones, but I pushed it away, like I was swallowing back the urge to vomit. Henkhisesui rumbled in my head like the roaring wind of a spring storm, and I shook my head.

"Arty?"

"Just some... noise," I said. I didn't want Wes and Irina to know that I had a god in my head–they'd lock me in a museum to be studied and dissected.

"We're gonna talk about that noise real soon," William said.

"And the emerald," I added and that sexy, smirking face dropped back to stone. His eyes shot down to the necklace and now I was the one with the shit-eating grin.

"Aren't I supposed to be the one with the comebacks?"

"Not when you make it so easy," I said, trying my best to flash the same wicked smile. His eyes glittered.

"Oh, so I'm easy now?"

"Gentlemen, as much I love that this little love story has finally taken off, can we focus on the matter at hand? Namely my broken leg? Yes, hm? You can flirt once I'm being med-evaced," Wes gritted out, nervous laughter taking him before infecting the rest of us. It was good to see him laughing; I told myself that meant the break wasn't too severe and that he would be okay.

"Do you have your sat-phone?" I asked.

"Yes of course I do."

"Give it to Irina and start checking for signal."

"I really hope the winding stairs are like, ten steps and not fifty," William said.

"Do you really think we have that kind of luck?" I asked and the megawatt smile was back. He was so beautiful it hurt to look at him for too long. Not that he needed to know that; his ego was already barely tolerable.

"No signal yet," Irina said, holding the phone up like it was some miracle. The marvels of modern technology didn't hold a candle to wonders in this temple. I didn't want to leave; not that I knew there was a way out. Would it still be here? Or would Henkhisesui bury it again to protect Kheti's resting place? There were piles of gore where Rami's men were eaten by the scarabs. The bone and blood was enough to make my gag, but I did my best to look away.

The artistry of the temple was enough to keep me mostly distracted from the gore.

Kheti had to be here, it was the only reason that Henkhisesui would even care about this damn temple. A god of destruction and creation wouldn't care about the preservation of history; he'd wipe it out and create it again. But the final resting place of his lover that he hasn't been able to let go over for thousands of years?

That was worth saving.

We hobbled across the throne room. There were two thrones both cast in gold; one was much larger than the other, and that had to be where Henkhisesui sat. Kheti's more delicate throne looked like it was fit for a reigning queen, but there was no queen here.

"There," I said, pointing to an opening around the corner, leading to a hallway. The hall was another ornately decorated piece, but the opening looked accidental, like it was part of the collateral damage of the temple being rediscovered.

"Are we taking bets on how many steps there's gonna be?" William asked, but the joke fell flat for me. He'd gambled enough, and even though there were no stakes at all behind his words, it still struck me. This all started because of his poor choices. Anger welled in my chest but it wasn't the time for it. Wes needed medical attention. We needed to get out before the temple collapsed or someone else showed up wanting to kill us.

"Too many," Wes said as we limped through the empty hall. Murals lined the walls here too, and they were more tender scenes. Henkhisesui and Kheti embraced and their faces were so serene, I wondered how long their love story lasted. What was a mortal lifetime to a god? The loneliness from Henkhisesui crept into my mind, and I realized how long he waited for Kheti to be born and to live, just for him to fade away so soon. We climbed the stairs but I kept looking back at the temple.

Leaving suddenly felt wrong. How could I leave this place when there was still so much to see?

"I know what you're thinking, and no," William said.

"How could you possibly know what I'm thinking?"

"Because you look at me the same way you're looking at the hall and we can't go back, not yet."

"Oh, don't worry, we are absolutely coming back to this site, Arthur. I just need to get this leg in a cast first," Wes said, and his weakened voice nearly broke my heart. Irina's steadying hand on his back as we half dragged him up the steps was all that seemed to keep him from slipping back.

"Absolutely. This is the biggest discovery in a century, maybe more. The art style alone is worthy of decades of research," Irina said. I heard the awe in her tone, the reverence, and I saw why Wes cared for her so much. They were twin flames, even if they couldn't have figured that out years ago.

My thighs ached from the climb; falling into this place was a lot easier than climbing out. The temple stretched on forever. Even though we felt more and more of the sun as we climbed, it didn't seem to matter. The steps were unending, and Wes was losing strength.

"I've got signal!" Irina shouted. She dialed and switched to Arabic, speaking fast once someone answered.

"Who was that?" I asked. My lungs burned, and I didn't know how many more steps I could do either.

"I sent our coordinates to my lab back in the city. They're contacting help. We should hear from them soon, so let's keep going," she said. Wes leaned heavily on her, and they climbed together. The promise of help seemed to reinvigorate them both, but it didn't do a damn thing for me.

"You okay?" William asked. He was three steps ahead, waiting for me.

"Dandy," I wheezed and he walked over to me. William didn't even seem winded, and jealousy burned in me. Probably just asthma, but still.

"Aside from being a horrible liar, you're also not great with sarcasm, Arty. It'd be more believable if I couldn't hear you wheezing."

"I'm fine–"

"You're not, and I need you to just fucking tell me that you're not okay."

"Why?"

"Because I want you to trust me enough with your safety to actually tell me when you're struggling." The way he grabbed my arm shocked me. The jokes were gone now, and the seriousness around his eyes made my heart skip.

"I can take care of myself," I said quietly, not sure what else I should say.

"Yeah, I'm getting that," he said just as quietly. The energy shifted between us again–the tension and the heat switched to something more sober, more alone. Wind rushed from the temple and pressed against our backs, until William's shirt stuck to the outline of his body.

"I think Henkhisesui is trying to tell us something," I said.

"And to think, he's been so subtle recently," William said, flashing a grin.

"Maybe I'm not okay," I said.

"Yeah, I got that too." William wrapped his arm around me and we stood there for a moment. He was on the step above, making him another couple inches taller than me. The stairs were uneven and worn, and this one was shorter than the others.

"Why do you know me so well?" I asked.

"Because even while we fight, I like finding details about you. Who knows what will help me win the next spat?"

"We don't have *spats*."

"Tiffs? Spars? Arguments?" he said, a warm rumbling laugh in his throat. William's green eyes were so vibrant now, like the sun had realized he was here and needed the extra spotlight on him.

"Quarrels, conundrums," I added.

"See? I knew you'd have to get the last word in." William tugged me forward, but his arm supported my weight in case I needed him. My lungs struggled, and I wanted to say something more, but he would hear the wheezing and seeing the crease between his brows made my chest tighten even more.

"No quick come back? You must be feeling shitty," he said. I tripped on one of the uneven steps and his grip tightened so fast that it was startling.

"Ass," I said, and he laughed.

"Save all of the comebacks for later once we get your inhaler. It's more fun to piss you off when you can breathe."

"You're–"

"Insufferable, yeah, we covered that too. Cute as hell also." Now it was my turn to laugh, but it quickly turned into a coughing fit.

"Arthur, we're almost to the top! I can see the exit!" Irina shouted. Wes was practically crawling now, and they sat together on the top of the stairs. His leg had started bleeding more, and it left a trail for us to follow.

"Almost there," William said. His unwavering kindness was odd. William wasn't cruel, but this was different.

"I need a bath and my inhaler."

"Inhaler first. Then you can get all cleaned up."

"Good plan."

"A compliment on something other than my looks. You must be dying," he joked. I shoved his arm and he shoved back, but our hands stayed tangled together.

XV

William

ONCE WE MADE IT up the endless stairs, Wes collapsed. The pain, the blood loss–whatever it was, his body gave out and he collapsed. He passed out in Irina's arms as she cried but everything felt far away, like I watched the scene unfold in a movie instead of in front of me. Arthur's tight breathing consumed every ounce of my attention. His shaky hands and wheezing chest were all that I could see and hear, despite the noise of the helicopter incoming. Arthur needed to be treated also, but I knew he wouldn't speak up.

I just wasn't sure if it was because he was humble or because he couldn't speak at the moment. Rubbing circles on his back, Arthur leaned into my touch and I fought all of my instincts to wrap him in a hug. The blistering heat wasn't helping him breathe any better either.

The helicopter landed a ways away, and I was the only one strong enough to wave them down and bring them over to Wes. Arthur's soft brown eyes pleaded with me to go get help, and without a word I ran off.

Waving my arms like a madman, the occupants of the helicopter hopped out and followed me back to the temple opening. Wes was unconscious, Irina was hysterical, and Arthur stood like a statue.

I asked one of the paramedics if they had anything for asthma in Arabic, but I didn't know the word for it. I tried to explain, words feeling like another faraway thought. The language that I felt so confident in now felt like I was a fledgling student again. I remembered how Zahra would laugh at my accent, how I'd stumble through the sounds, and struggle with the text.

What was happening?

The paramedic—a young guy with a sunny smile and kind eyes—pressed an inhaler in my hand and continued on to look at Wes. The moments stretched into hours; time felt so altered for me that I didn't process how they moved Wes onto a stretcher or how they quietly treated our scrapes and bruises.

The same kind paramedic inspected my ribs and split lip, applying antiseptic and prodding gently.

"Can you hear me?" he asked in perfect English.

"Yes, sorry."

"Adrenaline crash. You will feel out of it for a little while. We don't have space in the heli for you and your friend. The woman is requesting to go with your injured friend."

"Arthur is staying here?"

"Yes, with you, I'm afraid. I'll send more help this way–"

"We need a car," I said, turning back to the deserted camp site. The expedition was over before it even started, and guilt ripped through me. I'd brought this disaster to Arthur's feet.

"There was a bad sandstorm a couple days ago and the roads were wiped out. It's too long to walk back to the city; we will come back tomorrow to get you, okay? The doctors said there are enough supplies for you two for a few days at least, but we will be back tomorrow." He handed me Irina's satellite phone and trotted back to the helicopter. It was still surreal that Irina could get a helicopter out here, but maybe she was more important, more connected than I realized. The paramedic, his partner, Irina, and Wes loaded themselves into the helicopter, and we watched as they flew off. The noise made Arthur flinch, covering his ears, but I was still motionless.

Maybe it was just the crash of adrenaline. Maybe I was exhausted. Maybe it was the way Arthur looked at me, like there was something worthy of his attention.

"How long do you think it'll take us to get back to the site?" he asked, his words sharp and clear, no trace of the strangling, wheezing grip the asthma had on him.

"Twenty, thirty minutes? I'm beat, and climbing through these dunes is gonna suck. A leisurely stroll is about all I have in me," I said, and Arthur smiled.

"Thank god, because if you were about to jog again, I was going to die," he said, taking a long drink of water from one of the several bottles the paramedics left.

"Never expected to see a helicopter that up close and personal," I said, and Arthur nodded.

"Wes was already looking better before they left," Arthur said. He was looking better too, but I didn't want to mention it. The glow in his cheeks from the heat made him radiate health and I was so damn thankful.

"Yeah, now once we get back to camp, I'm going to make dinner. A huge dinner, I feel like I could eat for days."

"Have at it, I'm terrible at cooking," Arthur said.

"At least you can admit it. Those sausages were... something," I laughed and he shoved against my shoulder. Night slowly crept in, and I had no idea what time it was. My phone had died at some point in the temple, and I didn't have a watch. Arthur didn't either, and Irina's satellite phone seemed to have the wrong time, unless evening crept in at two in the afternoon.

"I told Wes not to put me on kitchen duty," he grinned.

The rest of the walk back to camp was quiet, but not the kind that made my skin itch or feel the need to fill it. Arthur's companionable silence wrapped a comforting blanket around us, and as we walked, our hands would brush. Our arms pressed together with each step we took, and when we finally made it back to the site, our hands were linked. I wanted to say something, but what if I broke this moment?

The site was still intact, a little worse for wear from the sandstorms, but everything was as it was. The tents were up but empty. No lights came from the large research dome, or from the professors' shared tent. No sounds of people stirring or working. The only sounds came from Arthur and I as we settled in for the night.

Arthur peeled off his shirt, tossing it on the seat next to him at the main camp fire. The stars were out already, even though the sky was still dusky. The camp would be pitch black soon, and realizing that we would be back in the dark, forced me into action. I wasn't ready to face the darkness again, and as we worked together to get the fire going, Arthur seemed to be on the same page with me.

His bare chest felt like an invitation, but I stayed quiet. Once the fire picked up, he laid back on one of the benches, stretching. His long, lean torso and arms curled with each stretch, making his pants sink lower across his hip bones.

"Looks like it's gonna be sausages again tonight. And spam," I said, and Arthur laughed.

"Fine dining at its best." Arthur took his glasses off and sat them on the back of the bench. They were dirty enough that I could see the filth from my seat next to the fire.

"Maybe once we're back in town, we can find some vegetables. Looks like we've still got a few apples though."

"Apples and spam, the food of the gods. I wish we had a beer," Arthur said as he sat up.

"Arthur Lewis drinks beer?"

"Shocking, I know. One day I'll acquire the taste of bourbon or something, but honestly it makes me sick."

"Beers will have to wait until tomorrow." I cooked our simple meal over the open fire and Arthur came to sit next to me. His leg leaned against mine, and soon all of Arthur leaned against me.

"Arty–"

"No more words, for a while, hm?" he said, as his head rested on my shoulder.

I nodded, and kissed his forehead. The way his breath hitched gave me butterflies, but I didn't push any further. We were building to something, and I needed Arthur to take the reins. I needed him to lead this silence dance, and I'd follow wherever he took us.

I was in so far over my head with him, with the feelings that bubbled up in my chest.

He plucked a piece of spam off the plate and took a bite. We sipped water and ate quietly as the fire crackled. Night had descended on us, and the sky sparkled more brilliantly than I'd ever seen before. The only light came from the fire, and I held his hand as we traced patterns in the sky.

Moonlight made his freckles shimmer. We laid back on the bench, my arm around his shoulders as our legs tangled together.

"I love how small the sky makes me feel," Arthur said, and I pulled him closer.

"I love how the sky makes anything seem possible," I said, and it felt like we both confessed something here, something tender, precious.

"We should get cleaned up," Arthur said. He sat up, and his back showed the subtle knobs of each vertebrae. The tattoo was back to all lotuses, peaking over the top of his shoulder.

"I'll start on the dishes," I said, and he shook his head.

"*We* should get cleaned up, Will."

Just the way he said my name, *Will*, not William or Ford or asshole, sent longing and need jolting through me, lighting up every nerve. I followed Arthur through the camp with our little flashlights to the showers. There was no one else waiting, no one needing the hot water, and when Arthur peeled out of the rest of his clothes, I was so damn thankful for the peace. He turned the water on, shivering at the contact but grinning ear to ear.

I shrugged out of my filthy clothes, remembering the last time we showered together. Remembering how his hands felt against my cock and round my neck. Remembering how he pressed against me, until our bodies were aligned for a deeper connection.

Stepping in the spray of the water, it was still cold but it didn't phase me. I pressed Arthur against the shower wall, running my hand along those sexy, narrow hip bones.

"Will," he breathed, and I nodded, trying to respond to my name.

"Arty," I said, my voice so husky and thick, it sounded foreign.

"We're alive," he said, and I nodded again, this time capturing his lips. A kiss that said so many things that neither of us was ready to say. A kiss that begged for connection and more, more, more.

Arthur was every breath I took. The water heated up, and we truly were filthy. I broke away long enough to reach for the soap, lathering the bar in my hands to scrub away the day from us both.

He washed my hair, kneading at my scalp to get all of the sand buried in my hair out. I massaged the expanse of his back, raking the bar over his skin.

When he lathered up his hands and wrapped them around my length and down my thighs, washing between my legs and back up, I nearly bucked against him. I did the same, spending more time caressing the sensitive skin between his legs. Arthur pressed his back to me, and I let my hands roam. His head leaned against me, and our cheeks touched. We swayed under the water, letting it wash away all of the sand and grim, all of the tension. All of the words we'd said, and the ones we wanted to. That *I* wanted to.

The water faded from hot to tepid to cold, but we didn't move. Arthur turned so we faced each other, his pupils dilated and lips parted.

His fingers tangled in my wet hair, and with him firmly tucked against me, we both knew where this moment was heading. The water off, we toweled off at record speed, and headed for our tent. The small lanterns that cast the desert in soft, warm glow. Our bare feet trudged through the cool sand, and with just towels around our waists, the night was cold.

Arthur flipped on the small fairy lights he'd hung in the tent to give us just enough light to see. I placed the lantern on his makeshift desk, and held my hand out for him.

Sand from our feet got tracked inside, but I didn't care. The soft grit of it grounded me in reality that Arthur was here, naked and wanting me.

"Arty–"

"Yes, to whatever you're asking. Yes to whatever you're willing to give," he said, and I swallowed hard. There was so much I wanted to give him, but that conversation would wait for another day, another moment.

Touching himself with long, lingering strokes until he was erect, then Arthur kneeled before me. Arthur pulled off my towel, and it was a different kind of feeling exposed. Stripped bare, Arthur placed experimental kisses on my stomach, working his way down, down, down.

"Ah," I hissed when he took me in his mouth. He swirled his tongue around the tip of my cock before moving further down until he had his lips around all of me. As good as this felt, I wanted to kiss him. I wanted this night to last before we woke up and whatever clarity came with the rising sun.

Arthur found a pace and a rhythm that had my blood humming to life as my body bucked and begged for release. His cock dripped with a drop of his arousal, and as he stroked and guided himself closer to the edge, I cupped his face.

"I want you," I said between breaths, and he nodded.

"You were close–"

"I want *you*, Arty," I said again and pulled him up to kiss him. We fell back on the bed rolls shoved together. Our oversensitive bodies brushed, until I wanted to rub myself against him.

He read the question in my eyes, and smiled. "I want you, Will. Do you have protection?"

"Yeah, in my bag," I said, and he laughed.

"Always prepared, aren't you?"

"Got the lube too," I said, and his eyes glittered. He was so fucking beautiful, and I doubted he even knew it.

"What do you prefer?" I asked, kissing along his collarbones. I loved his collarbones; they were so elegant, so defined but still delicate. Arthur's lithe body was full of delicate lines that demanded attention, and I needed to explore every one of them.

"Get me ready," he said, opening his legs. That coy smile and I knew I was gone; Arthur was going to guide every moment of tonight, and as he spread legs to let me closer, I felt my resolve slipping away.

"I'll make you feel good, Arty," I said, just barely over a whisper and he nodded. Pink cheeks and blown pupils, Arthur's kiss-bruised lips and the sheen of sweat on his brow–I never wanted to forget this moment. I popped open the small bottle of lube and put some on my fingers, letting a little drop down to his entrance before I started massaging him there.

He squirmed, trying to move closer.

"I already feel good," he said.

"Then let's make you see stars tonight," I said, kissing the sensitive skin on his upper thigh, rolling it between my teeth. He'd have a mark tomorrow, but no one would know it was there except me.

Gently, slowly, maddeningly, I pressed one finger in him and let him adjust to the pressure, the stretch. Moving deeper and deeper until I hit that sweet spot that made Arthur moan. I loved seeing him come undone, lose control.

"There, there," he said, trying to press himself down more on me.

"I'm gonna add another finger," I said, trying to keep my own release in check. He was so damn sexy, glowing from pleasure. Adding more lube, I pressed a second finger in him, slowly working him open. The tight ring of muscle clenched against me, just imagining how good he would feel had me struggling to breath.

"Don't stop, Will," he said through ragged breaths, and I pedaled my fingers just enough to rub his prostate until he was so close to coming, that I had to stop. Arthur panted and writhed, trying to get closer as I slowly withdrew my fingers.

"Easy, baby," I said as I tore open the condom and rolled it on. As I lined myself up to his entrance, I asked him, "This okay?"

"Yes, for chrissake, *yes*," he huffed and I leaned forward to kiss him as I pushed in.

"Oh fuck," he mumbled against my lips and I nodded, moving so fucking slowly that I thought I was going to die.

"Feel okay?"

"Perfect, more," he breathed, his arms around my shoulders, my neck. Arthur grabbed and pulled, trying to bring me closer. "I need you, Will, more."

I moved again until our bodies were flush, and he was grinning and breathing hard. He was so free, so relaxed and happy that I couldn't stop myself. I angled my hips so I hit that sensitive, swollen spot and Arthur moaned my name. It was the best sound I'd ever heard, better than any song or symphony was hearing my name on Arthur Lewis' lips.

We found a rhythm until we were blissed out, nerves overheated and sensitive. I felt my release coming, and Arthur gripped himself tight, stroking and stroking until we both came undone. Arthur's release spilled on his belly, and I felt himself squeezing around my cock until I saw stars.

"Did you see any stars?" I asked, reaching for the towel to clean his stomach. Slowly I pulled out of him, peppering his heated chest with kisses.

"A whole sky full of them," he laughed, and turned to me. I wiped him down quickly and with our bodies loose and blissed out, Arthur cuddled into my chest. I didn't care about the sand that would inevitably get under the covers, and tossed a blanket over us. He was warm and I had everything I ever wanted in my arms.

"We should have done that years ago," I said.

"Hey, I tried to get you to notice me."

"You mean you tried to pick a fight with me."

"Same thing. It worked this time, didn't it?" he said, that smug smirk tugging at his lips. I flipped him over, pulling him on top of me and he laughed.

"You trying to pick another fight with me?"

"Depends, what am I gonna win?"

"Give me about twenty minutes and you'll find out," I said as he kissed me, deepening the kiss until I was panting again.

"Tomorrow, and this time I get to play with the lube." My dick twitched at that, and he grinned. "Tonight we sleep. I'm spent."

I opened my mouth to make a joke and he shushed me, "Don't ruin the moment with a terrible joke, Will. Cuddle me."

"Who knew you were so demanding?"

"You did, and that's why you like me."

"Is that so?"

"William Ford, we both know you need someone to keep you in line and I'm happy to put you in place." He stretched, the scent of our lovemaking in the air, and rolled over to sleep.

"Good night Arty."

"Good night, Will."

XVI

Arthur

William's arms were wrapped around my middle, his hand resting against my heart, when I woke up the next morning. Our legs were tangled together; we were utterly wrapped up in each other, and all of the emotions of last night came rushing back to me. William's even breathing told me he was still asleep, so I stayed as still as I could, just soaking this moment in.

Would it be weird when he woke up? Would he regret last night?

I'd never regret it, not for as long as I lived.

I'd had plenty of nights with other men before, but this was different. I knew it in the pit of my stomach that this was different, and judging from the way that William clung to me, I think he did too.

I wasn't looking forward to that conversation. The nagging fear in the back of my mind whispered the truth though; I wasn't afraid of gaining William as a more... permanent part of my life. I was afraid of just the opposite.

"Arty, the sun is barely up and I can hear the wheels in your head turning."

"I thought you were asleep," I said. He hugged me tighter to his chest. Of course William would be the big spoon.

"I was until you were thinking so loudly."

"About last night–"

"Yes, it was great. No, I don't regret it. Yes, I'm planning on doing it again. Does that about cover everything in there?" William asked as he tapped the side of my head.

"Most of it."

"And the other items on the list?"

"They can wait until after breakfast," I said, turning to face him. William's beard was thicker than it had been and I loved the feel of it against the sides of my face, my neck.

"What's on the menu? Are you on the menu?" he asked, rolling so he was on top of me.

"Judging from all of the meals thus far, I'm going to guess... spam."

"So no to you being part of breakfast?" he said, nudging against my ear. He was hard, and saying no to him felt like a crime, but there were things to do and we hadn't heard from Wes–

"It's less fun when you're thinking," he laughed and got up.

"I didn't say *no*," I protested.

"Your brain did. Let's get the day started so I can get you naked in a proper bed tonight."

A flood of emotions rushed through me–tonight, bed, me–the words he said replayed until I heard the message I wanted to hear: William wasn't leaving.

He stood up and stretched, with the lightweight sheet falling away. He was naked and with the sun filtering in, he could have been mistaken for a god. William's sun kissed skin and chiseled body were something out of a classic painting, and I wanted to touch him. *Mine, mine, mine*, my mind whispered.

He saw something on my face and his eyes softened. I hated how unreasonably good looking it made him.

"Yeah Arty, I'm planning on taking you to bed tonight. But like with a real bed, my back is killing me." We laughed and threw on some clothes. The tent was entirely too sandy, and despite William standing naked in broad daylight to shake everything out, my skin felt coated in sand already. "You're barely even thirty and your back hurts already?"

"Technically it's from the *multiple beatings*, but sure, let's blame my thirties."

"I didn't mean–"

"It's fine. I'm more mad that you know I'm already thirty."

"You look great," I found myself saying and my cheeks heated. He grinned, pulling me in for a kiss.

God, I didn't even care about the morning breath. I was screwed.

Before he could kiss me, he slapped his hand over my mouth and stood ramrod still. His eyes darted around and that's when I felt the prickling, tingling feeling on my arm of the tattoo. They shifted again, and I glanced down to see what they were now. The words scrawled across my skin in English with long looping letters and lotuses on the back of my hand. He reached in the tent to grab his clothes, throwing them on as fast as he could.

"Did you hear that?" he asked in hushed tones. I shook my head no; I hadn't heard a thing, but my focus was on him.

"I heard something," he said. That's when the golden wind came, swirling through the sand.

It howled and groaned, the sand kicking itself up and up until it was a funnel larger than us. Henkhisesui was back. We needed to run before he trapped us somewhere else–

The sand twisted and shaped itself until it formed a four legged animal. A long neck and snout formed with two ears poking out of it, a large, thick middle, before the rear formed with a long, thin tail.

"Is that a fucking camel?" William asked, and the creature spit at his feet.

"What are we supposed to do with this?" I asked, and William reached to pet it. The camel tried to bite him and he threw his hands up.

"Yeah, no, I'm not dealing with the biting asshole camel. A helicopter will be here soon to pick us up."

Don't be so sure of that, a voice rumbled. Henkhisesui.

"You heard that, right?" I asked. William nodded. He pointed at the camel and it *smiled* at us. Its yellowed teeth drew my attention until I noticed that the animal's lips were moving.

"The fucking camel is talking," William deadpanned.

"No, it can't be–"

I will take any form I choose. You will help me. Your lover has what I want, the east wind god said.

"William–"

"I'm not having this conversation with a camel."

"William, for fuck's *sake*, just tell me what he's talking about." He opened his mouth to respond when the satellite phone rang. William practically bolted to our tent, pulling it out. He covered his other ear, trying to hear.

"They aren't coming," he said, and I paused.

"What do you mean? We have no vehicle and we're running out of clean water," I said, trying not to let panic infiltrate my thoughts.

"There's another sandstorm, and it's not safe to fly," William said as he stared down at the camel.

"They aren't coming," I repeated. Technically, we would be okay for another day or two. Hell, we could survive for a few days really if we pushed it. A few less showers and–

Give me Kheti's pendant, Henkhisesui said.

"What pendant? I can't take this off," I said, tugging on the necklace still around my neck. I'd gotten so used to its weight that I didn't notice it. I did notice how William stood too straight, how his shoulders were too squared, the tightness around his eyes.

My lover's emerald, he said. Those camel lips twisted with each sound, the language sounding even more foreign.

"Why would he just give that to you?" I asked, and the camel's strange golden eyes narrowed at me.

Because aside from keeping his *lover alive, I'm quite sure he would want the girl to remain unharmed.*

"What girl?" William said. He was barely breathing–it couldn't be Zahra, she was taken by those thugs that she was in bed with.

Not all treasures are made from gold, surely you've realized that by now, Arthur Lewis. Some treasures lie in the hearts of men and some treasures are the bonds you form.

"How could you have taken her?" William asked, his voice that deadly calm that made him seem so alien. Where was the warmth in his tones that made my heart melt?

I can take any form, human. It was not hard to capture her.

"So Rami–"

He believes she has returned to the oasis city, but she has not. She is in my temple, where she shall remain unless you give me Kheti's emerald.

"What's so special about this?" William asked, cool and indifferent.

I need it.

"And I want my best friend back, alive and well, and ready to nag the shit out of me for not shaving for three days. Take me to her," William demanded.

"Will, wait–"

I will make you an offer, William Ford. The emerald for Zahra.

"Done," William said. The camel sneered, spitting at his feet. William didn't flinch this time, and I admired the backbone but not the brains. What the hell just happened?

Return to my temple. This animal will guide you.

The wind stirred and swept through us until a gentle looking camel nudged at my hand. It's tail swung back and forth, little whining noises coming from it, demanding more attention.

"You realize this is a horrible idea, right?" I said. For so many reasons–Henkhisesui wasn't exactly reliable, Zahra could be literally anywhere, and we needed to get back to Fayoum to see Wes.

"Rami didn't actually say he knew where she was," William said. All of the bravado faded and he seemed like a shell of himself.

"He said she should be back in Fayoum," I said, remembering carefully the words that Rami said before fleeing. The little weasel.

"Should. He didn't know. Why would she just leave without telling me anything?"

"William, she's working for the Spice Traders. Why would she tell you if she was going to leave?"

"If you made a bad choice, would you just own up to it? Would you come clean?" he asked. I thought about it for a minute. I didn't know. I'd never made such a colossally stupid mistake. Getting a parking ticket for parking in front of a fire hydrant didn't compare to working for criminals, or getting into more debt than I could fathom.

"I don't know," I said honestly. What would have I done in William's shoes? In Zahra's?

"I think you'd ask for help. And I'm asking for help, Arty. Whatever her involvement in all of this, I'm the one that got the necklace. I'm the one that started this shit. She's collateral damage, and I can't live with that. Please, even if its trap, I'll make sure you get out–"

"Oh shut up, don't be so dramatic. We'll go, then we head to Fayoum."

"Thank you."

"Don't thank me yet, you're not going to like my plans once we get back to the city."

"As long as they involve you naked in a hotel room at some point, I'll take my chances." William smiled but it didn't reach his eyes. He tried to plaster on that charming grin, but he couldn't quite make it.

"She's either in the temple or in the city. Our chances are decent," I said. I didn't know why I needed to comfort him, but I did. I needed him to actually smile. The sat-phone rang again, and this time I answered it.

"Arthur? It's Wes. I'm fine. I'm in a damn cast, and I won't be able to return to the site. We're going to have to regroup in a few days. Hang tight until tomorrow. These damn sandstorms are something else. I haven't seen one like this in ages," he rambled, and I listened to his slurred words. He had to be on painkillers.

"We'll be fine," I said and he laughed.

"Have a bit of fun for me, will you? Ah to be young again," he said, and he giggled. Wes had to be utterly stoned. I'd never heard the man *giggle*.

"Everything okay?" William asked.

"Wes. He's in a cast and high as a kite."

"Jealous. The high part, not the cast part. I've broken a leg before, and can't say I recommend that," William draped his arm around my shoulders. The camel made another whining noise, and I realized we couldn't leave the animal here.

"Will," I said as I started petting the nose of the camel.

"No, you've got to be joking. No, Arty, no. I'm not a camel kind of guy–"

"We can't leave it here."

"Of course we can. Henkhisesui brought it here, he can take care of it."

The camel spat at William again.

"Also, it hates me," he said.

"I think we need to bring it back to the temple. Henkhisesui can teleport it somewhere. It'll just die out here," I said, and the camel nudged the side of my face. It had really lovely eyelashes, and despite the horrid breath, it was actually quite cute. "I think we should give him a name. Hank, maybe?"

"Arty, don't name it, you'll get too attached then."

"He looks like a Hank to me."

"How do you know he's a *he?*" I glanced down and the evidence was hanging there quite noticeably.

"Okay fine, it's a he. But I'm not riding it." Hank tried to bite William then, nipping at him until he got closer to the saddle. "Of course Henkhisesui possessed a fucking camel that already had a saddle," he muttered.

"William, just get on the damn camel."

"And where are you going to be?"

"We're going to ride together."

"Absolutely not," William said, throwing his hands up in the air.

"You'd like to walk those what, five miles, again in the heat of the day? I sure as hell don't," I said, climbing up on the camel's back. It took me a minute, but I got situated and comfortable fairly fast. The saddle's leather was worn but still supple enough that it was soft. The pommel had lotuses carved into it, and I felt the lingering magic of Henkhisesui in it. Could he make things, or shape the world around him? Goosebumps raised on my arms when I thought about it. A god, living and breathing in the world of men. It wasn't that I wasn't a spiritual person, but I'd never given it much thought. Logic was the comfort of my mind, not faith. It was hard to grapple with the existence of a being that lived outside the laws of logic and physics. It was hard to accept that maybe I was wrong about the world.

"I've never ridden a horse, Arty. How the hell am I going to stay on a camel?" William blurted out.

"How have you never ridden a horse? We went to an ivy league school. Horseback riding and golf were practically mandatory."

"Convenient illnesses or made up exams. You do realize that beast could step on you and you'd die, right?"

"How did you stare into the face of a god without flinching but it's the *camel* that pushes you over the ledge?"

"I never said I made sense. Just a hot oxymoron," he said, trying to defuse his fear with that dashing smile. It didn't work; I saw how his knees knocked but it was cute nonetheless.

"Get up here and just hold onto me. You will be fine, I promise."

"What if I fall?"

"Then you'll fall off the ass end, where you can't get stepped on. Just watch out for piles of shit."

"Sometimes Arty, you are so romantic that it's *astounding*."

The laugh bubbled up in my chest and I fought it hard as William struggled to mount the camel. There was plenty of room in the saddle; it was clearly designed to hold two people. I felt bad for the animal as William flopped and flailed, his arms swinging wildly trying to balance.

"This is a new level of pathetic, Will," I said, the laugh barely contained. I turned to help him up, and he yanked on my shirt, desperate for purchase as he slid back dragging me with him.

We both landed hard on the ground, sand spraying around us. The laughter tore out of me, and I rolled to hold my side. William looked positively flabbergasted that he was flat on his back.

"You're laughing," he said.

"That was the most pathetic thing I've seen in my entire life," I said, wiping the tears from my eyes. His sparkling green eyes danced with mischief, and I stood up, pulling him up with me. "We're trying again, but this time you get on first."

"What if I fall again?" he asked, and this time I didn't laugh. I wrapped my arms around his waist and he leaned into me.

"I'll help so you don't fall. Then I'll get on and you can just hold onto me."

"Shouldn't you get on first?" he asked, stepping back away from the camel.

"Typically yes, but we tried that and we ended up in the sand. So, up you go. One foot in the stirrup, then swing over. Easy," I said, and the doubt etched in the lines around his mouth was priceless.

William took a couple of steadying breaths and then hauled himself up and over. The camel huffed at his obvious struggling but didn't run. I didn't tell him that there was a chance of the camel running off. Once he was up and stable, I climbed up. I'd ridden horses for ages, and this wasn't a lot different. A camel moved differently but the basics of the saddle were the same. Before I could even get comfortable, William had his arms around me in a death grip.

"I do need to be able to breathe," I said and he kissed the shell of my ear.

"I don't like falling, Arty."

"Sometimes falling isn't so bad," I breathed, and I wondered where the conversation had turned. He leaned against my back, and even though the added heat was awful, being so close to him wasn't. Having William invading all of my senses was heady and surreal, and as I gently eased the camel forward, he didn't let go of me.

I motioned the camel to move a little faster and William tensed before relaxing.

"You're less likely to fall if you go with the flow. Relax. We're barely trotting," I said.

"If I fall, I'm bringing you with me."

I think you already have, I thought but didn't dare say the thought out loud. Feelings for William had grown and shifted to something deeper, more connected. We fit together like two pieces of a puzzle, and all of his hard edges matched against mine. Now when we moved, our bodies found the same rhythm, syncing our steps until we moved as one. Until our hands met. Until we were nose to nose, lips to lips, heart to heart.

It was more terrifying than falling off of any camel.

"Do you think Henkhisesui actually has Zahra?" he asked, breaking my thoughts.

"It's possible. I think it's more likely that he wants whatever trinket you stole."

"Do you hate me for it? For looking for an easy way out from the Spice Traders?"

"Hate you? No. I don't like it, but–" *But what? This was against everything I ever believed in, and I was suddenly okay with him robbing a temple?*

"I hate it, but they said they'd target my mom. I can't take that change. And now Zahra–"

"I get it, Will. There's got to be another solution though. If we can sell it to a reputable museum," I trailed off. But how long would that take? Authenticating and dating the piece, inspections and insurance, before it was even possible for a museum to take it? Assuming the grants for the dig didn't claim it once we went public with the emerald. "Let me see it," I said, holding my arm up for William to hand me the jewel. I didn't want to see the struggle on his face for handing it over to me. Last time he gave me a necklace, things got weird. It was hard to imagine how it could get worse.

William fished the emerald from his pocket carefully and handed it to me, all the while not letting go of me for a second.

"It's stunning," I breathed. The emerald was nearly the size of my palm. There were two lotuses etched within it, the stems crossing. It was fastened to a long gold chain with thick links. The chain alone would be worth a fortune. William handed me a million dollar–likely more–jewel like it was nothing. Like it meant nothing.

Like I was worth more than it.

"It is, yeah. Arty, there's more treasure down there than the modern world has seen in an age. I found an entire room full of gold."

"We aren't treasure hunters, Will. We're archaeologists."

"Didn't you dream of finding the treasure? Like Indiana Jones?"

"Yes of course, but I'm happy with just seeing the past. All of that feels like it's far away now though. I'm holding this emerald like it's a common stone," I said.

"I'd trade it for you or Zahra in a heartbeat, if that's what Henkhisesui really wants."

"I don't think we can trust what he says," I whisper, trying to keep my voice soft enough in case he was still connected to the camel somehow. At this point, I was waiting for Henkhisesui to reappear at any moment.

"I can't say I trust anything that takes over your mind like you're some kind of puppet," William added.

Henkhisesui taking a stroll through my head wasn't comfortable for me either; I knew what was happening but I didn't. The world was cold and black with little bits of light and information filtering in. I heard William calling for me, and I remember Henkhisesui retreating, but I knew it was only temporary. Zahra or not, I needed to return to the temple to find a way to release Henkhisesui from me before he decided to stay permanently.

"What're you thinking?" William asked.

"I'm thinking that we're gonna have to do those stairs again," I lied, trying to sigh to really sell it.

"Maybe Henkhisesui will be so tired of us, he'll give us a lift back up. With Zahra."

"Your optimism is really quite lovely," I said, and William hugged me closer to him.

"That's all I got left Arty. Reality is too real right now," he said, resting his head on my shoulder. William hugged me tight, and it wasn't for balance.

We rode under the hot sun, and my skin was sticky with sweat, but this was probably the best afternoon of my life. With William holding onto me, the vastness of the desert stretching out for what felt like forever–it felt like my life was beginning. Like I was finally awake, finally seeing the world the way it was meant to be seen, through rose-colored glasses.

I'd have to tell him this eventually, but not today, not when the day was perfect and the ruins were closing in on us.

The stairs we escaped from were practically hidden by the sand, but I saw the glittering magic of Henkhisesui rising up like steam from a teapot.

"Well that's not ominous," William mumbled, and I stifled a laugh.

I felt the pull of Henkhisesui's magic though, the connection that he had wormed in my head. I hated that he was there constantly, like some kind of parasite. William ran his fingers through my hair, and it grounded me in the present again. The camel grunted as we approached the stairs, refusing to get any closer. When I tried to nudge him forward, Hank hummed and snorted before promptly sitting down in the sand.

"Don't be so dramatic, Hank, the sparkles aren't going to hurt you," I said, patting his nose. Hank spit in the sand.

"Finally, someone agrees with me," William said.

"So now you're friends with him?" I asked, and William was already dismounting. He stretched his legs, doing a few squats. I needed to do that too; my inner thighs were sore, not to mention my tailbone. Probably also had something to do with how the evening went too... but it was best not to think about that right now. Last thing I needed was a hard-on trying to explore this temple.

Again.

"Going down can't be as bad as going up, right?" William asked.

"With all of those muscles, I was sure you wouldn't complain so much about a little physical activity."

"I can think of a dozen other *physical activities* I'd prefer to engage in with you, Arty. Shockingly, stairs are not involved in any of them."

"I brought my inhaler this time," I said, waving it at him. I wasn't going to take the bait; William wanted me to play, but see the above point: no hard-ons in the temple.

"Now who's the boy scout?" He cupped my face, and the heat from hands was nearly unbearable with the sun beating down on us. I didn't move, and William tilted my head back to kiss me. "Arty, your glasses are fogging up."

I shoved his hands away playfully, swatting at him. "Well, stop breathing on them!"

"Is it me? Or am I just getting you all hot and bothered?"

"The *sun* is getting me all hot and bothered–"

"Whatever you say, Arty." He kissed my forehead and started for the stairs. Hank rolled over like a dog, grunting and humming some more.

"I don't think normal camels do that," I said.

"He was possessed by a god, Hank is by default *not normal*," William said. I needed to sharpen my mind; William had bested me too many times in little verbal spats recently. Sleeping with him or not, there were lines that I wouldn't cross. Letting him win at anything, was one of them. I rubbed my glasses on my shirt and let my unfocused eyes scan the desert. It was so striking: the way the dunes were endless, the shifting sands, and reflection of the sun in the distance. It had a kind of melancholy that reminded me of sad poetry. An air of loneliness hung in the air, and I knew then that it was from Henkhisesui.

"Can you feel that?" I asked, and I searched William's green eyes. They were faraway too. Could he feel the depth of Henkhisesui's sorrow here?

"Yeah," he said, and he reached for me. Our fingers interlaced like they were magnets, and as we held each other, we descended the stairs.

The ancient murals slowly became visible. It was like an entrance to a river with the soft blues and the depictions of reeds. Then as we walked deeper into the temple, the murals shifted to their lives. The ram-headed god and his lover in a soft embrace.

I noticed how the air changed, like we were experiencing everything that Henkhisesui had felt all those years ago. My heart raced as I watched the murals, and watched Kheti become more and more prevalent. His serene face looked so impassive that it was hard to tell how he really felt, but Henkhisesui's features were always painted with such joy. Was Kheti stern and hard-faced, while Henkhisesui was the free, chaotic spirit? No wonder Henkhisesui didn't want to spend a lot of time in my head; I was the opposite of carefree.

William wasn't though–he was a free spirit if I'd ever met one.

"Do you think they were happy?" he asked, breaking the silence. William's voice echoed deep into the temple.

"I hope so," I said, and I found that I really meant it. I wanted their happiness to be real, just as much as my own.

"Kheti looks so serious," he said, and I nodded.

"He does, but he doesn't look unhappy. Maybe he was the even-keeled one."

"Maybe," William said. He thumbed over the emerald in his pocket before handing it to me. "There will be other ways to get out of this debt. Take this."

"Will–"

"Before I change my mind about being heroic and shit."

"Now who's the romantic one?" I asked and we both laughed.

"Keep up that charm and I'll have you naked against that wall in two minutes flat."

"You would *never*–"

"Absolutely I would," he said, and that wicked grin played on his lips. God, he had such beautiful lips. It should be criminal, honestly.

"You will *not* risk damaging the art!"

"Fine, the stairs won't be as fun, but hey, maybe I can think of a few physical activities here." He winked and I was undone.

"Will!"

Wind rushed by us, and we stilled. "I think Henkhisesui is a cock blocker," William grumbled.

"Even the god of the east wind is telling you to back off with the bullshit, honestly William."

"I love it when you chastise me."

I nudged his arm, but we still held hands as we went deeper in the temple. As the light faded, a lump formed in my chest. We didn't have any flashlights. Why didn't we bring flashlights? Or anything, really?

Like Henkhisesui was listening, the wall sconces lit up with that faint, golden glow. William's grip tightened, and we slowed as we stepped into the throne room. The large golden thrones dominated the eastern side of the room. Looping swirls that reminded me of Japanese art covered the walls that sparkled with gold.

The room. The walls.

It was made of *gold.*

"Do you–"

"See all of the insane amounts of gold? Yep, yep, glad I'm not imagining that." He stepped in front of me, trying to lead the way, but I wandered off toward the thrones. I needed to see what they looked like; I had to see what story was engraved there.

"Henkhisesui, great god of eastern winds. Kheti, most beloved," I whispered, as I traced over the hieroglyphics. The lyrics that haunted my thoughts were etched in the gold as well.

"The East Wind rises again, a storm without end, a lover in search of home. A lover, lost and alone, feels the East Wind caress his face and knows he will never stop searching," William said as he joined me.

"I thought your skills were rusty."

"Turns out seeing the same passage tattooed on me is a great way to learn something."

I had to find a way to catalog and preserve all of this; there was so much to see and learn from this temple. God, I'd give anything to spend more time here. Years. As I surveyed the throne room, turning to really take in the grandeur, I realized this temple would be my life's work. This was what I was meant to find, meant to study. I'd never been a believer in fate, but that was changing. Everything was changing, and I was ready for it.

Give me Kheti's jewel, Henkhisesui demanded. Dust fell from the ceiling, and William instinctively wrapped his arms around me, cradling my head.

"Where's Zahra?" I asked as more dust and dirt fell.

She is in Kheti's resting place.

"What–" William started, but I shushed him.

"Where is that?" I asked, but I would have known without the east wind god responding. Now that he mentioned Kheti, I felt the tug, the pull from the necklace to bring me closer to him. William pulled the emerald out and dropped it, like it had burned him.

When I scooped it up, there was an alignment of energy in me. The necklace and the emerald seemed to hum to each other, and when I strained to listen, the words were clear.

"The East Wind rises again, a storm without end, a lover in search of home. A lover, lost and alone, feels the East Wind caress his face and knows he will never stop searching," over and over in the gentlest tenor.

They called out to each other. Thousands of years had passed but still their souls, their spirits–whatever remnants of Henkhisesui and Kheti were left shouted in the ether to be together.

"You want to rest," I said, and a sigh of wind brushed against my cheek. William walked in front of me, his hand raised to touch me, but stopping.

"Arty," he said, his voice soft and reverent. His skin reflected light, and I tried to find the source, but it was me. Henkhisesui's golden wind had lit me from within, and I saw it reflecting on William.

"This is... bizarre," I said, studying my hands, my arms. The light grew stronger the closer it got to my chest, where the necklace was.

"You're magic," he said, and the awe in his voice was enough to leave me speechless. I'm magic? I was just a guy, a normal guy with bad eyesight and asthma, but when William looked at me like that, it felt like maybe I could be made of magic.

"Henkhisesui is," I corrected and he huffed at me. He didn't hesitate then to reach for me, to pull me against his chest and bring our lips together.

"No Arty, it's you," he breathed, and I knew that the truth bubbling up in my chest was going to boil over soon.

"I-I-I think we should keep going," I stuttered out, and he pressed our foreheads together.

"Yeah, let's find Zahra before," William's words trailed off as he swallowed back the tears that threatened to fall. I prayed that Zahra wasn't dead.

"This way," I said, as I felt for the connection between Henkhisesui and Kheti. The emerald tugged harder to the east, and we followed. There was so much to see, so many details to take in, but I couldn't stop this force.

This was a new tunnel. The walls were still gilded, and the small lights along each wall bounced light off each other. The ceiling was so tall the light didn't reach it, so I kept my eyes down, watching each step.

The mosaics in the floor were made of blue and green tiles, painting a landscape that shifted from grassy green to the cornflower blue of the sky until it darkened into night. A doorway lined with black onyx glittered in the low light. The emerald practically pulled itself from my hand, and the necklace tried to pull me under.

"I've got a bad feeling about this," William said, and the pit in my stomach only grew with every step we took toward the doorway.

"Yeah, that makes sense. This has to be the worst idea we've had yet," I said.

"Worse than trying to impress you with that thing?" he said, gesturing to the necklace.

"Maybe the second worst idea we've had," I said and he shot me a quick grin.

Henkhisesui stood in the center of the room, his hands placed on a sarcophagus. It was solid gold with emeralds everywhere. That had to be Kheti.

"What the actual fuck," William said, backing up to flee when he saw Henkhisesui. The ram head, the wings, the large, muscled human legs and arms. Henkhisesui was about ten feet tall, and he snarled at William.

You woke me and left me to wander this plane without my beloved, he shouted and we both covered our ears to shield the noise. The words shook the organs in my body, rattled my bones. William's knees buckled and he went down to one knee, his hands on the sand-covered tile.

"We didn't know," I said, hands raised.

Ignorance is no excuse, Henkhisesui thundered. His steps shook the tomb, and I stepped in front of William, shielding him.

"Before this necklace, I didn't even know you existed. The old gods have been forgotten by the modern world, Henkhisesui," I said, my temper flaring. William thrusted a hand for me but I stepped out of his grasp.

The ram-headed god towered over me, rage barely concealed within him. This was absolutely stupid, but there was no backing down now. I pulled the emerald out of my pocket and he sucked in a breath. More dust fell from the ceiling, and it stuck to my glasses. The slight loss of visibility made my heart rate spike; I didn't want to lose sight of him for even a moment.

How dare–

"But, they could remember. I could study your temple, catalog every detail, and share with the world what a marvel it is. But you don't actually care about that, do you? You care about Kheti. That's what this is about," I said, letting the words bubble up as I babbled. Henkhisesui nodded.

Everything I have ever done is for Kheti.

"You miss him. You want to be reunited with his spirit. I can feel it, you know. It's so strange, whatever you did to hang out in my mind, I can feel Kheti's presence now too."

Henkhisesui placed a hand on the golden sarcophagus. Oh god, if a mummy popped up I would lose it. That was too far into the paranormal for me. Believing in fate was about as far into the unknown as I was willing to go.

Kheti lies here. His soul lies there. Henkhisesui pointed at the emerald.

"How did you bind his soul to this?" I asked. William crept up to stand beside me.

He did not wish to leave my side when Anubis called for him, and I am deathless. This was our solution.

"So you... bound him to the emerald?"

As he wished. I would have never done this without his consent.

"And now you want to..."

Release him. Release us both. I bound myself to the necklace at your throat. If we cannot walk this realm together, then it is time to move on to the next.

William and I were both speechless. There was so much sorrow in the room that we were suffocating with it. Henkhisesui sank to his knees, the large wings resting on the tiled floor, as he laid his head on the sarcophagus. The way he caressed the masked face was the way that William held me. I saw all of the love in Henkhisesui's tender expression and when I turned to William, his eyes were damp with tears.

"You're ready to go," I said, and he didn't respond. Henkhisesui's eyes were closed as he knelt before the body of his beloved. How beautifully tragic: love that lasts through centuries even when it's only carried by one soul.

I have begged Anubis to return to the underworld. This half life is worse than death, and now that I am awake, I will not bear it any longer.

"How can we help?" William asked. His voice trembled but his shoulders didn't. He bumped against me, quiet, solid support, and I swallowed down my own emotions.

I need you to release us. It's time for this to end.

"Tell me what to do," I said and when the lid of the sarcophagus shifted, I nearly jumped out of my skin.

"Oh shit–"

I need to be with him, Henkhisesui said. The lid slowly opened and it took every ounce of courage, every recited mantra of "*what would Indy do*," to keep me in place. Even William looked pale in the wane light.

"Is-is that mummy going to sit up or something? Because I could really use a fucking warning," William said and I shushed him.

The dead do not rise without command and I do not possess such power. Kheti's body will remain here, just as this form will once I lay down with him.

"You can't mean for us to lock you in there," I said, and there was so much grief climbing up my throat that I couldn't breathe.

Yes, Arthur Lewis. You will release me and my body will return to his. Heart to heart, flesh to flesh, soul to soul. In every way, we belong together.

"But the necklace–"

You know how to take it off. You've known all along. The rage that surrounded him had faded completely and all that was left was the weary soul of one drowning in sorrow. With the emerald in one hand and the necklace around my neck, the answer seemed to come to me all at once.

Together. They needed to be together, in every way, in every aspect of life. Together.

"Wait, Henkhisesui, where is Zahra? You said she was here," William blurted out.

Yes, your friend is here. She waits in the chamber beyond, in Kheti's antechamber. No harm will befall her.

"Why are you being so kind now?" I asked, remembering how he took possession of my head, how the rage made him inconsolable.

Because even a god gets tired of his own wrath.

I nodded, and knew it was time. I knew it was time for Henkhisesui to leave this plane and enter the afterlife–whatever that looked like. I prayed they were headed for the Land of Reeds, where everything was plentiful and peaceful. They deserved that–everyone deserved that kind of joy and eternal rest. I hoped to hell that's what awaited me at the end of this life.

The emerald had a faint glow that got brighter the closer I brought it to the worn pendant with Henkhisesui's name on it.

The words etched on my skin and etched in their hearts came to my lips, except I knew there was another line:

"The East Wind rises again, a storm without end, a lover in search of home. A lover, lost and alone, feels the East Wind caress his face and knows he will never stop searching. One day we will rise again and there will be no storm, no force that will stand between the East Wind and his lover. Until they find their rest in the Land of Reeds, the land of love," I spoke in Egyptian, the language of Henkhisesui and Kheti.

The glow from the pendants grew brighter until the chain fell from my neck. I dropped them both and watched them shatter as they hit the sand-covered tile floor. It hit me then what the scene was–the Land of

Reeds. The gentle blue and the evergreen tiles were paradise, and they led directly to Kheti's resting place.

Henkhisesui's ram-like body faded first. The head transformed into a human and his wings fell away. Bones shortened until he was about the same size as William. Honey brown eyes searched my face and smiled. This was Henkhisesui's soul, I realized. His golden magic feathered off of him in waves, like he was fading away.

Kheti's soul sat up from the sarcophagus and I heard William swear–*oh sonabitch*–but I just watched the two of them.

Kheti was strikingly beautiful. Jet black, straight hair cropped to his shoulders. Dark, lovely onyx eyes, and deeply tanned skin. Henkhisesui cupped his face, and tears ran down their faces. He pressed kisses to his eyelids, his forehead, his nose, anywhere that Henkhisesui could get his lips to.

"My beloved," Henkhisesui said.

"My beloved," Kheti replied. His voice was softer than what his figure would suggest; Kheti was strong and solidly built, and not at all a match to the gentle, whispered voice.

"We are free," Henkhisesui whispered back.

"I have been waiting for you to come home, Henkhisesui."

"Will we be judged worthy?"

"I am prepared to beg, great one. You deserve to rest."

Henkhisesui helped Kheti's soul rise and they stood in an embrace before turning to me. Kheti's head nestled against Henkhisesui's chest, and their arms were wrapped around each other so tightly. Their magic faded and faded, and soon they were mostly transparent.

"Thank you, Arthur Lewis. Thank you, William Ford. The Great Determiner has guided your footsteps to us, and to one another. No mere lifetime can bind what lies in the hearts of men, remember that."

Henkhisesui and Kheti held hands as they reached forward to William and I. Palm to palm, Henkhisesui and I stood until he faded completely. Kheti's soft smile tugged at my heart as they faded away.

"Cherish the love you find, it is worth more than any jewel," Kheti said.

As the magic faded, I leaned over the sarcophagus and sobbed.

XVII

William

FOR ONCE IN MY life, I was at a loss for words. The passing of Henkhisesui and Kheti struck a chord deep in my heart. I felt their sorrow and their loss. Watching them share the joy of just holding each other, being together again, hit me with the truth that I couldn't–*wouldn't*–hide anymore.

Arthur collapsed against the sarcophagus, crying so hard I was worried he'd need his inhaler. It was like he cried for every moment they were apart, every tear another piece of their sorrow and loneliness.

I pulled him into my arms, into my lap, and let him cry.

Henkhisesui said that Zahra would be okay, and I actually believed him. Right now, the only thing I could focus on was calming Arthur's crying, trying to rub reassessing circles on his back. The sobs wracked through his slim shoulders until there were no tears left in him. We sat on the ground, leaning against Kheti's tomb. Arthur climbed into my lap, his head in the crook of my neck. He looped his arms around my neck, pulling us closer. The tattoos on his arm started to fade, and so did mine.

"Arty, look," I said, and held out my arm.

"No," he protested, rubbing at his skin. "No, they can't be gone–"

"Arty," I said gently.

"Please stay," he whispered, and the tattoos stopped fading. They reformed into a single lotus on his forearm and mine did the same. The words from Henkhisesui and Kheti's love song printed in fine, detailed, English script.

"The East Wind rises again, a storm without end, a lover in search of home," scrawled across his arm, looping and beautiful.

"A lover, lost and alone, feels the East Wind caress his face and knows he will never stop searching," in the same fine font along my arm.

The lotuses were opened and in bloom, and I held my breath. This was the time. I felt it in my core, and as I searched Arthur's adoring brown eyes, I saw the truth reflected there.

"I love you," we said in unison. The words tangled together, and our voices merged so it was one confession, one declaration.

"You do?" he asked, that utterly befuddled look on his face. I took his glasses off, placing them on the ground beside us, just so I could see him even more. The dirt and grime on his glasses hid the color of his eyes.

"Not all treasure is made of gold, Arty."

He cracked a smile, so pure of joy that I couldn't help but grin. "We were having a moment, and you hit me with that line?"

"What? It was *perfect*. You are a treasure, and as far as I can tell, you don't have a drop of gold on you."

"I could get a gold tooth," he said, the eyebrow arched in competition. His tear stained cheeks were flushed with color, but now it seemed to make him lighter. The grief had loosened its hold on him and he was smiling. And he loved me. Somehow he loved me, and that felt like the greatest gift I'd ever been given.

He loved me.

Was I dreaming? *He loved me*. I wanted to shout it from the rooftops, but if I woke the dead again, he would absolutely kill me.

"Maybe let's pass on the gold teeth. I don't know if you could pull it off, not with the hat."

"I wish I had worn it. I think my scalp is burnt," he said, touching his hair like even the gentle pressure ached. I tugged a lock and he swatted at me.

"I love you, Arthur," I said again. I needed to say the words again; I needed him to hear them on their own, without the chorus of his own admission. He leaned back, taking in the details of my face. Likely assessing if I was telling the truth or not; can't blame him, I'm not sure I would believe me either.

"I love you, William, against my better judgement, I'm sure. But I do. I think I have for a while, and that's possibly even more ridiculous."

"Loving me is ridiculous?" I teased.

"Have you seen the messes you get into? I must be crazy."

"Let's see if we can find Zahra. Henkhisesui said she should be nearby," I said and he nodded. His glasses were a mess, so I wiped them down with my shirt and handed them back.

"Appreciate the gesture, but I'll have to teach you how to clean glasses properly," he said, kissing my shoulder. The tattoos were bright even in the low light, and Arthur studied my arm. "I'm glad these aren't gone."

"Yeah, me too."

"Hate to interrupt the moment, but my head is killing me, and I want to get out of here," a voice said. I turned so fast I nearly knocked Arthur over as I bolted to scoop Zahra up in my arms. She had a massive cut on her forehead, but I didn't see any other injuries.

"Where the hell have you been!" I said, hugging her to my chest.

"Knocked out. I don't know where we are, or anything. I was at the camp and then I just... wasn't. Look, William, we need to talk about the... thing I told you."

"About how you're working for the Spice Traders?" Arthur cut in, his tone lethally sharp.

She had the good sense to wince, and when they're eyes met, there was so much fire in Arthur's stare I was worried he'd set her ablaze. "My cousin, Rami, got me in with them. It seemed harmless at first, but it escalated. And then William got involved and it just spiraled."

"Was it your intention or Rami's to sabotage my dig?" Arthur asked.

"I–"

"Answer the question. You've already admitted that you dragged William into this nonsense. I want to know how black your core is before I decide if you should be turned over to the authorities too."

"Arty, wait–"

He held a hand, and he was every ounce the intimidating professor he'd be in a couple years. The stern face and drawn brows. It was weirdly hot, but that thought stayed as an inside thought.

"It was Rami's. And someone named Lavender. I was supposed to meet her here, but it never happened."

Something flashed across Arthur's face but it was gone within a second. He reached for my hand and I squeezed his fingers.

"We're dating now. Boyfriends. I'm going to see if the sandstorm has cleared so we can be airlifted back to Fayoum, and then we're going to get to the bottom of this," he declared, and pride swelled me in.

Dating. Boyfriends.

"How long was I out that I missed all of this?" Zahra asked me, and I smiled.

"Feels like forever, honestly. Long enough to discover a long lost temple and for Arthur to fall in love with me."

"God, have I gone for a century? It's hard to believe Arthur Lewis sees you as anything other than target practice."

"He's got his good sides," I said. Arthur was already fumbling down the long, narrow hallway leading back to the throne room. "Come on, let's get out of here."

"William, there's so much to see–"

"And we will, but not today. Arthur is going to be studying this temple for years to come, I know it."

"And you?"

"I'll be here too. Can't let him do all the discoveries."

"Wait, William Ford is planning for the future? Not ironically?" Zahra laughed. She winced when she laughed, the cut on her forehead pulling together. She stepped closer for a hug and I squeezed her tight. I thought she was dead. I thought she was gone. I thought she had betrayed me in ways I couldn't fathom. Her hair still smelled like her favorite coconut shampoo, and it steadied me.

"Miracles happen. Wait, if you worked for the Spice Traders, what spice were you?"

"Nope, not going there."

"Zahra, come on–"

"Coconut. I was Coconut, okay?" she stammered, desperately trying not to laugh again.

"That's not even a spice–"

"Right?"

"Are they that dumb?" I said, wiping a tear from my eye from laughing so hard. I pictured her on a walkie-talkie with someone saying, *Coconut, Coconut, can you hear me, Coconut?* It didn't help stem the giggles.

"I think there's just that many of them, William. This isn't a little network. Rami told me how deep they are. They're everywhere. They've got police and politicians and even museums and scientists on their payroll. I don't know we'll ever escape them."

The laughter died as I saw the look on her face. She belonged to this group and she saw no way out.

Good thing my new boyfriend was more relentless than any other person I'd met in my life. If the Spice Traders weren't willing to let go of us, Arty would pry our freedoms from their grubby hands. Like a dog with a bone, once Arthur Lewis set his sights on something, he never let it go.

The stupid, romantic part of me wondered if that applied to his boyfriends too; would Arthur be the relentless man I knew him to be when it came to us?

"Will, as much as I want to stay and study the art too, we need to go. I was able to get enough signal to call Irina. We've got a helicopter on the way. ETA is an hour. We can poke around the throne room," Arty called.

"Reunited with your best friend and he thinks you're looking at art?" Zahra said, the smirk firmly back in place.

"He's a romantic at heart," I said, and as Arty's head popped around the corner, I saw how true that was in his warm brown eyes.

As I left Kheti's resting place, I heard the words of their love song on the wind.

"The East Wind rises again, a storm without end, a lover in search of home. A lover, lost and alone, feels the East Wind caress his face and knows he will never stop searching. One day we will rise again and there will be no storm, no force that will stand between the East Wind and his lover. Until they find their rest in the Land of Reeds, the land of love," they sang from wherever their spirits had gone.

I stopped to listen to them singing, and I turned back to see their spirits again. This time Henkhisesui tilted Kheti's face up in a soft, loving kiss. The golden wind wrapped around them, and brushed my cheek.

I wish you every happiness, William Ford. Protect your beloved, enjoy your lives. Kheti and I will be watching over you. The East Wind will forever guide your steps, protecting the path you walk.

"Thank you, Henkhisesui. I hope you and Kheti will be at peace."

Peace is wherever love is.

"William? What're you looking at?" Zahra asked, and she pulled me along.

"Just looking," I said, as the sparkling wind faded again.

XVIII

Arthur

THE WISTFULNESS ON WILLIAM'S face reminded me that we needed to talk about whatever had brought that reaction on. When Zahra and him emerged from the mountain of stairs, we were all winded, but William looked utterly at peace.

It was strange.

The helicopter would be here in about ten minutes, and I wanted to be outside when it arrived. The temple called to me, and I wondered if William felt that same pull. Judging from how he kept looking back, I'd wager a guess it did.

Hank, our trusty camel, greeted us at the stairs with some delighted grunts and hums. He was an oddly intelligent camel; not that camels weren't smart, but he seemed *more*. Even after Henkhisesui had let go of him.

Hank butted his nose against my hand, demanding some affection. Very strange. He took one look at William and Zahra and promptly spit in their direction.

"Now, now Hank. Be nice. She's not that bad."

He blinked twice, looked from her to me, as if to say, *yeah right, whatever helps you sleep at night.*

"What a cute baby!" Zahra cooed and Hank huffed at her. "Oh, don't be like that. I love camels. They're just cuter horses." She scratched behind his ear and Hank huffed, but this time he seemed content.

Maybe she isn't so bad, the look said.

I was dying from a heat stroke, imagining that the camel was speaking to me.

William slung his arm around my shoulders and yanked me into a hug. "I haven't forgotten about my plans for you the next time we're in a real bed."

"Naked and moaning, something like that?"

"Mmm, indeed."

"Did something happen back there?" I asked, watching the emotions flicker on and off his face.

"Zahra said the Spice Traders are a bigger issue than we thought. And I got to see Henkhisesui and Kheti again. They were saying goodbye," he said, resting his head against my forehead.

"I'm sorry I missed that."

"I think they had said their goodbye to you, but this one was for me. It was... really something."

"Do you want to talk about it?"

"Is this what boyfriends do? Open and honest communication?"

"Typically yes. At least according to all of the romance novels I've read," I said, watching the information register.

"You like romance novels?"

"Smutty ones. I'll be providing you with a reading list." William grabbed my chin and kissed me, a tangle of tongues and joy and love. I could get used to this. I already had.

"Also," he breathed, "Zahra's code name was Coconut."

"That's not even a spice."

"Exactly what I said."

"We were clearly made for each other," I said, venturing out a little past boyfriends. A little closer into *I love you as in, forever, as in, this is it, you're mine, I'm done.*

"Obviously, Two halves of the same coin. Whatever the saying is." He kissed my forehead as the helicopter came into view, ready to land. "What are we going to do about Hank?"

"I'm going to tell him to go back to the excavation site," I declared and William waited for me to elaborate. "He's a very smart animal. I think Henkhisesui made him more intelligent. So, I'm going to tell him to go there and then we will have to bring him back to Fayoum in a couple days."

"You're serious."

"Afraid so. Go get Zahra on the helicopter. I'm going to give Hank his marching orders."

"I love you, Arty. You bizarre, adorable man."

"I think that was a compliment," I said, kissing his cheek.

"Wait until we get back to the hotel. I'll show you how much of a compliment it was."

"Gross, please stop. I'm not used to William being... normal. You two can play kissy face later. I think I need stitches," Zahra said. Hank waited for me, and before I could speak he nuzzled my hand and took off galloping across the sand back toward the site.

The helicopter landed about fifty feet away and sand still flew everywhere. I covered my face as much as I could, and the same technician came to help us. The helicopter seemed larger, but maybe it wasn't; maybe I just didn't look properly because Wes was bleeding.

"Come on!" he yelled, and William held my hand as we made our way to the copter. They got us situated with headsets and helmets, seatbelts fastened, and we were in the air almost instantly.

***

Wes was awake and cursing up a storm in the hospital. He was not happy about being laid up with his leg in a cast. I was just so damn thankful that he still had a leg. The break looked terrible, and I never wanted to see that part of his body again. The doctor told me that they needed to put three steel pins in his leg, and Wes complained that now his leg will "know when it rains like an old man."

He was going to be insufferable for the next six months, but it was worth it.

Wes Carrington was alive, and that was enough for me to endure the whining. The man redefined the patheticness of man-flu, but aside from being selfishly glad my mentor was still around, Wes had become my family.

"Now tell me how your night was. Better than leg surgery, I'm guessing."

"William and I ate more sausages and then went back to the temple." His raised eyebrow made my cheeks flush.

"Aha! So you two finally figured it out. Excellent. I saw how you both were mooning over each other during your grad years. Glad you finally worked it out."

I filled Wes in on the rest of what happened, including watching Henkhisesui and Kheti say goodbye and how the tattoos shifted once again. Wes turned my arm this way and that, looking at the designs and reading the words. *The East Wind rises again, a storm without end, a lover in search of home,* covered my forearm, elbow to wrist.

A lover, lost and alone, feels the East Wind caress his face and knows he will never stop searching, wrapped around William's arm in matching placement and script. Just touching the words, I felt the gentle stir of Henkhisesui's magic brushing across the letters. I knew that it would always be there, and that settled the unrest in my heart.

I was going to uncover and show the world every inch of their temple, showcasing a love that lasted centuries.

"Hope I'm not interrupting," Irina said as she knocked on the door, letting herself in.

"Thank you for sending help to us. Zahra and William needed to be checked over," I said. My words were clipped and short, but I forced a smile on my face. Wes noticed the friction but said nothing; the concerned look on his face screamed *you will tell me about what's going on later*, but he remained silent.

"Are you alright Arthur?"

"Fine, thank you. Lovely tattoo, you've got there," I said, letting my tone slip down an octave, like William did when he was trying to seem dangerous.

Except I was: Irina Romanova was the connection, and I was so fucking angry at myself for not putting it together sooner. The funding. The fucking *helicopter*. Allowing and welcoming William to the site. That could have been Wes' insistence, but Irina held the money and she could have shut down any other involvement. But she didn't.

And she wouldn't either–not when she was supposed to be meeting someone that Rami knew.

Not when she was Lavender.

XIX

William

Zahra and I were back in the same hotel that I'd run into Arty not long ago. It felt like ages, like no time had passed between college and seeing him again. We were in the same room, and Zahra told me that Rami had paid for it for the next two months. She had little desire to stay here; after what happened at the site, she couldn't stomach dealing with Rami or the Spice Traders anymore.

I thought back to Rami pretending to be so shocked when I mentioned them, or how he forced me into a card game for him. I thought about how he tried so hard to pretend that he gave off weird, desperate vibes. Everything about Rami had been an act; the only real reaction I'd seen from him was in the temple when he was terrified that I was going to shoot him.

Part of me hated that I didn't. A larger part hated that I lifted a gun at someone to begin with.

"Have you heard from Arthur?" she asked.

"Yeah, Wes is doing better. He said he'd be back soon."

When my phone rang again, I was expecting the call. Zahra paled when she saw the blocked number. Annatto. It had been a good three days since he called to harass me again; it was overdue.

"William, William, William. Where have you been? Better yet, do you have the money?"

"Annatto–"

"I don't care for excuses. I'll be in Fayoum tomorrow night. You will have it."

"And if I don't?"

"Let's not talk about such things. Such dire things. Rest well, William."

"Was it Rami or you that gave Annatto my information?" I asked, and instantly regretted it. Zahra averted her eyes and it was enough of an answer. "Did you know that I'd lose?"

"No. They cheated; that last hand when you lost? They cheated. I know they did," she pleaded.

The last game was bullshit–cheating or not, it was normal for luck to run out. I knew I was pushing it, but I kept going. That need, the allure of just one more hand when you were up was hard to resist. The Spice Traders didn't need to do much to push me over the edge.

"Why did Rami get me to play for him?"

"He makes so many stupid choices it's hard to keep up with. The last he told me, he was in serious debt to Cardamom. He probably heard about your winning streak and wanted to capitalize on it. I mean, if you lost, he'd just tell them it was all you and you'd end up with even more debt. But then you won that necklace–"

"Don't mention that necklace to anyone. Or the temple. Or anything you saw there–"

"Yes, William, I got it. Shut the hell up."

"Zahra, it's just, I need a minute. The trust was broken."

"How can I make it up to you?"

"I don't know yet," I said honestly. I wanted nothing more for things to go back to normal, but that seemed so far beyond the realm of possibility. How could I look her in the eyes and feel like she wasn't hiding something from me now?

"I am sorry, I hope that you know that. Truly." Zahra turned toward the bed and paused. The room was a single bed, and the idea of pretending to be her boyfriend or whatever made my stomach sour. She plopped on the bed, not looking at me. Zahra felt the energy shift too. I walked over and folded her into a hug.

"I love you. I'm pissed at you, but I love you. I'm gonna stay in Arty's room tonight. I need to check in with him anyway. Still figuring out this boyfriend thing."

"He's good for you," she said, and the tinge of sadness in her tone made my heart lurch.

"Yeah, he really is."

I kissed her on the cheek and grabbed my backpack on the way out. There weren't any more words to say. It took me a minute to walk away from Zahra, and I leaned heavily against the wall. Arthur's room was only a short walk away, but my steps were heavy. Everything just felt so fucking heavy; regardless of how I ended up here, the debt was still a problem I needed to solve. Shuffling down the narrow, dimly-light hall, I knocked on Arthur's door and he opened it almost immediately.

"Hi," I said.

"Hi," he said. Arthur was in a towel again; his wet hair dripped on his bare feet. Arthur wasn't wearing his glasses and that made him more vulnerable than standing in just a towel. The freckles on his face and across his nose were pronounced. All of the sun exposure gave him a warm, ruddy glow. Arthur was warm and alive and I really wanted to kiss him.

"Can I come in?"

"Will, I just assumed that this was your room now too. Of course you can come in," he said, holding the towel for dear life again. The almost-not-there shake in his fingers told me he was just as nervous as I was: this whole *together* thing was new and beautiful, and neither one of us was known for gentleness.

"Because we are boyfriends now," I said.

"Sorry, I should have run that by you. We should talk about it like adults–"

"Or, you can take that towel off, and I can keep that promise I made to you in the desert."

"Remind me, my memory isn't very good," he said, the sarcasm and desire dripping from his words like the water droplets from his hair. I was going to lap them off his collarbones. I closed the door with my foot and Arthur let the towel fall.

Standing in his hotel room again, but this time welcomed, felt different. Arthur turned around, completely bare for me to take in. It was an offering, and I understood everything he tried to say with the shifting of his weight, the blush creeping up his neck to stain his cheeks. All of my things were on the floor now, and my arms opened for him. Arthur stepped into me, and I breathed in the scent of his freshly washed skin, the mint and cedar of his soap. It was the same he'd used in college; I remembered it from spending the odd night at his place on the couch. How many times were we an arm's length away when we could have been hand in hand? He nestled into the crook of my neck and comforted me like I'd never known. The heaviness from moments ago felt lightyears away, like it didn't matter at all.

It did, of course. Annatto would be a problem to solve tomorrow, but tonight it was just Arthur and I in this hotel room, locked and secluded.

I guided Arthur to the bed, and pulled my faded t-shirt up over my head. It landed on the turned down bed with a soft plop. Arthur's eyes followed the motion of the shirt and he swallowed hard, looking back to me.

"I love when you do that," Arthur said.

"Do what?" I asked, working on getting my linen pants off. They were crumpled all to hell, but that was also a problem for tomorrow. Thank god I showered before Zahra and I had our heart to heart.

"How you take your shirts off. You just move so fluidly, like the fabric will bend to your will regardless of heat or sweat or–"

"I think you just like watching me strip, Arty."

"Oh. Well, when you phrase it like that–"

"It's allowed. Boyfriends right?"

"Boyfriends," he said, tilting his chin up just a hair for a kiss. I was learning all of Arthur's tells, all of the little ques he gave for what he wanted and how. He responded with little gasps when our tongues met, and he pressed into me when I threaded my hands in his hair. Anytime I brought us together, Arthur wanted to be closer. Every inch of him craved connection, and as we laid together to kiss, our legs curled around each other.

"It's been a long time since I've had a boyfriend," Arthur said.

"Same. Too long. I might need to be housetrained again."

"Were you ever house broken?" he challenged.

"Cute," I said with a nibble along the sensitive skin just below his ear, until he shivered.

"Yes, you are," he said, and pulled me into a kiss. Heaven. This had to be what heaven felt like, wrapped up in Arthur's arms with the steady, rising beat of his heart pounding against my chest.

"This snappy, one-liner Arty is new. I like it," I teased.

"Hmm, he's always been here, but was too shy to snap back."

"Arty, I don't think you've ever been shy in your life." The conversation flowed between kisses: lips and cheeks, foreheads and collarbones, hands and sensitive skin of bare chests. The aircon cooled the room and our overheated skin just from existing together.

"I was once. But then I realized that having a voice was the only power I'd ever truly have. I wasn't strong or athletic; sure I excelled at school, but my voice was the only weapon I could hone, so I did." Our hands roamed over each other, learning the contours and dips of each other.

"I want to hear all about your shy days."

"Later, I feel like I remember something about being naked and moaning? That sounds like a good plan."

"Really, I should be in charge of more things, I've got a knack for plans," I said, and Arthur laughed. My hands rubbed down his bare shoulders and he shivered, leaning into my touch. Arthur was hard and ready; when our bodies touched, it was electric. Little shockwaves rocketed through me, and just this was enough. Just him with his hand on my belly, our cocks brushing against each other in what felt almost like a kiss. His body was magic, and he was mine to explore.

"Will," he said, voice strained. I nodded as he led us to the bed. The very large, very soft, very clean bed. He hadn't even turned down the covers yet, and it was such an Arthur thing to do. I imagined him sitting on the less-comfortable chairs because they were *sitting* and the bed was for *laying*, and god help him if he mixed that up.

"I love you," I said with the image of him eyeing the bed in my mind's eye. I couldn't keep the smile from my face, and he lit up in response. I nudged him to lay back, but he stopped, nudging me down instead. Arthur kissed me like I held the only oxygen in the room, in the world, in the universe.

God, he was *magic*.

Flat on my back, he settled across my hips. The warmth of his skin seeped into my thighs and hips and belly. Arthur's hands roamed from my cock to my face, touching and touching like I might suddenly disappear. When he rocked back, his entrance rubbing across me, I sucked in a breath.

"We've covered the naked part," he said, the sparkle of mischief in his eyes that made my chest tight–love and desire twisting in a heady mixture.

"So it seems," I said, rolling my hips in response. Arthur braced his hands on my chest, and I knew he had to feel how wild my heart beat. I sat up to kiss him, and Arthur wrapped his arms around my neck. With our chests pressed together, I felt the wild thrum of his heart too, as he guided my hands to where he wanted them. In a swift–clearly planned–motion, he reached for a condom and a small bottle of lube. Those slim, deft fingers had the condom and bottle opened in record speed, and it was me who was moaning when he rolled it down my length with his teeth as he knelt next to me.

"Wasn't I supposed to be the one moaning? Did I misunderstand you?" he asked, the glitter in his eyes positively sparkling.

"You're playing dirty, Arty. I just got here, barely a chance to *see* you and you've already got me where you wanted me."

"You're right, this is exactly where I want you. Here, with me," he said, his voice dropping low as he reached between his legs. His fingers were slick as one pressed against his entrance. It slipped in easily and one of us grunted–I think it was me.

"Arty–"

"I might have had my own plans," he said, as he worked himself open. Arthur laid back, knees falling open, as I got to take in the view of his body. One hand wrapped around his cock, and the other at his opening was the hottest thing I'd ever seen in my life. This primal, needy version of Arthur might have been my favorite. With the way he looked at me to the way he *needed* me, it was addictive and I couldn't get enough of it.

I wanted to touch myself just to ease the pressure building, but I didn't. My eyes were glued to him, watching him please himself, and when Arthur let out a little cry, a little moan, I nearly came.

"The next phase of this plan involves more work on your part, Will," he said, too breathy to sound like he was in control. I fucking loved watching the control slip away from him as he gave in, told me what he wanted, what he needed.

"Glad the audience gets to be involved now," I said, gently pulling him back to straddle me again. Arthur slowly removed his fingers, and lined me up to his entrance. He sank slowly around me, and I didn't dare breathe until I was in him fully. He set the pace, rocking until I was driving into him, hitting that sweet spot. Arthur cried out, crying my name, and hearing my name on his lips covered in bliss was nearly too much. He came on my stomach, and I rubbed his back through his release, trying my best to keep the rhythm going until my own threatened to ignite.

"Will," he pleaded, his whispers against my ear. His loose, boneless body was warm and limp in my arms, and pressed back against me until my release hit. Now it was me crying out his name, but he pressed kisses to my mouth like he was swallowing the words coming from me. Spent and warm, I held Arthur until he was ready to move. It might have been minutes or maybe hours. There was bliss and love here, and I didn't want to let go of him even for a shower.

"Let's get cleaned up," he said between kisses and groaned, squeezing him to my chest.

"Not yet," I said, and he relaxed back into my arms.

"Two minutes. Then shower." I bit the shell of his ear and he shuttered, swatting me away. "Okay, ah, moment is ruined. Shower. Now. You smell like sex."

"I think I hate this plan," I said, and Arthur rolled over, clearly done with my protests. He started to get up but I pulled him back for one last kiss. "And who's fault is it that I smell like sex?"

"Definitely yours."

***

Arthur slept like the dead, and his light snoring put me out too. I dreamt about the temple and saw Kheti smiling at me. I hoped they were happy now; it seemed like it, but where did their spirits really go? In the dream, the lotus on my hand opened even further and on the petals Arthur's name was etched as the lines to create the bloom. It was beautiful and odd; the more I tried to examine the soft, curling letters of his name as the lines of the flower, the more the lotus changed.

Slowly the lotus shifted to something else, and I watched the lines on my hand dance until I recognized what they were becoming.

It was Arthur.

Drawn in simple lines, the outline of his face with the details of his hair and freckles and glasses perfectly rendered how I pictured him in my mind.

Now the tiny lines changed from spelling out his name to different words.

I love you, I love you, I love you over and over as the fine lines of his face.

Was I crying? Maybe, the dream made my body feel far away but here in this little corner of my mind I was more connected to myself than I'd ever been. In the hidden parts of my heart, the recesses of my mind, tucked between my memories was Arthur.

Warmth bloomed in my chest, and when I opened my eyes, the dream sat heavy on my mind. Arthur's sleeping, snoring form next to me hugged my arm tight to his chest. Steady breaths and slow heartbeats felt like a lullaby, but I forced myself to stay awake to take this moment in.

"I feel you staring at me. It's weird," he mumbled, and I turned to fold him into my arms.

"You're cute when you snore."

"I do not snore."

"You do. I'll take a video."

"I do *not* snore, Will."

"Indignant and adorable. Go back to sleep," I said as I ran my fingers through his hair. The silky locks slipped through my fingers so easily, and he leaned into me.

"We'll talk about this in the morning," he said, already half asleep. Within minutes he was snoring again, and I reached for my phone to take a video. A message popped up on my screen from Zahra and my heart nearly stopped.

There's a game tomorrow night. All the big players are gonna be there. If you can win, you'll be in the clear.

Another game. Who were the big players? I knew Annatto was a mid-level idiot, but what about Cardamom? I'd heard whispers of others in the area like Paprika and Fennel, but I'd never met them. They were careful to not let too many people see them. I wanted to ask Zahra if this was another trap, but that felt shitty. We had to have moved past that now, right?

Time and place

I pressed send before I could talk myself out of it. I could win; Arthur wouldn't have to worry about me or anyone else robbing his research site. Maybe I'd be able to look at myself in the mirror again without being disgusted.

"I can hear you thinking," Arthur grunted out, his lips barely moving.

"Okay, okay, I'm laying down now."

"Mmppphhh," he said, the snoring resuming. I got my video of a few good ones and added myself in there kissing his forehead. Arthur grunted like a pig and twitched. I tried my best not to laugh and mostly succeeded. His arms wrapped around my waist in a death grip, and I tossed my phone on the nightstand.

Tomorrow.

He'd likely want to go see Wes again. I'll make my excuses and then slip out for a few hours.

Tomorrow.
It ends tomorrow.

XX

Arthur

WILLIAM WAS CAGEY IN the morning. He was a terrible liar, despite what he told himself. His tells were how he tried so damn hard to pretend that he was completely *fiiine*. He smiled too much, too wide, touched his hair too much, scratched at his beard. There were so many tiny details about him that screamed *I am lying!*

Now to narrow down what he was lying about.

This was the tricky part.

After he paced for the third time, I opened the conversation gently, "Are you hungry? You seem restless. I could go for some coffee."

"Coffee sounds great. My treat?"

"Aren't you broke?"

"Credit cards still work, babe." He kissed me on the cheek, and for a minute his misdirection worked. He called me babe. That was a first, and I didn't like that it was to mislead me.

"Babe?"

"Yeah, thought I'd try it out. You know, boyfriends and all." He wouldn't meet my eyes, and I decided this wasn't what he was trying to deceive me with.

"Sugar?"

"What?" he said.

"Honey? Darling? Baby? None of these really feel right," I said, the laughter edging into my voice.

"You look like a babe. I could see you being a babe."

"I think I'll need to work on finding the appropriate pet name... pookie."

William laughed so hard I thought his ribs might actually break. He wiped the tears from his eye, and grabbed my hand.

"Breakfast and coffee, *babe*. Then what?"

"Well, *pookie*," I laughed mid sentence, "Wes is raising hell at the hospital, so I'm thinking I'm going to help him out today before they kick him out for being such an ass."

"Good plan. What about Irina? Is he going to stay with her?" he asked, and now it was my turn for the deception. I shook my head, and shrugged.

"Arty, what's up?"

Apparently I wasn't great at lying either; not to him, anyway.

"She's been distant. She isn't really answering my messages," I lied, waiting to see if he would press it further.

"Maybe she's just processing. The desert was wild," he said.

And I was desperate to get back to the temple. I felt the stir of the lingering magic under my skin and in my chest, wanting me to explore and find all the details of Henkhisesui and Kheti's stories. I knew William wanted to too, but I didn't see the longing for the sands in him like I felt them. The howling wind of the desert nights was hypnotic and it still had its grip on me.

"Yeah," I said. My mind wandered away from the conversation, and it was too hard to pull the words together. His nervous energy set my nerves on edge, but he wasn't ready to talk about it. I wasn't sure I was ready to hear whatever he was clearly hiding. "Do you want to see him with me?" I asked, and I watched the panic flicker across his face in just a millisecond or two.

"Nah, maybe tomorrow. If he's in a mood, I don't want a lecture about going back to school."

"Should I provide one for you, pookie? I'm quite good at lecturing–"

"If you wanted to punish me, can you come up with something a little more fun?" his voice dropped low, sending desire shooting straight down my body.

"You are truly incorrigible," I said, and he wriggled his eyebrows.

"The one and only."

"Let's go. I've got a few errands to do too, do you want to join?"

"Arty," he started but swallowed. The debate of how much to say was written so clearly on his face. My heart sank; *don't lie to me,* I pleaded silently. "I'm going to spend some time with Zahra."

The words were so quiet that it felt like he had just admitted to a murder instead of wanting to work things out with one of his oldest friends. Perhaps I'd been too critical of her.

"Is that why you're acting weird?"

"I am not acting weird," he pouted.

"You are, and I'm glad you're going to talk to her. Work out what you need to so you can move past this. I don't *love* her, but you clearly do. That alone is reason enough to sort your feelings out."

"I love you too, you know."

"I know," I said, and he smiled. There was a genuine smile. It made me feel a tad guilty that I hadn't told him the truth, but sometimes we have to protect the ones we love even from themselves.

I was going to confront *Lavender* tonight. She was going to help me get William out of this mess before I ruined her life completely. Irina didn't know what was going to hit her, and it was going to be *glorious*.

But first I had to tell Wes. I couldn't do this without him being on board. William quickly dressed and we were out the door in the next ten minutes. The cafe that he favored was nearby and as long as I had some coffee, I didn't care where we went. I needed caffeine to settle my nerves, and I needed time to convince myself that keeping the truth from William was different than lying.

It *was* different. He'd know the truth soon enough. I just couldn't tell him yet; not when he was still in danger. The lotus on my hand warmed as we held hands, and Henkhisesui's prayer on my arm was the reminder that I needed. Kheti's matching lines on William's skin confirmed my convictions: I'd do whatever I needed to keep him safe.

And right now that meant keeping him safe from himself.

That tender smile tugged at my heart, and I beamed back at him. We left the hotel and headed for the coffee shop walking down the busy streets of Fayoum. I didn't reach for his hand, but when they accidentally brushed over and over again, it felt like the same thing. I wasn't comfortable reaching for him out in public yet; everything was so new and we were still building the rules for what our normal would look like.

The other half of whatever he didn't want to talk about was evident during our awkward coffee date. We were overly quiet, and while the silence itself wasn't terrible, the energy in the air was charged.

He was waiting for something to happen.

So was I.

"Things will be okay with Zahra," I said, and watched as he fiddled with the ring on his finger. It was his fake wedding band that he wore when Zahra was around. He spun it around, the nervous energy rolling off of him in rushing waves.

"I know. One day, but when will that be? I just never thought I'd be here with her."

"People surprise us. Sometimes for the good, sometimes not," I said. I edged toward a confession, wondering how he would actually respond.

"Yeah," he replied, and stretched his legs so they brushed against mine. Any reason to touch–this was what I craved. This was the adventure I wanted. It was just him. It had always been him.

"I'd really like to kiss you," I said.

"Later," he said, smiling over the rim of his cup. His phone buzzed but I couldn't see the name from this angle. Sunlight poured in from the window hitting his phone just right so I couldn't see anything. This shop was old and cozy. The tables were older than we were, with tablecloths that were threadbare. Coffee stronger than most legal alcohols brewed and filled the air. I breathed deep, savoring the heavenly smell. For a moment I let myself be carried away in the ambiance, and just enjoyed this quiet moment with William. He picked at a lemon scone, pretending to eat.

"Are we truly okay?" I asked, and his picking stopped.

"Yeah Arty. We're okay," William said. I wanted to reach for him, but neither of us moved. This lingering felt like torture, but he winked at me and I took a piece of his scone. I should have ordered something too, but

I didn't want to drag this out too much. Now I regretted it; after tonight would he still want to kiss me?

I'd find out tomorrow.

His phone buzzed again and this time he picked up. "Yeah, yeah I'll see you soon. Bye." William hurried off the phone and I waited. It sounded like a male voice on the line, not Zahra.

"I'm gonna meet Zahra soon. We're going to go shopping and talk."

"Okay," I said. Was he lying about meeting Zahra? Anxiety curled in my stomach, but I pressed it down. Trust. That's what relationships were built on, and I needed to trust William. I needed to trust his words and that he'd still hang around after–

"I'm going to kiss you until the wheels in your head stop spinning later. I like it when you're love-drunk."

"Promise?" I asked before I could stop myself.

"Oh, absolutely. I didn't specify *where* I'd be kissing you, either, for the record."

"You're–"

"Delightful, wonderful, charming, incorrigible? Yes, yes, yes, so you've said."

"Pretty sure I've only said that last one." My coffee was nearly gone now, and I took the last sip, savoring every drop.

"You've thought the others," he said, flashing that wicked smile. God, I loved him. I loved every insufferable inch of him.

"I plead the fifth."

"Same as being guilty. I'll see you later? Text me?"

"I could call you," I said. He feigned disgust, a hand to his mouth with wide eyes. Those beautiful green eyes shone with that playful spark that made him William.

"You wouldn't dare. You're more civilized than that," he said.

"Zahra calls you."

"Zahra is a disaster of a human," he deadpanned.

"Not touching that one," I said, pushing up from the table. My own phone was ringing, and I knew it was Wes.

William kissed each of my cheeks in goodbye, and even though the gesture was meant to look innocent, he scraped his beard against my cheek to get my attention.

"Love you," he said, and was off. The others in the shop glanced toward us, but a couple of winks from William and they turned away. He paid the bill and slipped out of the shop before I could say anything else to him.

Wes' text was simple and to the point: *come over now*. He didn't ask for any special treats, but I knew better than to show up without some carbonated lemon water. After a quick stop at a convenience store and a short taxi ride, I was back at the hospital.

The fact that he hadn't broken out was a miracle. Wes was fully dressed in shorts and a t-shirt that clearly came from the gift shop. I couldn't imagine him willingly buying an *I love Egypt* shirt, even though he did in fact love Egypt. The bright white shirt with the black and red letters was obnoxious in the harsh fluorescent lighting. His suntanned skin made him seem much older. Wes had lost weight in the last few days, and it showed on his now-gaunt face.

"I'm leaving," he declared.

"Are you allowed to leave?" I asked as I handed him his water. Wes popped open the can and started chugging.

"Allowed! Am I a prisoner?"

"No, but you are in a hospital. Where there are medical doctors that actually know what they're doing–"

"I'm a doctor too!"

"Wes."

"Oh I know, but this place is dreadful. I've been cooped up for too long."

"Wes, it's been like three days."

"Yes, and I am patched up and ready to get back to work–"

"Wes–"

"First I think we should–"

"Wes!" I shouted and he stilled, watching me like he just realized I was truly here for the first time. "There's something I need your help with."

"Oh, yes, I'm sorry, of course. The site. It's going to be a paperwork *hell* but I'll help you through all of it."

"I meant something else. With William."

"Love trouble already?" I shook my head and Wes settled back into his wheelchair. He had crutches, but

I saw those lasting all of twenty minutes before he tried to walk without them. I explained to him about the Spice Traders and the debt. I watched as disappointment and disgust registered on his face, but he nodded along, listening intently. I walked him through Rami and Zahra's deceit, and then I brought up the gut-punch that I wished I never had to.

"And she was going to meet someone called Lavender," I said, and then stayed quiet. I paused, waiting for Wes to connect the dots. He was a brilliant man, he'd see the connection soon enough.

"Lavender," he repeated.

"Yes." I swallowed hard, suddenly regretting ever asking for his help. This was too much to ask of him.

"And you're sure it's her?" he asked, but I saw as he scanned through his thoughts, sorting the evidence in his mind. He had this same look when he was researching, mentally cataloging everything he learned.

"Yes," I said again.

"And you plan to–"

"Yes," I finished. He nodded once, reaching out for my hand.

"Then you have to get me out here, and off of these damn crutches." He squeezed my shoulder in affection and I let go of the breath I'd been holding since this morning. "You should have told William."

"Not until it's over."

"Wear the hat. I think Indy would be proud." He clapped my back and I helped Wes back into his wheelchair. The day was already slipping away from me, and I needed to get ready for the game tonight. After doing a little research on Irina, it wasn't hard to put together where she would be. It helped that Wes had her location too; she shared her location with him, so we could watch her every movement.

It felt invasive, but I wasn't the criminal here. Not yet, technically.

"I need some bourbon," Wes muttered.

"You're not mixing bourbon with your pain meds."

"Party pooper."

XXI

William

I EXAMINED MYSELF IN the mirror of Arthur's hotel room—our room? I didn't know if that was official, but it didn't matter at the moment. The split lip was mostly healed. The ribs weren't, but no one would see that. My hands were covered in knicks and scrapes, but those were easily explained away.

Overall, it didn't look like I'd been in a bar fight and that was the look I was going for.

After a couple more swipes at my hair to make me look appropriately roguish, I met Zahra in the lobby of the hotel. She was back to wearing her classic all black outfits even with the blazing heat. My linen pants and top looked odd next to her, but her heat tolerance was better than mine.

"You ready?" she asked.

"As ready as I'll ever be," I said, and I sent a quick text to Arthur. A couple hearts, just to let him know that I was thinking of him. He immediately replied with two more hearts.

"I'm happy for you," she said.

"So you've said."

"It's just a little gross watching you be all lovey-dovey."

"Maybe I just needed the right man," I said, knowing it was the truth. I needed an Arthur. A stubborn, brilliant, pain in my ass.

"The game is in the same place you went with Rami."

"You know about that?"

"He told me, yeah."

"Will he be there?"

"I haven't heard from Rami since the desert. I'm going to guess no. I'm betting he's going to lay low and try to disappear."

"Good luck with that," I muttered and she nodded.

"He's a rat."

"How big is this game?"

"Five players, including you. I don't have names other than Annatto, Cardamom, Lavender, and Fennel for who will be there. I doubt any of them will be playing."

"A bunch of unknowns, great."

"It's a high buy-in, William."

"How high?"

"Ten thousand. Cardamom is only agreeing to let you in because she likes watching you play. Also she's going to add it to your running tab."

"Peachy, no pressure."

"You don't have to–"

"Yeah, I do Zahra. I've gotta play, and I've gotta win. Then I'm walking away, and you are too."

"If they let me," she said, turning away from me. We walked through Fayoum, weaving between people as we passed them on the streets. Even as the sun started to sink, there was so much life in the city. It buzzed with energy and action, people going to and fro, heading home or out with friends.

A few were headed to this game too. But who? I tried to pin down the lives of the strangers we passed, wondering if I'd see them again soon. Was it that guy with bloodshot eyes and crumpled suit? Or the woman that darted through the streets like she just stole something valuable? Would I be shocked by the teenager scowling at his phone popping in to clean house?

The museum I visited with Rami was closed again, and this time Zahra got us in. The huge, lumbering doorman made my ribs ache. If he decided to kick the shit out of me again, this guy's massive feet would hurt like hell. I stamped down those thoughts and held my arm out for Zahra. She curled her hand in the crook of my arm, angling her hips and shoulders. She switched from Zahra to this lethally sultry version that I didn't recognize. I raised an eyebrow and she shook her head subtly. I'd be asking about that later.

All of the lights were off except in a narrow hallway. The ogre of a doorman led us through, and Zahra's nails dug into my arm. She was anxious, and I wondered which part was giving her nerves. Being here, pretending she was still with them, or leading me back to another game?

It didn't matter.

I just had to get through the night, win enough to pay back as much as I could, then walk away. Annatto had sent another text that I owed close to fifty-thousand now. It seemed impossible, but I doubted his integrity would suddenly kick in with his accounting abilities. That thought made my stomach churn–would he ever let me go then? Even if I somehow paid it all back?

It wasn't the time for that thought, especially as Annatto came out of a small, smoke filled room. It clogged my nose and cluttered my thoughts, but I tried to push it away. Zahra coughed lightly, and I knew the smoke bothered her too. Thick, heavy cigar smoke clung to my pores and clothes, and I'd need a shower before seeing Arthur later.

He hadn't texted me in a while, but that didn't matter now either.

There were three players sitting around a semicircle card table. Cardamom was at the dealer's table with a very low cut top. Whatever bra she had on pushed her modest assets up and the other players were only staring at them instead of paying attention, like normal. I recognized one man; he wore shades and a suit, but it was the same man with the salt-and-pepper hair that was a plant for Cardamom. The other two players–a woman with pretty blonde hair in a braid, and a man in what appeared to be his forties. He was clearly a local but his sharp eyes made me antsy. He scanned and searched everyone in the room, but his eyes were continuously drawn back to the blond.

"Hello William, so glad you could join us," Cardamom said. Annatto's smoker-laugh was raspy, cutting through the relative silence. The other players turned to look at me, careful assessments. I took a seat next to Shades, and he nodded like he remembered me too.

I should have checked if he had a knife to pull on me.

"We have one more player and then we can get started," she announced, and as I got settled with Zahra standing off to the side, the door opened again.

"Shit, Will–" Zahra's hushed words rushed out before she calmed her neutral mask. When I looked up, three people had entered the room, and I knew all three of them.

Dr. Romanova looked miserable and guilty, staring at her feet.

Dr. Carrington in a wheelchair with rage in his eyes.

And Arthur, dressed in a three piece suit with that damn hat from Wes. The dark brown suit played to his eyes perfectly, and the cream pocket square with a lotus on it sent heat down to my cock. He wheeled Dr. Carrington into the room, and stopped when our eyes met. I tried to smile, but he beat me to it. He grinned ear to ear, stunning and sexy as he turned his attention to the rest of the players in the room. With squared shoulders and a take-no-shit air about him, Arthur had never looked more alluring.

"Good evening, my name is Arthur. I'll be the fifth player in this game. I understand there is a buy-in of ten thousand? Lavender here will vouch for me."

Dr. Romanova stepped forward and opened her bag, pulling out several large wads of cash before dumping them on the table. "He will start with thirty thousand," she said weakly.

The other players stood to greet him, but I didn't. When he made his way over, Arthur held out his hand in greeting.

"I'm Arthur, pleasure to meet you. This will be a fun game," he said. That cocked eyebrow was a challenge to engage, and I smiled back.

"Most games are fun, I'm William."

"Shall we?" he asked as he took the seat directly across from me. He sat next to the shifty-looking local, who stared between us, trying to sort something out.

"Yes, let's get started," Cardamom said, clapping her hands. "For anyone not playing, you're allowed to watch, but no talking is allowed. If we believe that you are trying to communicate or assist the players in any way, you will be *removed* from the game."

Arthur leaned back in his chair, that familiar battle-calm settling over him like he was ready for a debate.

Let's fucking go.

XXII

Arthur

OF COURSE. OF FUCKING course this was what William didn't want to talk about this morning. Some stupid grandstand to get away from them–

His eyes caught mine and I watched them dart to my lips.

"Everyone okay with blackjack? It's just a fun game," Cardamom said. She introduced herself and all of the players, but their names were irrelevant. She had four decks in a card shuffling machine. Cardamom made a big show of revealing each deck, opening each sealed box, before putting them in the shuffler.

It would make calculating more difficult but not impossible for counting cards. Even though the buy in was ten-thousand, bets started at one-hundred dollars. Everyone starts conservative, trying to learn the feel of the dealer and the other players. I knew how William played; he was reckless and he went by the emotions of the others to judge his next move. They didn't matter. All that mattered was the count, so I threw the first four hands. William's creased brows during each hand had me worried but I forced myself to look away from him. The guy next to me fidgeted with every hand as his ten-thousand stack slowly dwindled. He was too aggressive out the gate, not watching or concerned with what anyone else was doing.

Stupid.

The woman, Carla, was too terrified to make any actual power moves with the game.

The man next to her refused to give his name, but it was clear to me that he was a plant; Cardamom kept looking at him and staring at his cards before he made a decision. Cardamom was actually playing that hand and it was obvious.

And then there was William. He assessed the cards around him, briefly looking at me, before his attention returned to the king and six before him. Realistically, he was going to lose this match, but passing at a sixteen was hard when you were desperate for a win. If I was right, he would be safe this round.

I drummed my fingers on the felt-lined table and he looked at me.

Do it, I tried to tell him, but he looked away. I kept drumming.

"Well, hit or stand?" Cardamom asked.

"Hit," he said, and I wanted to smile but I didn't.

He got a four. Twenty.

Cardamom showed a seventeen. Irritation lined her face as he won the round. I busted on purpose, trying to feel out the way the other players would respond.

Within three more hands, William and I were consistently winning. I upped the bets each time, forcing the players around us to be more and more aggressive, and that's when I hit my stride.

Blackjack.

Twenty-one.

Five cards under twenty-one.

Twenty. Twenty. Twenty-one.

Blackjack.

Cardamom opened the shuffler and reshuffled all of the cards, while the other players watched.

"You have beginner's luck," she said to me.

"Is that so?" I crossed my legs and doubled the initial bet. A few groans at the table made me smile but William scowled. He was down three-thousand. The other players were much worse off, with the grumpy local and Carla down to their last thousand.

I upped the bet to seven-fifty. This wasn't the kind of game that you left; you left when you were escorted out after losing all of your money. They wanted everyone to bow out slowly, losing it all, so they could leave in debt to them.

"You're feeling more confident," she said, gesturing to the amount I bet. All of the smoke in the room made it harder to think, but I blinked it away.

"I'm here to play," I said. I hadn't counted my chips, but I was over fifty-thousand now. I didn't want to take all of William's money, but I didn't even know where it came from. He struggled to buy coffee, much less buy into this game.

Zahra wrung her hands in the background, staring a hole in the back of his head. Of course she provided the funds. I didn't want or need to know where it came from. As much as I wanted to help William each hand, I couldn't. They would notice soon, and tensions were already high. Annatto said something in Arabic to Cardamom, and while my Arabic wasn't perfect, it was something along the lines of *what the fuck is happening.*

I stopped at nineteen. I knew the next card would be a face card, and I wanted to win this round. It would eliminate the cranky guy, and likely Carla. She clearly had never played with this much money before.

I pretended each of the chips were pennies; it didn't matter the amount. The money was Irina's from whatever shit she was into, and in exchange for my silence, I was going to buy out William's debt with her money.

Cranky guy busted. He swore in an Arabic accent I didn't recognize, and the giant bear-man dragged him out. Carla whimpered but said nothing. I felt bad for her; what shitty thing brought her here? What could she possibly have gotten into to think this was a good idea?

Glancing at William, I thought the same thing.

Carla had a fourteen–quite possibly the worst hand in blackjack. The deck was split then and the odds of getting what you needed were nearly fifty-fifty. She hit, and got a ten. Bust.

Cardamom's puppet had a fifteen and he hit. Nineteen. Stand.

William's turn came up and he showed an ace. I folded my hands on the table, trying to communicate that he needed to hit without bringing attention to myself again.

"Hit," he said and he got a jack. *Yes!*

This round brought him back up to ten-thousand, and the three of us played for hours. I didn't know how much time passed as there were no clocks, but it felt like I had been sitting in this shitty fold up chair for hours.

I alternated between dominating for a while and throwing hands to avoid suspicion. Irina paced, and Wes was silent as the grave behind me. After a quick count, I was up to sixty-three thousand. I still have the majority of Irina's money, and I had no qualms about asking for more.

"You found an excellent player, Lavender," Cardamom said and the words were sharpened like knives.

"Yes, he's quite good."

"Indeed." They eyed each other, until finally Irina looked away. She couldn't meet Wes' eyes, and I didn't blame him. William was almost in the same boat–so fucking close–and I felt just as disgusted. If he had truly chosen to rob the temple, I wasn't sure that was something I could get past. Especially now that Henkhisesui and Kheti were at peace. Judging the expression on his face, William felt the same way looking at Irina.

The game resumed after a short break for everyone to stretch. I stayed at the table, mainly because I wanted to see what Cardamom was going to do with the decks.

William took his phone out and typed away.

I waited a minute before I pulled mine out and read his message.

You're here

Of course I am

Did you know I'd be here?

No, but in retrospect I should have

Why are you here?

Would you be mad if I said this was my grand gesture?

Saving me from a mountain of debt? Hot

Full of surprises, Will

You'll be full of something later

Do not make me blush! They will know we know each other!

Kick ass, Arty

By the time I tucked my phone away, the game was ready to resume. William played on his a little longer, scrolling through something that made him smile. Had to be cat videos. Cardamom didn't touch the decks, and that made me more leery than if she had; if I were trying to rig a game, I'd mess with the decks as much as possible.

But she didn't. Cardamom made a phone call, sent a couple of messages, but otherwise did nothing else. She didn't even excuse herself to the bathroom, wherever that was.

Something was wrong–something had to be wrong.

William and I locked eyes at that exact moment, and I knew he felt it too. Energy filled the air, and I felt everyone around us shifting back and forth. Irina had taken several steps back, closer to Wes, but he didn't react to her.

A man in a black suit walked into the room. His salt and pepper hair was cropped short and his beard neatly, tightly trimmed highlighting his jawline. The lapels of the suit were sharp enough to cut, and judging from the confusion on the players' faces, everyone was curious about this stranger.

"Hello Saffron, to what do we owe the pleasure?" Cardamom said.

"Stopping in to check on my investments. It seems like you are doing well," he said, lightly kissing her cheeks. Cardamom grimaced but recovered, planting a smile back on her face. They exchanged a few more words in hushed tones and Saffron locked eyes with Zahra. She practically melted into the floor under his gaze. Rage edged over William's face, and I prayed that my thoughts of *don't do anything fucking stupid* radiated loudly enough for him to not react.

When he caught my eye again, the fire in him died down.

Saffron smirked at the room, took a bow, and left just as quickly as he arrived. Cardamom settled back at the dealer's seat, the playful facade finally gone. Her icy glare assessed each player that was left.

"Shall we up the minimum bets to, say one-thousand?" she said.

I was ready to finish this shitshow too. I pushed a grand into the center, my signal to deal me in. Her planted guy pushed his money into the pot. When William searched the faces of everyone at the table, his pile of chips was higher than when he started. I'd made sure to throw enough hands to ensure he got a better hand. It helped throw any suspicion off of me, too.

"I think I'm out, a grand is too rich for me," he finally said, standing.

“I think you misunderstood, dear. You’re going to keep playing,” Cardamom said, and the icy demeanor slipped into her voice until all of her words were edged with steel.

“This is a friendly game, isn’t it?” I added, raising my eyebrow, feigning concern. I placed my hand on the table, and tried to wrap my arm around the pile of chips.

“Of course, of course. But you will come back next time, and do be sure you bring my little Coconut,” she said. Zahra flinched, stepping back, and William wrapped an arm around her shoulders. I stood too, signaling my exit from the game. The thousand dollars in the pot would be lost, but it was Irina’s money so I didn’t give a shit anyway.

“I want to cash this out,” I said, and Cardamom snapped her fingers. Annatto returned with a cash box. He did the math, pulling out insane amounts of cash.

“Eighty-four thousand, four hundred,” he said, wrapping ten thousand in thick wads with rubber bands. The remaining was tucked in an envelope and handed over to me. “A pleasure to play with you, I hope we see you again. You had a good run tonight,” Annatto said.

“Mmm, yes, I’ll be back. Lavender was right, this was a good time.”

“Very good,” Cardamom said. Wes rolled over to me and opened a small backpack. I placed all of the cash in there, and we each took turns saying goodbye. My heart was ready to explode, but I kept calm. I pictured how Henkhisesui persevered for Kheti and suddenly I was the one made of steel. I placed a light kiss on the back of Cardamom's hand until she smiled again. I shook hands with her player and then with William, nodding a goodbye to Zahra. He didn't want to let go of my hand, but I pulled away before anyone noticed how he lingered with me.

"Lavender will keep me informed when the next game is?" I said, and Irina quickly agreed. William and Annatto talked in harsh, hushed tones but I didn't turn back around. I had to walk away–he had to get out of this building, and then I'd give him all of the money and he would be free. Everything would be fine, as long as he just walked out of the damn building.

I pushed Wes' wheelchair and we walked in silence until we were back to the main street.

"You weren't joking, you are a good player," Irina said.

"It's less impressive when you know I can cheat with the best of them. Where the hell is William?" I asked, finally turning around to look for him.

My phone buzzed, and I opened his message.

See you in your room <3

Relief rushed through me, and then I dialed another number: the local police. Who knew what would happen, but knowing that someone was on the way to bust up what remained of that game was satisfying enough. There were too many pieces to dismantle at once, but cutting off the head of one snake was enough for me. At least for today.

"Wes, can we talk?" Irina asked.

I stopped, and turned his chair toward her. "I didn't tell you to stop!"

"Hear what she has to say. I can't imagine whatever excuse comes from her will change your mind on how you feel, but I know you'd regret not at least listening. You're too damn curious for your own good," I said. Wes chuckled, and I hugged him tight.

"You're right. Is this how it feels? God, this is dreadful. The lecturing. You should have stopped me ages ago."

"I need to make sure that William is okay," I said. I didn't want to leave Wes with her, but there was still so much love in his eyes. Maybe they could work it out, just like with William and Zahra. Wes handed me the backpack, and I felt like the entire world knew I had eighty-thousand dollars on me as I walked through Fayoum. It was dark out, but the lights from all of the stores and cars and just the noise of life filled the air. I walked with purpose heading straight toward the hotel, desperate to get back to William.

When I got into the lobby, Zahra was there, tears in her eyes as she launched herself into my arms.

"Thank you," she said between her sobs, and I held her awkwardly. "Thank you, thank you, thank you."

"I didn't do this for you, I did it for William." I flinched at the harshness of my words, but it was true: ultimately, Zahra was collateral damage in whatever played out for him.

"I don't care who or what motivated you to help. William will be free, and for that I will never be able to thank you enough."

As I let go of her, she stepped back like she was going to retreat, but I held her steady. "He loves you. Please work things out with him."

"I'll try. Work on him for me, okay?" she smiled and I smiled back. I didn't know if I'd ever truly *like* Zahra, but she was William's person and there was no changing it.

"How much does he owe, do you know?"

"Around seventy," she whispered. I had enough. I had more than enough; he would be okay. *We* would be okay.

"See you around?" I asked and she nodded.

"Yes, I'm heading back to my room now. I need to sleep after all this crap," she said, nervous laughter tinging her words. She retreated toward the elevator before I could say anything else, and that was for the best; I had nothing else to say to her. All of my words were stored in my chest for one person.

"William," I said as I opened the door to my hotel room. He was there and he was in one piece, and he was *smiling*.

"You reckless, ridiculous, insane, incredible man. How?" William wrapped me in the best hug of my life. My hat fell off my head and landed on the floor with a light thud. He was warm and safe and absolutely *fine*. I clung to him like he was a life raft, and all of the nerves, all of the anxious energy–it all came out. I trembled in his arms, shaking so violently I nearly knocked him over.

"I did tell you that I was better at cards than you," I said, and his laughter filled the room. Loud and warm. He cupped my face with tears in his eyes. Our foreheads touched, and I held his wrists, desperate to hold any part of him. "I love you," he whispered and I nodded. The lump in my throat felt like it was trying to choke me, so I just nodded again and again, as William held me.

When he tipped my chin to bring our lips together, everything in the entire world melted away. The magic from Henkhisesui was gone, but the magic between us wasn't. I don't know if it was the tattoos or just us, but it felt like we were glowing.

"I love you," I finally said back. William pressed kisses to my eyelids and my cheeks, my lips and my nose. Any and everywhere he could reach.

"This might be the best day of my life, even though I was convinced you were going to break up with me this morning."

"I thought you were going to break up with *me*," I countered and he laughed again.

"You're stuck with me now, Arty. It would look a tad silly to break up the matching tattoos. How would we explain that at a removal appointment?"

"Who knows if it can be removed," I countered and he nibbled on my lip.

"You just *have* to argue, don't you? Just gotta have the last word."

"Yes," I said and he scooped me up before tossing me on the bed.

"Or, instead of arguing, we could just–"

"Excellent idea," I said, guiding him to lay next to me, our limbs tangled together. "What about Annatto?"

"I told him we'd meet tomorrow to work out the terms of my payment plan. He seemed happy enough about it."

"No thievery involved either," I said.

"Well, I did steal one thing," he said, taking my glasses off to place them on the bedside table.

"I swear to god if you say my heart–"

"I stole your heart, didn't I?"

"The worst. The *absolute* worst line–"

"You love it."

He was right, and that was probably the most infuriating part of it all. I loved every line he said. I loved how his eyes sparkled before he delivered a doozy of a line, and how he always had another one ready. William pulled his shirt up and off, and I grinned. I loved that too.

"Yeah, yeah," I said as William pulled me into his arms. I glanced over at my hat and smiled to myself; William would be the adventure of a lifetime and he was mine.

Epilogue

William

Nine Months Later

IT WAS EARLY SPRING but the desert was plenty warm. Arthur directed traffic like he was born to be a traffic cop, ordering people left and right to get the site set up. He'd been working with Drs. Carrington and Romanova for the last six months to get the site ready for excavation again.

Wes walked with a cane most days, but he got around just fine, only whining when it was going to rain. Luckily for everyone involved, that was rare here. Irina fussed over him like a mother hen and for as much they both pretended the other drove them nuts, there were hearts in their eyes. After Irina agreed to provide more evidence against Cardamom and Annatto, that seemed to warm Wes' heart right back up.

Of course this didn't happen until after I paid off my debts to Annatto. Between the money I had won at the game–around twenty thousand total–and all of Arthur's winnings, we had enough to pay him back and then some as a *go away and never come back* incentive. Annatto seemed to vanish, but not well enough. He was picked up by local police not long after our meeting.

Life had been easy, and happy. It was terrifying how easy things were; I was constantly waiting for something to fuck up, but it never came.

Arthur finished his degree. He was officially Dr. Lewis now, and watching him graduate pushed me to start my PhD program too. I doubted I'd ever be as motivated as him, but I wanted to study languages more.

"Will, come on, we're going to reopen the temple," he said. Arthur beamed at me and my heart nearly stopped. This was all still so new, so wonderful. Our small apartment in Fayoum was everything I wanted a home to be, and our tiny tent in the desert reminded me of good times past.

Our hands laced together like they were meant to be together, and we approached Henkhisesui's temple. It had been nine months since we had been back, and I knew how badly he wanted to return. Arthur still dreamt of the god of the East Wind, swearing that Henkhisesui was telling him to come back. I'd never dreamt of Kheti, but it didn't bother me. Arthur and Henkhisesui had a deeper, creepier bond and even though he denies it, I think Arthur missed him.

As we approached the staircase leading down, Hank the camel came galloping toward us, spitting and huffing.

"You're not coming with us," I said, and Hank stomped a hoofed foot.

"He's right, sadly. You'd hate being underground. Stay here and we will come back soon," Arthur said, petting Hank's nose.

"It's odd how much he likes you," I said.

"Don't be jealous. It doesn't suit you."

I shoved his arm, and Arthur tipped his hat. The hat was finally more worn in, and it seemed to be molded to Arthur's head. The toolkit that Wes gave him was on his belt, and together we headed down the stairs into the temple.

Arthur lit one of the wall sconces and the rest of them lit up. He gasped, squeezing my hand tighter, as we gazed at the open throne room. The art was the same as I remembered it; covering every surface and still in near-perfect condition. I ran my hand over their names etched into the closest pillar.

When we stepped into the temple, a familiar, wonderful song danced on the wind.

The East Wind rises again, a storm without end, a lover in search of home. A lover, lost and alone, feels the East Wind caress his face and knows he will never stop searching.

Dear Reader,

THANK YOU SO MUCH for reading Shifting Sands! I sincerely hope that you enjoyed watching Arthur and William begrudgingly fall in love and bond over ancient magic.

If you enjoyed it, please consider leaving a review and spreading the word! This helps other readers to find this book; chatting and posting about it on social media, blogs, and forums is an absolute blessing for indie writers. This is how we connect with our readers, and every review is so appreciated!

Also, if you'd like some exclusive content and teasers you can always sign up for my **NEWSLETTER** too!

Love,

Jana

Acknowledgments

As always, my love, thanks, and gratitude goes to my dear friends, family, my awesome husband. I am so incredibly blessed to have such wonderful humans in my life.

This book feels a little different for me. It's the first book I wrote fully without HRH Prince Babar, and that was hard. It was hard to sit down to write without his fuzzy little self demanding attention and huffing when I didn't reach for him fast enough. It was really, wretchedly hard.

Shifting Sands is also a new genre for me, and one I've loved for a long time. Queer romance is near and dear to my heart, as I strongly believe in telling all kinds of love stories.

I felt different too, in that this time, as this book reaches your hands, that I'm actually worthy of the title *author.* I'm not sure why exactly; maybe it's because this is the 6th book I've released, maybe it's because I'm finally stepping into some confidence, but I'm not shying away from calling myself an author anymore.

So for that, I'll give myself a shout out here: You did it, Jana. You made your dreams come true, and you should be damn proud of yourself.

And last but certainly not least, thank you to all of my readers. Thank you for spending your time and energy with me and my characters. Thank you for choosing this book. Thank you for everything.

About the Author

Writer. Wife/Mom. Servant to 4lb Chihuahua with a Napoleon complex. Avid coffee drinker. Travel junkie. Book devourer. (Not, *literally*—too much fiber.) HRH Prince Babar, my beloved chihuahua, passed away in November 2024, but he will remain in my bios and pictures, because he will always hold a very special, very large part of my heart.

I've been writing most of my life, but my heart has always been drawn to magic. Urban Fantasy--mixing magic with real life--became the perfect genre for me.

Born and raised on the Southeast Coast of Virginia, when I'm not writing or momming, I'm heading for the ocean.

Come join my newsletter called **"The Magic Shop,"** where I'll send you (hopefully) monthly emails to tease upcoming books, provide flower, crystal, and character bios.

Feeling social? I'm on Facebook and IG, and I'd love for you to come say hello!

f facebook.com/profile.php?id=100091558147127

instagram.com/jana_sun_books/

tiktok.com/@jana_sun_books?_t=8nZvXwxUsCV&_r=1

a amazon.com/stores/Jana-Sun/author/B0CLSBT8VH?ref=ap_rdr&isDramIntegrated=true&shoppingPortalEnabled=true

g goodreads.com/author/show/42798427.Jana_Sun